FREDERICA SUMMER

FREDERICA SUMMER

A story of love and cultural conflict during
the Spanish incursion into Georgia

Dody Myers

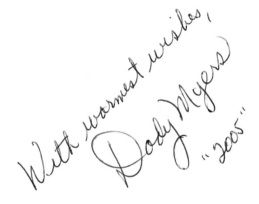

FREDERICA SUMMER

ISBN 0-9747685-4-5

First Printing: December 2004

Library of Congress Control Number: 2004115959

Printed in the United States of America on acid-free paper.

Cover painting and interior graphics by Joyce Wright – www.artbyjoyce.com
Book design by Bella Rosa Books

BellaRosaBooks and logo are trademarks of Bella Rosa Books

Dedicated to Constance Daley and Susan Alou
with thanks for their wisdom and candid advice.
—Dody

Author's Note

Although the main characters in FREDERICA SUMMER are fictional, the historical facts are true. The Calwell family, Anna Meyer and John Henney, Beatre Hawkins, and the numerous tradesmen mentioned were all actual residents of Frederica Town during the summer of 1742. General James Oglethorpe commanded the Forty-Second Regiment of Foot stationed at the fort and both John and Charles Wesley served as chaplains at differing times.

A visitor to Fort Frederica National Park can walk along Broad Street amid the beautiful live oaks and view the ruins of the Fort, the Soldiers Barracks and the foundations of the Calwell and Hawkins homes.

I would like to thank Ranger Patricia Barefoot for giving me access to the fort's archives, to Chief Ranger Kim Coons for answering my unending questions, and to Bridgett Mathues for helping me to research the Calwell family.

The battles of Gulley Hole Creek and Bloody Marsh each lasted less than a day and are seldom mentioned in the annals of American history but they stemmed the tide of the Spanish incursion into the British colonies and perhaps changed forever the course of our history.

Chapter One

Today was her birthday!

It was the fifth of April in the year 1739 and she was thirteen years old.

Tabitha Plummer stood at the open window of a room in her grandparent's home, where she had come with her father, gazing out at the tender new green of spring in the side garden. Shafts of sunlight filtered through oaks strung with silvery moss. Magnolias, camellias and azaleas grew in profusion and Tabitha drank in the simple smell of freshly turned soil. There was a gentle breeze and tiny oak leaves floated to the ground in their ever-changing life cycle. It was radiant and sweet-smelling, a day to be treasured and remembered.

Father had brought her to Savannah to celebrate this important entrance into young womanhood. The problem was that today she was dressed in a frilly pink dress more suited to a ten-year-old and her grandmother insisted she wear English shoes instead of her more comfortable moccasins. Her feet hurt.

Tabitha lived in the village of Tustacatty along the Oconee River in inland Georgia with her father, George Plummer, and her Creek mother, Windwhisper. She had been very excited when her father told her of his plans for her birthday. Now she wasn't so sure. Although she had been educated in Savannah she felt out of place in the white world—as out of place as she sometimes felt in the Indian world.

Leaning her head against the window frame Tabitha thought of the difference between her two worlds. Unexpectedly her throat tightened and she felt tears gathering behind her eyes as sadness at the feeling of not belonging welled up in her. With a bleak, wintry feeling she blinked and issued a soft cough to clear her throat. It was her birthday. She would not allow negative thoughts to mar this day, she would not feel sorry for herself. Tabitha hated self-pity in others, considered it to be a sign of weakness. *She was strong.* Her mother always told her she was, and her mother was the wisest person she knew.

Turning away from the window, she walked over to the door and twisted the knob. Resolutely she let a smile curl her lips and stuck out her chin. She would not be sad. Not today. Not on her birthday.

Her father, a man of medium height with the distinctive long nose and high brow of the English, was waiting for her in the entry hall and he watched her descend the spiral staircase with a look of tender love on his face.

"Oh, Princess, you look lovely," he said softly. "And your hair . . . what a difference."

Self-consciously, Tabitha lifted her hand to pat the shiny black tresses that her grandmother had loosened from their customary braids to cascade across her shoulders.

"Thank you, Poppa."

"Are you ready for your big day?" he asked as he took her arm and moved her toward the door. "I thought we might visit several of the shops that have opened on Bull Street and find a special present for my special girl."

"Do I get to pick it out?"

"Indeed you do."

Together she and her father walked out into the brilliant April sunshine. They wandered slowly along the tree-shaded streets admiring the beautiful things displayed in shop windows.

Her father seemed attracted to a jeweler's shop where he

pointed out several baubles that caught his attention. "Just look at that," he cried pointing to a broach of blue stones. "It matches perfectly the blue of your eyes."

"But Poppa I would have no use for that at Tustacatty. Besides, I have many strings of beads from the Trading Post."

"Those are only Indian trinkets. This broach is meant for a lady."

Tabitha giggled.

Ten minutes later, as they were passing the last shop on the street Tabitha spotted a dress hanging on a form just inside the open door of Madame Elaine's Frock Shop. She fell in love with it instantly. Unlike the childish dress she wore, it was a grown up gown of airy, gossamer muslin. It was highly impractical, obviously very expensive, and very, very, beautiful. She could not take her eyes from it. Tabitha knew she would never have a place to wear it and yet she ached to own it.

Her father did not miss her halting footsteps and the look of longing in her eyes. He took her hand and drew her into the small shop.

"No, Poppa. It will be far too expensive," she said, pulling back.

He obviously had no intention of being thwarted. He took Tabitha's arm in a vise-like grip and marched her into Madame Elaine's.

The shop girl immediately took charge, removing the dress from the form, leading Tabitha into a dressing room and helping her into the gown. When all was in place Tabitha reluctantly looked at her reflection in the cheval mirror. The color was captivating, a clear bright blue, the color of the delphiniums in Grandma's garden. It suited her to perfection.

She studied herself in the mirror and for the first time in her young life acknowledged that she was rather pretty. Not beautiful, but then neither was she plain. There was a hint of stubbornness in her face reflected in the determined set of her chin and resolute mouth. Her skin had a rosy tint that spoke of her Indian heritage, her hair was black as ebony, but it was her eyes that were her best feature. They were large, thickly fringed with long black lashes and blue, deep and vivid, unusual for a girl of mixed-blood.

The blue of the dress intensified the color of her eyes and its cut hinted at the curves of her newly blossoming figure. Tabitha was tall and her height was a constant source of irritation to her. *Although,* she thought as she twisted and turned before the mirror, *I am slender and rather shapely.*

"It is perfect for you," the shop girl cooed as she steered Tabitha back into the showroom where her father waited.

His gaze swept her from head to toe. "You must have it," he said, nodding his approval.

"But Poppa, wherever will I wear it?" She glanced at Madame Elaine hovering nearby and dropped her voice to a whisper. "It's very expensive."

"And it is worth every penny. Today is special, Princess. Business has been good this spring. You can wear it this evening for your birthday dinner. Mr. Otterbridge and his fiancée have been invited. You remember him, don't you? He's a good friend of your former teacher, the Reverend John Wesley."

He turned and winked at Madame Elaine. "We'll take it."

Later, they stopped for lunch at a lovely little tea shop and then, hand in hand, took a leisurely stroll through Johnson Square. Newly planted pansies and bluebells formed a tapestry of brilliant color beneath the shady oaks. Her father found a bench in a shady space under the trees and motioned for her to sit down.

"Wait here for me, Tabitha. I've business across the street with a fur broker that will be of no interest to you. I'll only be a short time and then we'll return home. You'll have time for a nap and a bath before dressing for dinner. Will you be all right?"

"Of course I will, Poppa. Go tend to your business." She settled herself on the bench and placed the bag containing her new dress beside her, then flashed him a smile. "What possible harm could come to me here?"

However, only five minutes later Tabitha watched a trio of boys saunter by, then turn to stare at her. They were dirty and unkempt and they stood close together snickering and making lewd gestures with grimy fingers. She heard one of them say, "That red-skin look to her means only one thing, boys. That gal's a half-breed. Come with me." He ambled over to her and the others followed.

Tabitha kept her eyes downcast trying to ignore their presence.

"What you doin' all alone out here, half-breed?" the boldest asked.

Tabitha made no reply.

"Hopin' for some company ain't you?" another said with a smirk. "All dressed up in a pretty pink dress."

"We got jest what yer lookin' fer," the bold one said. He reached out a hand to touch her arm when a loud oath from a short distance away caused all of the boys to whirl around.

A tall, well built Indian brave glared down at the boys. He was naked to the waist, bulging biceps gleaming with oil, wearing a breechclout and leggings. "Move on," he commanded in a tongue Tabitha recognized as Cherokee. The boys did not seem to comprehend so he repeated the order in broken English. His coal black eyes shot signals of danger as he moved menacingly closer.

The boys turned tail and ran.

The Cherokee looked at her sternly. "Savannah rough town. No place for girl alone," he said.

"My father is just across the square." Tabitha stuck her chin out. "He'll be back shortly. I can take care of myself . . . but thank you for coming to my aid."

His thin lips quirked with a hint of a smile. His gaze swept over her and he rocked his weight from side to side as though unsure whether to stay and talk or move on.

Just then Tabitha spotted her father running toward them. He skidded to a stop, glaring at the Indian. "What is going on here?" he gasped, out of breath. "Tabitha, you know better than to speak to strangers."

Quickly Tabitha told him what had happened and how the brave had come to her assistance.

Mollified, Mr. Plummer twirled around and grasped the hand of the surprised Indian. "George Plummer," he said, "of the Tustacatty Trading Post. And this," he added, "is my daughter Tabitha. I believe I owe you my gratitude."

"Broken Arrow, of the Antelope Clan of the Cherokee Confederacy," the brave replied. He dropped his hand to his side and his gaze darted to Tabitha. There was a look in his eyes that unsettled her. He hesitated, obviously unsure what to say.

"Thank you, again," she said, fidgeting slightly under his intense stare, suddenly aware of her femininity. He was unbelievably handsome, his skin a rich coppery color.

Mr. Plummer put his hand on her elbow and guided her to her feet. "We must be on our way. Come, dear." He nodded to Broken Arrow and began to walk away with a firm hand on Tabitha's arm.

Broken Arrow stared intently after her and as she glanced over her shoulder she saw his hand rise slightly in a gesture of farewell.

After returning home from the park Tabitha took a short nap, then, refreshed and eager for the evening ahead, she bathed, dusted her body generously with her Grandmother's talcum and began to dress for the evening ahead. Her face flushed with happiness as she pulled the new blue dress over her head and settled it about her shoulders. She hardly dared look in the cheval glass, a long mirror mounted on swivels in a mahogany frame, standing in a corner of her grandmother's spare room. What if it wasn't as pretty or fit as well as she recalled? Slowly she turned, first one way, then the other, to view the dress in its entire splendor. Oh, it was just as she remembered. It was beautiful—undoubtedly the loveliest thing she had ever owned.

With a perky swish of her skirt she moved to the tiny

dressing table set with an array of powders, perfumes and brushes. She brushed her hair until it shone, and then with a slight giggle she applied a dab of cologne behind her ear.

Satisfied at last with her appearance she descended the spiral staircase and joined her grandparents and their guests in the drawing room.

The room was furnished in excellent taste, with a few mahogany Hepplewhite pieces, and several needlepoint chairs. The walls were stenciled with vines of green ivy, the color repeated in the silk drapes and upholstery of two circular sofas facing one another. Louvered doors leading onto a covered logia stood ajar admitting a faint breeze that carried the scent of magnolia and mimosa.

Reverend Otterbridge rose from a chair and strode across the room to greet her. Tabitha was delighted to see him. He was a good friend of Reverend John Wesley, having served with him as assistant pastor at the Savannah church where two years earlier she was introduced to the Christian faith. Tabitha had spent that summer with her grandparents receiving both an education and tutoring in English from John Wesley.

"Tabitha!" Otterbridge exclaimed raising her hand to his lips. "Happy Birthday, my dear."

She felt heat flood her face. No one had ever kissed her hand before. *It must be the grown-up gown,* she thought with delight.

A young woman had joined him and he turned to introduce her with a look of adoration. "Let me introduce my fiancée . . . Tabitha Plummer . . . Miss Adele Lefebvre."

Tabitha liked her immediately. She had a look of sense and elegance, a petite figure, soft, light-brown hair and intelligent hazel eyes. Her gaze, when it lingered on Mr. Otterbridge, showed the same adoration. For some crazy reason Tabitha's thoughts flickered to the young brave in the park that afternoon. How wonderful it must be to be in love.

"Tabitha, what a pretty name," Adele said. "It's from the Bible, isn't it?"

"Yes, from the Book of Acts. My Creek name is White Blossom, but when I was to be baptized Reverend Wesley told me to just open the Bible and look for a Christian name I liked. It fell open to Acts 9:36 and the first name I saw was Tabitha. I like it. It means *full of good works and almsdeeds.*"

How lovely. And White Blossom is delightful too. You are lucky to have two attractive names."

But not to live in two different worlds, Tabitha thought ruefully. *Next week I will go back to being White Blossom again.* She wondered if that was why her father always called her Princess. Was it because that way he did not have to choose one name over the other?

She set a smile on her face as they walked over to join her family. Her father was standing in front of the fireplace, one hand resting on the mantle, a glass of sherry in the other. *How handsome he is*, she thought. *No buckskins tonight.* Tonight he was dressed in a figured waistcoat, a ruffled shirt with a white cravat, short breeches buttoned to the knee and long boots with white tops. He was talking animatedly to her grandfather, a tall man with bristling gray hair and a sizeable pouch.

Grandmother Plummer rose from her chair with a rustle of brocaded silk and gathered her granddaughter in her arms. She smelled of lavender. Tabitha fondly placed a kiss on her rouged cheek.

Conversation ebbed and flowed as they awaited the announcement of dinner. When it came her father took her arm and escorted her to the dinning room. She walked with her head high, her shoulders back, aware of every place the blue dress clung to her slender body.

How out of place Mother would feel in these surroundings, she thought with a sudden pang. *She is wise to stay in the village among her own.*

The table was set with her grandmother's best china and silver and there was a tall vase of flowers in the center. Tabitha was seated between Mr. Otterbridge and her grandfather. Adele was directly across the table from her and as they were being served she leaned forward and said, "I suppose you know that both the Wesley brothers . . . John and Charles . . . have returned to England."

"No, I didn't," Tabitha said with a start of surprise.

"Well, of course, Charles suffered from fever and dysentery, but mostly it was a case of mental agony and depression. He served as General Oglethorpe's Secretary at Fort Frederica for about nine months but he felt the soldiers were undisciplined heathens." She laughed. "And he claimed the people at Frederica were unsettled, in a constant state of alarm from the Spaniards, and completely unreceptive to his message. He was very unhappy."

Mr. Otterbridge nodded. "Then, of course, his brother's main design in coming to the colonies was to preach to the Indians. John took the appointment to the Savannah church only after his plan to go to the Choctaws, the least corrupted of all the Indian nations, was thwarted by General Oglethorpe."

"Why did General Oglethorpe object?" Grandmother Plummer asked.

Mr. Otterbridge turned to her with a smile. "There was considerable danger of him being intercepted or killed by the French who are in control of the Choctaw, but more importantly it would leave Savannah destitute of a minister."

"But you are here in Savannah," Tabitha said.

"Ah, but I had been appointed to serve the congregation at Ebenezer. Now, of course, I am here filling John's post."

"He was a good schoolmaster," Tabitha commented. "He had great patience with women and children."

The soup was served and for awhile everyone was busy eating the delicious chowder. Adele finally laid her spoon aside and said, "I don't mean to be a gossip but John Wesley had an unhappy love affair with a Miss Sophia Hopkey. When she up and married a Mr. Williamson, John refused to give her the Sacrament of the Lord's Supper because he believed her guilty of conduct which he judged to be reprehensible. He was brought before the court. Later he was acquitted but this was the final blow to his self esteem and he asked to be relieved of his duties as minister to Savannah and in December last he sailed for England."

"We lost a good man," Tabitha's grandfather observed sagely. "But you, sir, have filled in admirably in the interim."

"Thank you," Mr. Otterbridge said. "And now that I have become engaged to this lovely young lady I will undoubtedly stay in Savannah."

Conversation lagged as the meal progressed. Finally dishes were cleared, and desert brought in. As Tabitha began to spoon her bread pudding Mrs. Plummer looked at her with an affectionate smile. "You look very pretty tonight, dear. That dress is most becoming—it brings out the blue of your eyes. Won't you stay with us another week? Susan Alou is having a birthday party next Saturday and I feel certain she would be glad to invite you."

Tabitha looked hopefully at her father.

"We must get back to the Trading Post," he said regretfully. "When I spoke with my factor this afternoon he encouraged me to make the trip to Spanish Florida this fall to trade with the Yemassee. I have been planning it for some time. Alligator skins are more plentiful there and of larger size. I want Windwhisper and Tabitha to accompany me."

"Oh, dear! Isn't that dangerous, son?" Tabitha's grandmother said. "I hear the Spanish are quite angry with us for expanding the boundaries of the Georgia colony and taking possession of land that they claim belongs to them."

"I'll take a number of Creek braves with me for protection. For some time now I've been thinking of setting up another post in Florida, where competition with other traders is not so keen. Nothing will happen to us. And Tabitha is looking forward to it."

Not really, Tabitha thought. She felt a sudden chill, a strange foreboding of danger. But she wouldn't tell her father that. He would be ashamed of her childish fear.

Chapter Two

Scottish Highlands - 1739

They carry with them their language, their opinions,
Their popular songs and hereditary merriment:
They change nothing but their place of abode;
And of that change they perceive the benefit.
-Samuel Johnson, Journey to the Western Isles of Scotland

Ian's head emerged from the depths of his bed into the steamy darkness of the tiny sleeping loft. Beside him his younger brother snored softly. Slowly, objects in the loft took shape as the first flush of dawn colored the single window open against the July sky. His stomach lurched as he became fully awake. This was the last dawn he would ever watch from this room. The day had come much sooner than expected.

He groaned with a mixture of excitement, apprehension and sadness.

Today he would leave everything familiar to him, everything that had shaped him into the man he had become. He stretched, his long limbs jamming against the footboard of the bed long ago grown too short for him. Feeling a pressing need he swung his feet over the side moaning softly as they hit the rough bare floor. With his toe he maneuvered the chamber pot from under the bed and watched the vapor rise from the china as he directed his stream into the bowl.

In the farmyard a rooster crowed. Ian's father was up, the

aroma of coffee from the kitchen fireplace crept through a crude hole cut in the wooden floor.

"Time ye get up, Mitchell," Ian called as he reached down to shake his brother.

Mitchell opened his eyes and yawned. "'Tis barely light," he muttered, burying his head under his pillow.

"I leave within the hour," Ian reminded him as he grabbed trousers from a peg on the wall. "If ye want to bid me farewell ye need to get up now." Hastily he tucked a new shirt of homespun into his pants and pulled the cloth sack he had packed the night before from under the bed. He slung it over his shoulder. "I'll see ye in the kitchen," he said with a chuckle as a half-awake Mitchell stumbled to the chamber pot to take his place. "See ye hurry now. I want to be on the road by full light."

Ian's father shuffled back and forth from the fireplace speaking not a word as he ladled porridge into bowls and then took his seat on one of the wooden benches that served the table. Time had turned his once red hair a shock of white and he sat hunched over, tall and spare, with a squared off face and glaring eyes, a shell of a man ravaged by imprisonment. Ian's heart ached for him in his role as both mother and father to his two sons and his spoon stopped in midair as a wave of guilt swept over him. *Was he doing the right thing by leaving his homeland for the promise of America?*

His father leaned forward and cleared his throat. "Be careful Laddie and remember ye home 'twill always be here if the tales that recruiter spoke are not true."

"Da, it isn't only what that Captain Mackay says. I've read ye the glowing articles in the Edinburgh Echo about the success of the Georgia colony. The MacDonalds have a foothold there and our clan has already furnished several strong men to clear the free land and build homes. Scootlan' is changin'. Industry has coom ta Scootlan' and our way of life is different. We're simple sheepherders, Da. An' the strong ties of families to clan are disappearing. Ye suffer that as much as I."

His father shook his shaggy head. "I could never leave the Highlands. 'Tis our home . . . has been for generations."

Mitchell twisted nervously on the bench, refusing to meet Ian's eyes, eating mechanically.

They were not making this easy.

"We've talked and talked 'til there's no more to be said," Ian said, suddenly angry. "I'm tired of living with a half-empty belly. Our people are starvin' after years of bad harvests and dropping cattle prices. If land rents continue to rise 'twill be no farm here for you or your future generations and ye know it well. Scootlan' or no, I'll not spend my life eking out a bare living and fearing being put in prison for my political beliefs, as they did to ye."

Neither father nor brother responded to his outburst.

The sound of hooves, the jingling of harness chains and the rumbling wheels of an approaching wagon broke the heavy silence and Ian jumped to his feet in relief. "'Twill be Cory coomin' for me," he said inclining his head toward the door.

Mitchell rose and joined his father. Both stood with hands clutched at their side, their faces uncertain. Ian strode to his father and held out his hand. He swallowed a sob and closed his eyes to forbid the tears. It would not be manly to cry.

The old man had never been demonstrative—except with his wife, and then in the utmost privacy—and now he could do no more than hold onto Ian's hand and clasp him on the shoulder. Ian was overcome with a deep feeling of desolation as he looked into the eyes he would probably never see again. Once a bright penetrating green, as his own were, they were now faded and weary with defeat. A tear trickled down his leathery face.

"Da . . ." Ian choked on the words that would not come. He gathered the old man in his arms and clutched him tight.

His father returned the pressure, then shook his head and pulled away.

"God keep ye, my son," he said huskily.

Ian tried to answer, there was so much he wanted to say

and again the words caught in his throat. He turned to his brother. "Mitch, Mitch," he said brokenly, grasping his brother by the arms. "'Tis sorry I am ye choose to stay behind. Ye know I wish ye were going with me."

Mitch nodded. "And ye know Sarah Petrie and I plan to wed next year when we are of age. She'll have no thought of leaving her family and Glencoe. Besides, ye well know Da cannot run the sheep alone. Who will tend the fold if not me?" He lifted his mouth in a sardonic smile and Ian did not miss the smoldering resentment in his words.

The doorknob turned and Ian's friend Cory MacGrath stood in the opening.

"I'll be waiting outside," Cory said sensing the farewell taking place. He picked up Ian's sack of belongings. "Take yer time, Lad."

The door closed and Ian grasped his father's hand once more. The old man's shoulders began to shake. "Go then if ye must," his father muttered reaching in his pocket to withdraw a small bundle of dirty cloth tied with twine. "Heather seeds," he said, handing them to Ian. "A new country waits ye. Plant a bit of Scootlan' in her."

Ian released his hand with a nod, then pushed the packet into his pocket, fist clenched. He turned to his brother and clasped Mitch about the shoulders to give him a quick hug. "'Tis goodbye, then. God keep both of ye well." He turned to the door.

Ian stood with his hand on the latch for a moment, then pushed open the door and stared at the threshold. There was still time to change his mind. He hesitated for a brief second, and then moved through to the waiting carriage.

Cory had already placed his knapsack in the wagon and Ian scrambled up to the seat beside him. Cory clucked to their oxen and they rode along in silence for a while, a flush of embarrassment on Ian's face from the tears that smarted in his eyes.

The oxen's hooves rang loudly on the cobblestone lane as

they moved slowly through the quiet streets of Glencoe. Ian turned in his seat to peer over his shoulder into the early morning stillness. Looking back he could see lanterns beginning to glow behind windows in the village. The spire of the small kirk where he had been christened and took his first communion gleamed whitely in the fading moonlight. The village, its neat houses snuggled together in the small valley under the towering protection of the nearby mountains, faded into the distance. His pulse quickened. How was it possible to feel such eagerness to throw the familiar aside and rush blindly toward the new? Silently he said farewell and turned to the road ahead.

The tavern, one of dozens of similar ramshackle buildings lining the busy wharf of the Moray Firth, north of Inverness, was filled with raucous patrons, music, and smoke. The sour smell of ale mingled in the stale air with the heady odor of unwashed bodies and the cheap perfume of barmaids and prostitutes. Ian and Cory, clutching steins of potent beer huddled on a wooden bench placed haphazardly against an old stone wall at the back of the barroom.

Ian took a large gulp of the bitter ale, washing down the last bite of salted fish that had been his meager supper.

"If we don't soon get passage out of this rotten town our money will be gone before we get to America," he said, worry clouding his green eyes.

"Aye," Cory said. He made a Scottish noise of derision. "We've been a sittin' in this godforsaken hole called Cromarty for three weeks waitin' for favorable winds. The recruiters dinna tell us o' things like this. Or that the stinking ship we're to sail on is fit to carry only half the passengers meant fer it." He drained the last dregs of beer and wiped his mouth on the sleeve of his smelly shirt.

Ian looked at his friend thoughtfully. They looked much alike in kilts that showed sturdy knees above checkered stockings. Each had a ruddy complexion and red hair. Cory, usually the jolly one—a good counterpart to his own rather serious nature—normally treated adversity with a cocky smile. This display of animosity surprised Ian.

A girl, who Ian judged to be no more than fourteen, squeezed herself onto the bench next to him. A prostitute, he felt certain. Stringy blond hair framed weary gray eyes, wise beyond her years. Ian felt a profound sadness as he observed her used up youth.

"I have a friend, and a table we'd be willing to share, if you men would like some company," she said leaning against him. His ego swelled at the word *men,* he was after all only nineteen, and he felt heat flooding his body. It had been a long time since he'd had a girl. He could feel her warm thigh pressing against his on the crowded bench and found himself aroused at her obvious invitation. He glanced at Cory and almost laughed at the open lust on his friend's face.

Together they followed the young prostitute to a nearby table. Reluctantly Ian parted with several of his carefully hoarded coins to buy drinks for everyone. Cory lost no time making the acquaintance of the buxom young girl who had joined them and he already had his arm around her shoulder.

Despite his better judgment Ian also found himself enjoying the female companionship. He recognized the girls for what they were and he had been warned many times that bedding any of the harlots plying their trade along the teeming waterfront was fraught with the danger of disease. So far he and Cory had resisted temptation.

"We could go upstairs, where it's nice and quiet, and share some pleasure," his companion whispered, her warm breath caressing his ear.

Ian squirmed in his chair as his thoughts raced and his arousal became more pronounced. Cory had already disappeared with his girl. Perhaps because of his increasing despair over endless delays and dwindling funds, perhaps because he suspected the hardships still to come and needed some softness to blur the harsh reality of this journey, and perhaps only because he was young and in desperate need, his caution deserted him and he felt the last vestige of his resolve crumble.

"I only have one farthing to pay," he stammered, hoping she could not read his deceit.

"But surely, such a handsome man, has more that one farthing in his pockets," she purred. When he did not respond she shrewdly added, "One farthing it is, then. Follow me, my red-haired one," and taking his hand she led him up the stairs.

The only illumination in the room came from a shaft of fading light leaking through a torn and dirty curtain. Ian's gaze swept the dingy room searching for the prostitute. Only the girl's scent remained on the sagging mattress. He was alone.

His jaw tightened as he realized he had allowed himself to fall into a sated sleep. With an oath he swung his legs from the bed and reached for his kilt lying in a heap on the floor. Cold dread had already begun to gnaw at his belly. Frantically his fingers probed the pile of clothing searching for his money belt.

It was flat. Flat and empty.

He gaped in stunned silence. A vein throbbed in his temple and sweat beaded his forehead. He let loose a string of curses, his lips curled in disgust. He had been a fool, plain and simple. He knew with a certainty that he would never find the girl. She was gone and so was his money. All gone. All of the money he had carefully hoarded for the past year to get a new start in America.

Gone!

The next morning a chagrined Ian and a somber Cory sat on a piling along the wharf watching the bobbing of a large sailing vessel at anchor. "I hear we can expect to board today," Cory finally said.

When he got no response he turned and looked squarely at Ian. "I detect more than casual regret over last nights adventure, aye? I dinna care a fig for the lassie but it was good fun. We'll check ourselves carefully every day and douse ourselves liberally wi' whiskey." Getting no response he added, "Or is it something else worrying ye?"

"She emptied me *and* my purse," Ian answered dejectedly. "Darn fool that I was, I fell asleep and when I woke she was gone. I asked about but no one admits to knowing either of the girls. Whores! I should have known better."

Cory's brow furrowed in disbelief as he listened intently to his friend. "Ye mean the leddy let ye no money at all? Ye've not a penny to bless yourself with?"

"Aye, none!"

"What do ye plan t' do, then? I canna help ye much, Ian. I've barely enough to get meself started."

"Fortunately our passage is paid but I'll have to take service as an indentured servant once we reach America. I've been thinking about it anyway. Ye only have to serve four or five years and I may be lucky and learn a good trade. I'll be all right. Honest."

"Well, laddie," Cory said, with a nod of acceptance, "Let's hope that all the little lassie left ye wi' is empty pockets. An' let's hope the rumor's true an' the weather has cleared an' we can get out o' this rotten town before the week is out."

And so it was that on the 14th of July 1739, with favorable winds from the east-south-east, they stood out to sea.

Chapter Three

Once back at Tustacatty it didn't take long for Tabitha to settle into the rhythms of her village. In fact when she thought about it, it was truly amazing how adept she was at changing from one style of dress to another and one language to another. Here at Tustacatty she wore a doeskin dress and spoke Creek, the language of her mother. She was no longer Tabitha. Now, she was called White Blossom.

White Blossom carefully tied the ends of the stomach lining of a buffalo to four poles set over a fire pit. It would serve as a cooking vessel for several days until it became soggy and soft from the heat. The hide was considered a delicacy and the children especially delighted in tearing off hunks of it to chew. Today, though, she was going to cook stew and she filled the stomach with water and herbs and then added hunks of meat, turnips and onions. Using two leg bones as tongs she lifted hot, fist sized stones from the fire and dropped them into the stew to bring it to a boil.

Windwhisper looked at her approvingly. She and the other women in the camp were busy working with the meat the hunters had brought in from a buffalo hunt the day before. The men had left again before dawn for another day's hunt. It was summer, the high season for buffalo hunting, while the animals were fat and had not begun to grow their winter hair. Hides were at their prime and the trading post swarmed with activity. Despite the hard work—the animals had to be skinned and cut for drying, the hides tanned to make clothing and blankets—it was White Blossom's favorite time of the year. Dances were held nightly around huge campfires to celebrate the kill and there was great jubilation and gaiety.

White Blossom took a wooden cooking spoon and brought some of the stew to her mouth to taste. She rolled it around on her tongue, and then frowned. It was a little weak. She was just reaching for another handful of herbs to add to the broth when she heard Running Antelope, who had been left behind to guard the camp, call out. "They are back. And they have more kill."

White Blossom stirred the herbs into the stew, then laid aside her spoon and ran to the edge of the clearing to stand beside Running Antelope and watch the arrival of the returning braves.

Usually there was much shouting and bantering among the braves when they returned from a hunt but tonight they seemed unusually quiet.

"Look," Running Antelope cried, pointing to a riderless pony. "Someone is missing."

Just then White Blossom spotted another rider who seemed to be supporting the slumped form of an Indian brave. Running Antelope sucked in a deep breath. "That is Mokiska's pony. He must have been hurt in the hunt. Run and get your mother, White Blossom."

She took off at a run. Windwhisper was the village Shaman, known for her healing powers. Her father before her had been their medicine man and now she was teaching her daughter to take her place. But White Blossom knew she was far from ready to treat such a major injury.

She quickly located her mother and together they ran back to the hunting party. Gently they lowered Mokiska to the ground and Windwhisper bent over him. A dark stain spread over his skin shirt below the shoulder and blood dripped onto the ground.

"You're bleeding, badly," Moonwhisper murmured to him.

He dug his teeth into his lip. "It nothing."

With deft fingers Moonwhisper cut the shirt open to examine the wound. She grabbed a handful of weeds and grass and packed it into the laceration to slow the bleeding. "Help me get him to my hut where I can treat him properly," she ordered as she jumped to her feet. She grabbed White Blossom's wrist. "Come and watch carefully child, Someday you will need my skills."

With his good arm around the shoulder of a young brave for support, his other over White Blossom's thin shoulders they made their way to her cabin.

They laid Mokiska on White Blossom's cot where he lay with eyes closed, his breathing shallow.

"Good," he has gone deep into sleep," Windwhisper said. "It will make it easier to dress his wound." She hurried to a shelf on the wall and brought forth a large basket of herbs and bandages. She rooted through it until she found a large lump of pine tar. She handed it to White Blossom. "Put this in a pot and take it out to the fire to melt. Hurry now, I need it to pack the wound."

White Blossom ran to the fire pit where the stew simmered in its skin sling. She stirred the coals and put the small pot in their midst where the tar quickly began to melt.

As soon as it had become soft she returned with it to the cabin where she found her mother had already removed the temporary packing from the tear in Mokiska's shoulder and cleaned it out. Together they stuffed the pine tar into the wound and White Blossom watched carefully as Windwhisper ran the needle threaded with boiled horse hair through the torn flesh to stitch it back together. She showed White Blossom how to apply a compressing bandage and they were just finishing when Mokiska began to groan as he returned to consciousness.

"Now, he must eat," Windwhisper said. "Get a bowl of that stew you were preparing and feed it to him."

White Blossom returned to the buffalo stomach and ladled some of the fragrant stew into a clay bowl then hurried back to the cabin. Mokiska resisted at first as she spoon fed him but gradually she got him to eat a few bites before he fell asleep again. Gently she spread a blanket over him, tucking it in around his sleeping form, and as she did so she noticed a striking resemblance to the Cherokee who had come to her assistance in the park in Savannah two months ago. She had thought of him often. As she looked at Mokiska she saw the same strong lines of jaw, strongly muscled arms and thighs. He was wearing only a breechclout and as she tucked the blanket around him she found her eyes linger on his hard, corded thighs and the firm, sculpted flesh of his hips. White Blossom felt a strong stirring in her stomach and heat rushed to her face. As her body changed physically she was becoming more and more aware of the wonderful sensations that her body was capable of.

Her mother did not miss her lingering gaze and flushed face and gave her a knowing look. White Blossom turned away in consternation.

Windwhisper rose and placed a hand on her shoulder. "Your feelings are natural, child. With your show of blood last month you have become a woman. You are old enough to love and mate and you must not be ashamed of your natural urges. It is the Great Spirit's wish that woman join with man in the way of all nature."

White Blossom's face flamed and she rose to her feet. She had been thinking about her body a lot lately because she was not sure what these unbidden feelings meant. She wanted to talk more about it to her mother but she was too shy to ask. Still, she had always been able to discuss anything with her.

"I have no interest in Mokiska," she said quietly. "And I'm not sure what love is."

"No, but soon a man will stir these feeling and you will know because a spirit inside will speak to your heart and you will have no doubt." Windwhisper looked at the sleeping brave and smiled gently. "He is strong and hearty, he will heal quickly. Let him sleep." She looked at White Blossom and smiled sweetly. "You will make a good medicine woman someday when I am gone . . . an honor to our tribe."

Impulsively White Blossom threw her arms around her mother. "Don't speak of dying, mother. I could not live without you."

"Of course, you could, little one. You have a strength and wisdom beyond your years . . . I have seen it in you since you were a child. Now let Mokiska sleep and gather your scraping tools. We have much work to do before the festivities tonight."

Each day blended into the next and the months quickly passed. Early in the fall George Plummer turned over operation of the trading post to his wife's brother-in-law and began to make preparations for the journey to Florida.

White Blossom viewed the trip with mixed emotions. Her family had always traveled about and she was eager to see the country but for some reason there was a veil of apprehension surrounding her.

Early on a rainy November morning, using three Creek braves as pathfinders, George, Windwhisper, and White Blossom began to work their way southward on the obscure paths following the Inland Passage. Not far south of St. Marys her father ordered a change of direction to the west. After about ten miles of hard going they came upon a well-marked warpath that scouts told them began near Amelia Island and ended at St. Augustine in Florida. Wearily they trudged on to Amelia arriving late in the evening. It was a large fort, heavily fortified and garrisoned by sixteen Highlanders, a unit of twelve men from Oglethorpe's Forty Second Regiment and a dozen women and children.

It was here that George Plummer sought sanctuary for his party for the night.

Before dawn the next morning about a dozen Yemassee Indians, loyal to the Spanish, beached their dugout canoes on the ocean side of Amelia Island. The warriors cautiously crept through the woods until the stockade on the northwestern end of the island came into view. The war party concealed itself inside a stand of pines near the path that led from the fort and waited for someone to stray into their ambush.

Just after sunup White Blossom rolled out of her warm bed eager to be on her way. Only yesterday her father had stated that it should take just one more day to reach the St. Johns River in Spanish Florida where he intended to stop and set up his trading headquarters. She was tired and foot weary. It would be good to settle down again.

Her mother, squatting beside her, was already rolling up her bedroll.

"Where is father?" White Blossom asked.

"He left with Tomalchi to gather wood for the breakfast fire. Hurry now and secure your bear skin. It is already late." She smiled abashedly. "We lingered longer in bed than we planned."

Suddenly a loud volley of musket fire reverberated in the early morning sky. A chill ran up White Blossom's spine and Windwhisper rushed outside with a startled gasp.

Several soldiers were tearing down the sandy path that led into the pines where the explosions had taken place. Gun smoke hung in the heavy air.

White Blossom and her mother stood huddled together just outside the gate watching the path in stunned silence. "That is the direction your father took," Windwhisper said in a quavering voice.

Somehow they knew.

Minutes that seemed like hours passed and then soldiers could be seen walking up the path carrying the bodies of two men. The blood drained from White Blossom's face as the soldiers drew near, her gaze settling on the bloody clothing of one of the lifeless forms. She immediately recognized the fringed deerskins of her father. Windwhisper rushed forward, her face contorted in agony. She dropped to her knees with a high pitched keen of grief. The soldiers stood motionless.

White Blossom rushed to her side, and then recoiled in horror as she looked down at what had been her handsome father.

He had been beheaded!

Two weeks after her husband had been properly buried Windwhisper met with Captain Hugh Mackay, Jr. to discuss her plight.

They sat facing one another in his small office inside the fort and after polite introductions had been made, Mackay gave her a long, searching look.

"I understand you and your daughter were en route to Florida when this unfortunate tragedy occurred," Mackay said.

"Yes, sir. George planned to trade with the Seminoles there."

"And now what do you wish to do?"

"Return to our village on the Oconee near Savannah."

"You are far from home. It is not safe for two women to travel alone and as you know your two braves have disappeared." Mackay drummed his fingers on the arm of his chair. "General Oglethorpe fears the Spanish may be planning a major raiding effort to destroy Amelia Fort or Fort Saint Andrews. That is why the Yemassee scouts were here. So he is gathering his troops at Fort Frederica for a reconnaissance thrust into Florida. He hopes to raise at least two hundred regulars, some Highlanders from Darien, and several hundred Indians. It will take several months and I expect him to stop here for more recruits. I suggest you wait and accompany his forces to Florida."

"What would we do then? Florida is not our home."

"Take refuge at Fort Mosa and wait for the siege to be over. It was built to protect a village of runaway South Carolina slaves. It's about two miles north of St. Augustine with close to forty Negro families living there. You will be out of danger. Afterwards you can return with the army to Fort Frederica or Darien. You would be in friendly Creek territory and less than one hundred miles from your village."

Windwhisper fingered the long black braid that laid upon

her shoulder deep in thought. Finally she looked up and met Mackay's gaze, her dark eyes etched with sorrow. "It safest way for my daughter. We will wait for soldiers to come."

"Good. You are welcome to stay here in the fort. It may be several months but rest assured Oglethorpe will be here before spring."

"We wait."

White Blossom added another piece of pine to the campfire sending a shower of sparks into the night sky.

"No more," Moonwhisper warned. The woods are tinder dry and the wind is picking up."

"Yes, Mother," White Blossom said softly. She hunkered down by the fire, stretching her toes toward the flames. "I get such comfort from the fire." She ran a browned hand over the skirt of her deerskin dress. "I feel very lonely tonight."

Moonwhisper's face was etched with sorrow. "Your father's death bleeds in my heart as it does yours, little one." She beat her fist against her chest. "I curse the Spirits who took him from us."

White Blossom made no answer. Upriver an alligator bawled and the wind sighed through the cedars. In the flickering firelight White Blossom saw a tear trickle down her mother's cheek. *It was bad enough loosing one's father, but what must it be like to lose one's soul partner*, she wondered. She inched closer to Windwhisper and took her hand.

At least they had each other.

Chapter Four

After three months on the Atlantic, the *Prince Of Wales* sailed into the harbor of Savannah, Georgia. Ian and Cory crowded the rail together with a mixture of excited emigrants: a mariner, a surgeon, several tailors, laborers, servants, a minister and numerous women and children, all eager to make a start in the new world.

"Aye, 'tis a prosperous land," Cory said as his blue eyes swept the semi-circular bay and the bustling dock where ships of all sorts—galleons, trading vessels, stout men-of-war with tall masts, sloops, and three-masted schooners—lay at anchor. "An' smell that soft warm air, won't ye. Why in Glencoe we'd be knee deep in snow drifts."

Ian squinted in the gleaming sunlight. "I never quite believed the recruiter's promise of warm weather all year, but I guess he was right."

They hopped ashore on a dock teeming with activity. Shouts and curses rang out as men hoisted cargo on or off the ships. The clamor was unbelievable: hoists whined, mooring lines moaned, hardware clanged, carts rumbled over the ballast stone roadway, horses whinnied, venders sang out their wares and somewhere in the distance the gong of a bell sounded as a ship made for shore.

Ian and Cory climbed the steep rock steps that led from the wharf to a sandy street where tradesmen scurried in and out of public storehouses. Ian blinked with incredulity at the fever of activity and new construction going on everywhere. The ring of hammers and rasp of saws cut the air as the temporary palm-thatched shelters of the first colonists were replaced by substantial wooden or brick structures. A milkman was selling by the jug on the corner. Children played in a park where flowers bloomed. A dog barked.

"I don't know about ye but I've a powerful hunger for something that isn't dried or salted," Ian said licking his lips as he spied a vender with a wagon piled high with oranges.

"An' I've a mighty thirst," Cory said pointing to a tavern on the corner.

"First, the fruit." Ian walked to the wagon and picked up an orange. He fingered it with raised eyebrows. They were unusually small.

"How many?" The vender asked hopefully.

"Two . . . pick good ones now."

A girl came up beside him and began to carefully examine each fruit for a blemish before placing it in her basket. Without turning his head he watched her from the corner of his eyes. She was truly the loveliest thing he had ever seen. Her blond hair was pulled back and held by a tiny cluster of gardenia blossoms, soft ringlets tumbling to her golden-tanned shoulders. In a soft melodious voice she haggled briefly with the vender. She suddenly seemed aware of his interest and cast a covert glance in his direction. He touched his tam. The hint of a smile quickened her lips before she paid for her purchase and turned away.

Cory poked him in the arm with a wicked grin. "This new world is full o' wondrous things, aye laddie?"

Ian craned his neck to get a last glimpse of the girl as she moved down the street. "Aye an' I'll be on the lookout for that one, again," he promised.

Just then shouts from a nearby knot of people diverted Ian's attention. "Somethin' going on over there," he said nodding toward a nearby hut. The wooden sign read "Murphy's Tavern." Two drunken sailors were swinging their fists to the shouted encouragement of a half-dozen other sailors. Profanity rang in the air. A baker, his hands white with flour, rushed from his shop, patrons from the bar spilled onto the street and children stopped their games to watch the fight.

It ended abruptly when one of the hardy seamen caught an uppercut square on the jaw and sprawled unconscious on the street. One of his buddies slung him over his shoulder and headed for a nearby horse trough.

"I'm much in need of a tankard of rum to wash this orange away," Cory observed. "What say we visit Murphy's now that the fracas is over?"

"Aye . . . and maybe catch up on the current news."

Although early in the day the bar was crowded with sailors and dockworkers. Ian and Cory found a table and Cory strolled over to the barkeep. "Two mugs of rum," he ordered.

The barkeep snorted. "No rum in Georgia, Mister. That there's General Oglethorpe's danged orders. No rum, no slaves, and no lawyers."

Cory shook his head and grinned. "Aye, an 'I'll go along with the part about lawyers. Give us ale, then."

He and Ian were soon on their second tankard, greedily munching thick sandwiches of beef slathered with horseradish between two slices of warm bread. Ian's stomach growled at the richness of the food after months of shipboard fare.

One of two men seated at the next table caught his eye. "You fellows jest in?" the man asked. He was huge with heavy beard shadow, wild curly black hair, and a thick Cockney accent.

Ian dipped his head. "Only hours ago, and glad we are to have our legs on solid ground once more."

"W'ere from?"

"Glencoe . . . the Scottish Highlands. An' ye?"

"The British Cotswold. Been 'ere two mont's."

"What's yer trade?" Cory asked.

"Thatcher. Lots of work wit' all the building going on. Yours?"

"Sheepherders," Ian said. "But I'll be looking for

indentured service somewhere."

The other man at the table spoke up. "Go to the docks, then. Business men, wantin' to pick up indentured workers, interview ever' afternoon down by the river." He pushed lifeless yellow hair from his forehead. "They want five years o' your life."

"You boys look mighty 'ealthy," the black haired man observed. "I 'ear General Oglethorpe is recruitin' 'ard to settle men downriver. Gonna be a war wit' Spain that's for sure. T'ey's already buildin' t'em a fort at the mout' of the Altamaha."

"How far from Savannah is the fort?" Cory asked with interest.

"'Bout ninety miles. 'eard t'ey built a road. First 'ighway in Georgia . . . reaches way from Savannah to Darien."

"I'd like to know more about it," Cory said.

"Don't know much more."

A gray bearded, thickset man at the bar had been listening to their conversation and he picked up his mug and strode over to their table.

"Names, Argus McDermott," he said extending his hand to Cory.

"*Slainte-mhath*, Cory said raising his mug in a toast and motioning to an empty chair.

"I'm garrisoned at Fort King George," Argus said straddling a chair. "I heard ye ask 'bout it."

"I just might be interested."

"Weel, I'm here in Savannah with Captain Stephens to enlist Highlanders willing to man the fort and serve in the Regiment of Foot for the Defense of His Majesty's Plantations in America. We're looking for young, husky men to serve both as homesteaders and soldiers. They've already laid out a wee Scottish settlement named Darien. The fort serves as our southernmost outpost in the colonies."

"Hear tell the Spanish claim that land to be theirs," the yellow haired fellow said running his hand over a jutting chin bristling with stubble.

Argus brushed the comment away with a sweep of his hand. "Darien's good land for the settlin', high and healthy and verra fit for cattle. The wee village stands upon a hill on the northern branch of the Altamaha River and the timber is some of the best in Georgia. Each homesteader is provided a plot of five acres and a years ration of meat and staples to get going. The fort has a battery of four cannon, a guard house, a storehouse, and a place for divine services." He eyed Ian. "Are both of ye boys interested?"

"Not me," Ian stated emphatically. "My Da supported King James during the Jacobite Rebellion and spent four years in prison. If war comes I want no part in it. Besides, I like what I see of Savannah. I want to learn a gentleman's trade and stay here."

But Cory looked at Argus with sparkling blue eyes. "Would me service be indentured?" he asked.

"No, paid by the Crown."

For half an hour Argus talked and Cory asked questions. Finally Ian rose to his feet. "I'm going down to the dock to see what is being offered there," he said. "I'll meet ye back here at sundown and we'll get lodging for the night." He doffed his tam to the men at the table and went out into the bright winter sunshine.

Ian stood on the fringes of a small group of men gathered at the dock around Captain Dunbar, Master of the *Prince Of Wales*. Most arrivals from the ship had been indentured before they left Scotland and claimed by their new masters when their passage was paid. Ian's fare had already been paid when his unexpected turn of fortune occurred. Now he needed money and if he wanted to learn a trade he had to be taken on as an indentured apprentice and soon.

He snapped to attention as an elderly man, portly and bald except for fluffy white puffs of hair over his ears, entered with a girl on his arm. Ian drew a deep breath. It was the girl he had admired at the orange venders that very morning.

The man and girl approached Captain Dunbar and stood in

earnest conversation. The Captain suddenly looked in Ian's direction and his brow wrinkled in thought. Ian could see him purse his lips as the old gentleman waved his arm in agitation. The Captain frowned once more, and then said something to the man who stopped jabbering and turned to look at Ian.

The girl had been standing quietly listening to the conversation and she now turned her eyes in his direction with a small start of recognition.

Captain Dunbar raised his arm and motioned to Ian. He approached eagerly.

The Captain looked at him with speculation. "This is Mr. Gustav Bruner and his daughter, Charlotte. Mr. Bruner is a clockmaker seeking an apprentice. I don't recall your name young man but I believe I heard that you are seeking service."

"Yes, sir, I am. Me name is Ian MacDonald, newly arrived from Glencoe, Scootlan'.'"

"Haf you a trade?" Mr. Bruner asked. He spoke with a thick guttural accent.

"My Clan are sheepherders and husbandmen but I wish to learn a more cultured trade."

"Your age?"

"Twenty, sir."

Mr. Bruner ran a chubby hand over his baldpate and eyed Ian with interest. "Vell, I hoped to find someone younger, but my young apprentice got one of our servant girls in the family vay and ran off. Ya, vought a foolish fellow he vas. I find myself vit no help and a shop full of vork. Are you interested in learning to be a clockmaker? You have intelligent eyes."

Ian felt his heart soar. He struggled to keep from looking at the girl who seemed to be watching him intently. He was far more interested in her than learning to be a clockmaker but a position in the household would certainly suffice.

"What are your terms, sir?" he asked.

"Five years indenture, room and board vit a stipend of two shillings a week."

"That is more than generous. I would be happy to accept." He carefully kept his eyes trained on Mr. Bruner.

"Ya, vell come with us then. Mrs. Bruner vill have the final say but if all goes vell vit her you can start in the morning." He stuck out his hand.

Ian shook the pudgy hand, then that of the Captain with a quiet "thank you." He turned to Charlotte and swept his tam low. She smiled.

He watched them walk away, his heart soaring. God was surely with him on this day.

When Ian and Cory met outside of Murphy's later that evening they both had wide grins on their faces.

"Ye first," Cory said.

"I'm to apprentice as a clockmaker . . . room and board with a five-year indenture."

"A clockmaker! Never knew ye to have any interest in anything as fine as that."

"I dinna tell ye the best part. Remember the girl we saw this morning at the orange stand? Weel, my friend, she's the owner's daughter."

"Cory threw his head back and laughed. "Ye needn't say more, Laddie."

"And you? What about you, mon?"

"I'm to be a homesteader at Darien and a recruit in the Scottish Highlander Forty-Second Regiment of Foot. I leave at dawn."

Ian clapped Cory on the shoulder. "It's to be a partin' of the ways for us then."

"Not forever. Georgia is a small colony. Ye ken our paths will cross again."

"Ye will always be my best friend, Cory. Remember the blood pact we made as children—brothers as long as we live?"

Cory grabbed Ian and hugged him. "I remember. Now let's go into Murphy's and toast our good fortune."

"And our future . . . may it be as bright and full of promise as today."

* * *

It was at the dinner table in the Brunner home that the surreptitious glances between Ian and Charlotte began to take on meaning. Then Ian noticed that she seemed to find more and more excuses to visit the shop on small errands. He was always aware, however, of Mr. Bruner's watchful eyes and was careful not to show too much interest in the beautiful girl.

But it was very, very hard.

He had been indentured only a month when Charlotte appeared one afternoon with a basket on her arm. A frown creased her brow when she noticed her father's empty stool.

"Where's Poppa?" she asked. "Mother sent out some warm scones and clotted cream."

"He went over to the Fitzgerald's house to pick up a Grandmother clock that is not working." Ian gave her a crooked grin. "But I'll be only too glad to share the scones with you if you'll join me."

She gave him a pretty smile and readily lifted the checkered napkin covering the scones. With a flourish she spread the cloth on an empty table where she placed the scones, cream and a small pot of jam.

Ian pulled two stools to the table and after she had settled on one he inched his closer to where she sat. "Hmm," he said lifting a scone to his nose, "these smell delicious."

"Mother let me help with the baking." She smiled and dropped her gaze demurely. "She said I must know how to cook if I'm to make a man a good wife someday."

"You'll make some lucky fellow a bonny wife whether you can cook or not," Ian said with a smile as he slathered jam on a second scone. "I don't want to appear forward but I'd like to ask if anyone is courting you."

"Not at the present," she said looking flustered.

"Then I have a chance?"

Charlotte patted her lips with a napkin and looked him full in the eye. "You won't know till you try," she said with a mischievous grin.

Just then the door opened and Mr. Bruner walked into the shop. His eyebrows bunched as he looked at the two of them sharing the tea. It was obvious that he did not approve.

"Father," Charlotte said brightly, "mother sent some fresh scones out for your afternoon tea. Since you weren't here I offered to share them with Ian while they were warm."

"Ach, vell now that you have done so, young lady, I suggest you pack your basket and let the boy get back to his vork."

Charlotte blushed at his rudeness and jumped to her feet. As Mr. Bruner walked away she began to repack her basket and she peeked at Ian from under long lashes. "We'll talk again," she whispered.

His heart thudded in his chest as he watched her walk away with a voluptuous sway. *We certainly will*, he thought smiling jauntily.

Ian bided his time waiting for the right opportunity to speak to Charlotte again. From his bedroom window he could look into the garden below and quite often he saw her stroll among the roses just at twilight. One evening shortly after their repast at the shop he could withstand the temptation no longer and hurried outside to join her. He waited until she had reached a place on the path hidden from view of the house by a tall stand of bamboo before he approached her.

"Good evening, Miss Charlotte."

She jumped slightly and then dimpled sweetly. "What a pleasant surprise. It is a delightful evening for a stroll is it not."

"Aye, that it is."

"Are you interested in the roses?"

"No. You."

A faint flush appeared on her face and she gazed at him candidly, her eyes glinting with pleasure. Brown eyes, they were, framed by thick lashes, sultry and robust with life. Her golden hair glinted with fire from the last rays of the sun, the humid heat causing tiny tendrils to curl around her face. She was dressed in the latest fashion, a creation of deep blue silk with a scooped neck and mutton sleeves. The bodice was encrusted with little pearls and rows of ruffles.

Charlotte raised a paper fan and waved it back and forth. "It's very humid this evening. Have you become accustomed to our southern weather yet?"

"No, I don't know that I'll ever get accustomed to it. I think one only learns to tolerate it."

"Do you miss Scotland?"

"At times. Not the weather, certainly, but I do miss the beauty of the Highland's and I miss my family."

"I heard you mention a brother, once."

"William. I have only one. My mother died of milk fever shortly after he was born. Da raised both of us boys."

"How sad . . . not to have a mother I mean. A family needs the gentling influence of a woman."

Ian looked at her tenderly. "As does a man need a woman in his life."

Charlotte busied herself with her fan and did not answer but he noticed her face flush prettily. He moved closer to her so that they were almost touching and began to walk slowly along the path. "There is a party at Major Regor's next Saturday and I would like to take you if you have no escort. Do you think your father would give his permission?"

Charlotte chewed on her lip and her face grew pensive. "Oh, Ian, I'm afraid not. He had mother speak to me after he saw us eating together in the shop. Since you are bound in his service and we live under the same roof he thinks of you as an unsatisfactory suitor."

"And I'm poor," Ian said bitterly.

"In all honesty, I'm sure that is a factor."

Ian felt waves of disappointment wash over him and bunched his fists as he stared morosely at the ground. There had been rain earlier in the day and under his shadow the smell of damp earth was sweet where their feet had disturbed it. A robin called, answered by the sweet chirp of a house finch.

Charlotte broke the heavy silence. "I would like to get to know you better, Ian, whether father approves or not. Can we meet like this from time to time just to talk? There is a bench behind the arbor, shielded from view of the house."

Ian looked at her lovely face washed in pale moonlight and ached with an inner longing. He knew he couldn't say no. Whatever the cost to his pride he had to pursue this girl.

"When?" he asked in a tight voice.

"Father has a meeting at the German Club on Wednesday evenings and mother usually retires early. Wait for it to get dark and then meet me there."

He reached out and took her slender hand, raising it to his lips. It was all he could do to keep from gathering her into his hungry arms.

But if he read the look in her eyes correctly, dark and smoldering, that intimacy would come later.

Ian thought often of Cory and wondered how he was fairing. Ian was learning his trade and considered himself well on his way to becoming a master clockmaker. He often chafed at his indentured status and admitted that his temperament did not lend itself well to the confines of an indoor job, but Charlotte more than made up for any feelings of discontent.

He and Charlotte were meeting every chance they got. They were in love, very much in love. But it was necessary to meet in secret and that bothered Ian.

Mr. Bruner openly expressed his displeasure of the noticeable attraction of his daughter to an indentured servant from the Scottish Highlands. The affluent of Savannah were quickly reestablishing the elegant and sophisticated customs of London society and Ian was well aware that Gustav had high hopes for his beautiful daughter's future marriage to a man of wealth and position.

Chapter Five

Ian was tired of settling for a few stolen Wednesdays. Full of determination he dressed carefully and then crept quietly down the garden path that led to the secluded arbor tucked into a dark corner at the far end of the Bruner garden. It was their special point of rendezvous and it was here that he planned to propose.

Charlotte was sitting on a stone bench anxiously twisting a lace handkerchief as she peered into the darkness watching for him.

Nature could not have gifted them with a more perfect night. A full moon cast its silvery glow on the hidden arbor. A gentle breeze set the gray-green moss of the surrounding live oaks to sway in the cool night air scented with the sweet fragrance of late blooming roses.

"Darling," she whispered when she saw his shadowy form emerge from the darkness. She stood and reached out to draw him to her and he walked into her embrace his eyes shinning with pleasure. Her head nestled beneath his chin and he felt the slimness of her waist as his arms encircled her. He was acutely aware of her heartbeat, aware of his sudden unsteady breathing.

Her golden-blond hair was arranged with a mass of curls on top of her head, gathered into long ringlets that hung down to her shoulders. Tonight she wore a gown of rose brocade. The bodice with boned stays came to a point at her narrow waist and the overskirt was parted in the front to reveal a separate pattered underskirt. The neckline was low, cut square, and more than hinted at her ample bosom. Ian caught his breath and clenched his fists.

His hand slid down her back and lingered, pulling her tighter to his body.

"We had better stop, Ian," she said breathlessly.

"This feels right."

"This feels dangerous."

He kissed her behind her ear, then his lips worked their way down her throat. He kept his hand where it was. He could feel her pulse pounding and knew she was as aroused as he. "Charlotte, Charlotte," he murmured. "I want more than these clandestine meetings. We must find a way to meet somewhere more private. I need you. I want you."

"I want you, too," she said softly.

His mouth settled on hers.

Her lips parted slightly and his tongue slid along the seam of her mouth. She shuddered, then pushed against his chest with her fists and drew back. "What are you doing, Ian?" she asked breathlessly.

"I'm kissing you."

"I don't think I'm ready for that kind of kiss."

His lips curved into a smile. "I think you are." Their lips met again and held in growing heat. With a leaping heart he saw the longing mirrored on her beautiful face. Forcing himself to pull back he whispered, "I love you, Charlotte."

"I love you too, Ian."

He took her small hand in his and pulled her down on the bench. "I want to marry you, Charlotte."

"And I want to marry you too. But it's . . . complicated."

"Complicated?"

She pulled away and looked into his eyes. "Yes . . . complicated. Father has his heart set on my coming out in the fall. Savannah is planning its first debutante ball, similar to the one held in Charlestown last year."

"And you? Is that what you want?"

Her lips trembled and tears glistened in her brown eyes. "Oh, no, Ian. It's you I want. Kiss me, again. Hard!"

He lowered his head and she raised her mouth to his. He felt her shudder. It would be so easy to give way to passion. And so dangerous.

"Oh, Ian," she said when at last they pulled apart. I want us to be happy."

"We will be, if you'll say yes. We can leave Savannah. I can get a job in Charlestown or somewhere else in the colonies. Your father won't find us until it's too late."

"How can you be sure?"

He closed his eyes. How could he know the future? Nothing in life was certain. But they loved one another and love would find the way.

"Trust me, Charlotte. Trust our love."

"I won't run away, but I will pledge myself to you. Only it will have to be a secret . . . at least for now."

Ian swallowed hard. Was he willing to settle for that?

Yes, he thought, *if that's the only commitment I can get at the moment.*

He held her hand and drank in every expression that flickered across her beautiful face in the soft moonlight. The sky pulsed with stars, the night balmy and soft. Charlotte fell silent and Ian put his arms across her shoulders and drew her closer. "We are engaged, then," he said in a shaky voice. He dipped his head and his lips found hers.

The kiss started slowly, then her mouth parted slightly and his tongue brushed the opening. Ian felt a quiver of anticipation arc through him all the way to his toes and his arms crushed her to him as she responded with a groaning sound deep in her throat.

A sudden crunch of gravel on the walkway caused them to jump apart.

Ian froze. A large, hulking figure clothed in a flowing black cloak stomped toward them.

"*Mein Gott*! Vot is this?" Charlotte's father shouted as he planted his feet and glared down at them.

Ian took Charlotte's trembling hand in his. "I am courting your daughter, sir," he said.

"My permission you did not ask."

"Then may I court Charlotte, sir?"

"NO!"

Ian's face hardened and he gritted his teeth. "May I ask why?"

"Charlotte knows the answer. Ve talk many times."

"But, daddy . . ."

"No argument." He grabbed her arm and yanked her to her feet. "You come home vit me, now. Your mama vill give you a good talking to. You are much too young to be kissing a man in the dark." He wagged a finger at Ian. "My hospitality you have tested," he said coldly. "If I see you mit my daughter again you vill be gone."

With Charlotte in tow he stalked away.

Ian ran an agitated hand through his hair. Unable to sleep he had been lying on his cot for hours. Inwardly he trembled with rage. It was obvious that Gustav did not consider him good enough for his daughter. For an instant he was tempted to chuck the whole thing—to run away from his indenture and find adventure in this rugged new land. But this is where he needed to be if he wanted to claim Charlotte as his bride. And he did want her to be his wife. He wanted no other, could love no other as he loved her.

He did not worry that Gustav would dismiss him. Gustav would be hard pressed to find a replacement as good as he. As long as he and Charlotte kept their meetings secret all should be well. Ian clenched his jaw. He would show him. He would work night and day, if that's what it took, to become a master clockmaker. He would strive to lose his brogue and put aside the kilt that marked him as different, even though Charlotte seemed fascinated by both. When he finished his apprenticeship she would be of age to marry, his success would be complete, his independence assured. He could look Gustav Brunner in the eye and tell him in no uncertain terms where to go.

He punched the pillow into a ball under his head and tried to find a comfortable spot on the thin mattress. He doubted he would get much sleep tonight. But tomorrow he would tackle his job with renewed vigor—he would learn everything he could about his craft. It was important to him to make something of himself, to prove that he had been right to leave his homeland and come to America.

He and Charlotte would have to be more careful. They would have to find a new place to meet.

The next morning Ian scowled at his reflection as he combed his unruly hair. It was too long, hanging on his shoulders and curling over his ears. He didn't look so slick this morning, his eyes puffy and red from lack of sleep. He looked like he had a hangover.

Mr. Bruner gave him a curt nod when he entered the shop and without a word Ian walked to his workbench. He had been crafting a handsome grandfather clock for Major Regor and it stood complete except for the finish stain. He ran his hands over the satiny grain of the wood, amazed that his hands were capable of such fine work.

For the next hour he busied himself securing the proper rags and brushes, opening cans of turpentine and linseed oil, preparing the stain. Not a word had been spoken.

Several times Ian noticed Gustav staring off into space, his hands quiet, and a dark scowl on his face. It was mid-morning when his employer finally laid his tools aside, lifted his cap from a hook on the wall, and lumbered to the door.

"I haf business down at the docks," he said, throwing the remarks over his shoulder. "If customers ask for me, tell them to come back tomorrow." With that he slammed the door shut.

Ian became more and more apprehensive as he worked alone through the warm afternoon and Mr. Bruner did not return. Maybe he wasn't as irreplaceable as he thought. A cold dread filled his stomach. How could he possibly see

Charlotte if he were no longer employed at the Bruner's? At closing he locked the shop and, as was often his custom, walked the short distance to Murphy's Tavern for a pint before supper.

Ian stood at the end of a small bar staring morosely at his drink. The din of voices rose and fell like waves before an impending storm, washing the far corners of the murky taproom crowded with sailors and dock workers.

He missed Cory fiercely. What he wouldn't do to be able to discuss his thwarted love affair with his friend.

An Indian, dressed in fringed leggings and a tunic of deer hide pushed in beside him and ordered a drink. Ian noticed a furtive look pass between him and barkeep and wondered at it. Maybe they were not supposed to serve heathen Indians.

Around the tavern conversation ebbed and flowed. Curses and drunken laughter filled the room that reeked of unwashed bodies, yeasty ale and stale tobacco.

"Day mighty hot," the Indian said, wiping a grimy hand across his forehead.

Ian merely nodded.

The man set his full mug on the bar so close to Ian's they almost touched. Ian frowned. The Indian seemed to be standing closer to him than was necessary and his odor was repulsive.

A sudden altercation erupted at the back of the tavern and Ian turned away to watch. When he turned back to claim his drink the Indian was gone.

Thank heavens, he thought. He didn't really like Indians, in fact he detested them. And Mr. Bruner was always telling stories about their atrocious scalping of the enemy.

He downed his drink, grimacing at the bitter taste. It must be the bottom of the barrel. Nevertheless, he dreaded going home, dreaded facing the family at the table with forced conversation. So he ordered another pint. The noise level had increased as more workers, freed from their day's labor, stopped for a drink before going home for dinner. His eyes raked the smoky interior looking for a familiar face but found none. *Funny,* he thought, *the interior is more than smoky . . . it is downright cloudy.* Faces began to waver as though underwater. His knees felt like rubber and he grasped the bar for support.

And then everything went black.

The rhythmical snapping of sails and the screech of a gull slowly worked their way into Ian's consciousness. The air was filled with the pungent scent of seaweed and fish. As he blinked his eyelids and lifted his head to look about he dimly saw the figure of a man approaching.

Frowning, the man stopped and looked down at him.

"Where am I?" Ian croaked.

"Aboard the *Safire* bound for Fort King George at Darien."

Ian shook his head trying to clear the cobwebs. A wave of nausea rocked him and he clenched his jaw fighting the urge to vomit. "How did I get here?" he asked.

"'Tis a mystery, it is. We found you lying in a heap, amid a pile of discarded sail in the hold of the ship. We were well out to sea and had no thought of turning back. I assume you were shanghaied but by no man aboard this ship. We need recruits but that is not our method. I would guess someone harbors a huge dislike for you and decided to rid himself of your presence."

Suddenly it all made sense—Mr. Bruner's unexplained disappearance from the shop, the presence of the Indian at the bar, the bitter taste of the drink he was served. His employer had indeed decided to rid himself of a pesky problem.

Ian looked more closely at the man standing before him. He was a thin, wiry man, no more than fifty, with a goatee which he kept stroking. Ian noticed that he wore a black-watch tartan, the military issue of the Scots Highlanders.

He stuck out his hand. "Ian MacDonald," he said.

The man grasped it firmly. "Lieutenant Charles Mackay, commander of the Highland Independent Company of Foot garrisoned at Fort King George." His gaze swept Ian's well muscled frame from head to foot and seemed to register approval. "I realize you are here under duress but we are in need of men like you to fortify our presence in Georgia. Are you aware that war has broken out between Spain and England?"

"War? I knew that ownership of the land south of the Altamaha was debatable but I didn't know we had gone to war over it."

"Not specifically over that land. A pirate by the name of Jenkins was waylaid by the Spaniards. They cut his ear off and he took it and waved the danged thing in front of the fancy British Parliament. It was just the excuse the bloody politicians were looking for. They got all fired up and declared war on Spain." He laughed and pulled on his goatee. "They're callin' it the War of Jenkins Ear."

"I want no part of war," Ian said emphatically. "My father was imprisoned during the Jacobite Rebellion for his loyalty to the Stuarts."

"This is different though. It's not a matter of political infighting for power. The Spanish wish to invade the Carolina's and annex the entire coastal area south of Charlestown to Florida. We must defend our settlers. Strong defenses are called for."

"I have a friend who answered your call a year ago. Cory MacGrath. Do you know him?"

"Indeed I do. A fine man."

Ian's face broke into a smile. Distressful as this whole affair was he looked forward to seeing Cory, once more.

The Captain began to walk away. "I must leave you," he said briskly. "Talk to your friend and look around Darien. I think you will like what you see. The town sits on a hill on the northern branch of the Altamaha River. High and healthy, very fit for cattle. The land near the river is very fruitful with lots of game, particularly turkeys. In the meantime you can give us a hand as we dock. We can use help with the ropes. I'll talk with you later."

With that he was gone and Ian hurried to give what

assistance he could.

Ian climbed ashore at the little village of Darien and looked about him quizzically. Scots in their colorful Highland dress came to help unload goods and pick up mail from home. They greeted him in their heavy Gaelic dialect and it was good to hear the language of his homeland.

When all was unloaded the soldiers began a short trek along the edge of the marsh to Fort King George which soon came into view. The three-story blockhouse was square with diamond shaped bastions protruding from each corner, two on the landside and two on the marsh. It was surrounded by an earthen wall and stockade and seemed quite substantial.

Ian assisted in the stowing of supplies and then was shown to quarters in the bunkhouse. He freshened up as best he could, having no change of clothing, before setting off to find his friend, Cory.

He found him standing sentry at the north parapet. The look on Cory's face changed from one of incredulousness and surprise to one of joy and excitement. He leaped down from the parapet and grabbed Ian in a fierce bear hug.

"Great jumpin' Jehoshaphats," he cried. "What are ye doing here?"

"I came to join the army," Ian joked. At the look on Cory's face he hurried to add, "It's a long story. When do you get off duty?"

Cory glanced at the sun which was just disappearing over the horizon. "Soon." He pointed to a huge cedar tree just outside the wall of the fort. "I must get back to me post but wait for me over by that cedar. We'll walk into Darien. The Widow Leader operates a wee tavern there and ye can tell me yer story . . . which, by the way, I hope includes the news that ye are here to stay."

An hour later, over their third tankard of ale, Ian finished his tale of frustrated love.

"From what ye told me, Ian, I believe that the mon will

stop at nothin' to keep you from his daughter. Ye should stay here . . . join the Forty-Second Regiment of Foot . . . and give the situation time t' cool off."

"Aye, maybe."

"Do ye have a way to stay in touch wi' Charlotte?"

"She has a good friend who knows about our secret meetings and is sympathetic to our situation. We could probably exchange letters through her."

"I'd do that, then . . . at least for now. Why don't ye talk to Captain Mackay tomorrow and see if he canna use ye."

Ian ran his hand through his thick hair and downed the last drop of ale in his mug. He squinted at Cory and then winked. "I'll do that. I rather like the look of your jaunty Highlander uniforms. Maybe I've been missing my calling after all."

Charlotte settled herself on the garden bench and eagerly tore open the letter from Ian that had arrived in today's mail. She scanned it quickly and then reread it a second time more slowly. She had been so afraid of his reaction to her letter telling him of her father's part in having him removed from Savannah. But Ian seemed very understanding . . . not angry at all. In fact that worried her a little and she read his letter for a third time.

She remembered her own fury when she overhead Poppa telling her mother how he had arranged to have Ian's drink powdered and have him put aboard a ship bound for Darien. Poppa was determined to separate them before things got really serious and she was not surprised to find that her mother agreed. Even so, it was a terrible thing to do.

Charlotte's eyes misted. She loved Ian so much. At times she thought she would die with longing. She remembered every detail of the way his lips clung to hers, of the way his body felt when pressed against hers. How could she possibly wait two years for him to come to claim her? She pondered the possibility of running away and going to join him but, of course, that was impossible.

The thing that really worried her, though, was the fact that his letters seemed to indicate that he was actually enjoying the life of a soldier. Life on a military outpost was certainly not in her plans. Someday she intended to take her rightful place in Savannah society. She pictured Ian MacDonald at her side—handsome and intelligent—a full partner in her father's business. Poppa would come around once she and Ian were married.

She was sure of it!

Chapter Six

St. Augustine, Florida - 1740

White Blossom cowered behind a mutilated mattress, its moss stuffing splattered with blood. Her mother's head lay cradled in her lap, silent and waxen in death. Acrid smoke from the smoldering fort stung the girl's eyes, searing her nostrils and streaking her face. *Had the Spanish barbarians left anyone alive?*

For hours the St. Augustine sky had reverberated with the sound of pounding cannon and cracking muskets. Now, only her labored breathing broke the silence. From behind the mattress her wild eyes raked the room. Smoke shrouded the air, wrapping its ghostly tentacles around the lifeless English soldiers. Her eyes darted maniacally, picking objects out of the gloom. Should she try to reach the musket protruding from the hand of a dead Scots Highlander several feet from where she crouched on the floor? Could she fire it? Maybe she wouldn't have to. An enemy might back away from its wicked looking bayonet.

Tenderly, she stroked Windwhisper's hair, then gently lowered her mother to the floor. Fighting spasms of grief-stricken nausea she pulled the protruding shaft of an arrow from the motionless chest and threw it on the ground. Sobbing she edged herself from the protection of the ragged mattress and crawled toward the musket.

The Highlander lay face down, his kilt askew, a sun-bronzed arm outstretched, his fist clutching the musket.

White Blossom felt strangely disembodied as she reached with trembling fingers to unfold his hand, then, with a sickening wave of terror churning in her belly, she heard him groan and felt his fingers tighten on the stock of the gun.

He was alive!

She sank back on her heels, uncertain what to do. The Scots Highlanders were part of the invading British forces encamped here at Fort Mosa so not really her enemy. When the invading British forces reached St. Augustine she and her mother had taken refuge at the fort. Now, her mother was dead at the hand of a Yemassee scout for the Spanish and she might be too if the Highlander thought she meant to harm him. She knew that all Indians looked alike to the white man.

He was beginning to move and rolled over, struggling to sit upright. Blood gushed from a deep gash on his temple. Without thinking of the danger White Blossom removed her apron and pressed the soft doeskin firmly against his forehead.

He looked at her through bleary eyes, his face ashen, his head wobbling dangerously. White Blossom grasped it firmly and applied more pressure to the wound.

"Wha' . . .?" he gasped.

"Shhh."

"Who . . .?"

"My name is White Blossom. I am a friend."

He blinked with surprise. "You speak English?" His voice was strained, barely a whisper. "You look Indian."

She saw the disdain in his eyes. She had seen that look many times.

"I am half white."

"Yemassee?"

"No, Muskegon. My people support the British. The Yemassee led the attack against you. They are aligned with the Spanish, are they not?"

He did not answer. His green eyes were clouded with pain and he clamped them shut as he sagged against her. He was a large man, square of shoulder, with heavily muscled legs and she strained to support his weight. The bleeding had slowed, but he had lost a lot of blood. If the head injury was serious he would surely die without help. She chewed on her lower lip. Had any of the British escaped? The Spanish assault had come in the middle of the night when they were all sleeping and the sky was now beginning to lighten in the east. If she were to get help she would have to leave him and find the rest of the British army before dawn.

White Blossom dragged a blanket from a pile on the floor and covered the unconscious soldier. Then, with eyes brimming she took a second blanket and covered the body of her mother, kneeling to say a silent prayer. Slowly she rose to her feet and with a growing sense of urgency bolted out of the door and ran to the back of the fort. Stumbling in her haste she climbed the palisade, a six-foot high fence of cedar posts, and looked across the moat encircling the fort. Thankfully it was devoid of tidal water. She clambered down an embankment and slogged across the moat's muddy bottom until she reached firm ground on the other side.

White Blossom ran, fleet as her Indian ancestors, her moccasins silent on the leaf-strewn path. Branches pulled strands of hair loose from her long, black braid, prickly saw palmetto fronds slashed her arm, drawing blood, and her nostrils flared, tasting the scent of pine, leaf mold and lingering gun smoke.

Instinctively, she followed the St. Mark's River that coursed through piney woods as it snaked toward St. Augustine hoping to bypass the Spanish stronghold at the heavily fortified Castillo de San Marcos. It was here that the Negro inhabitants of Fort Mosa had taken refuge. Suddenly she froze. Loud voices shattered the stillness. She slid behind a stand of bamboo, struggling to quiet her breathing as her eyes scanned the forest.

Spanish! The voices were Spanish!

Bile rose in her throat. The enemy was near. Her heart was making such a loud thumping noise in her chest she feared they must surely hear her. She squared her shoulders and began to run once more through the dark forest, avoiding the path now, keeping to the cover of the trees and forcing herself through tangled vines and wild underbrush. Deerskin leggings protected her legs but her arms got a further lashing from cutbrier and blackberry thorns. Insects whined about her head and a covey of excited quail exploded from a nearby thicket.

On she ran, desperate now for friendly human contact.

The woods suddenly gave way to an eerie swamp and White Blossom stopped with a shudder. The swamp, lined with cypress pushing their knobby knees above the water, its seductive black water a labyrinth of secret passageways for alligators and snakes terrified her. Even so, she could see the smoke of a camp on the other side of the swamp and what appeared to be British Redcoats. If she wanted to secure help for the wounded soldier she had no choice but to forge ahead.

White Blossom picked up a fallen tree limb, using it to probe the water ahead of her as she walked. Her eyes scanned the swamp searching for the safest route. She would keep to the edge—if she crossed in the middle she would surely sink in quicksand and drown.

She bit her lip as she began to plod her way through the muck-filled, mosquito-infested mangroves, probing the water side to side with the stick before each step. The carrion-stink of decayed animals and the rotting vegetation made her stomach heave and she stifled a scream when something live and warm bumped against her leg. She debated closing her eyes and simply hurtling herself blindly toward the distant shore when she suddenly slid to a stop. Just ahead she saw the water move and two eyes gleam through the murky light.

At first she thought it was an alligator but when she could slow her breathing and focus her eyes she saw it was only a deer. The deer was submerged. Only its nose, eyes, and the tops of its ears were visible above the stagnant water in the slough. She had apparently spooked it when she emerged from the woods. She said a small prayer of thanks that it wasn't an alligator and biting her lips continued on doggedly.

A persuasive sun was rising, laying claim to a new day,

when she finally made the shore. The British encampment was dead ahead.

A guard sat astride a large horse blocking the road, rifle drawn.

"Halt!" he barked.

She jerked to a stop and stood before him, dripping mud and slime. He gawked in disbelief as his eyes took in her bedraggled appearance. She rapidly began to relate her story of the wounded soldier at Ft. Mosa.

"Please," she begged "You need to send someone at once. Let me talk to one of your generals."

"Come with me."

The guard rode beside her until they came to a tent where a group of officers were huddled around a map.

"Wait here," the guard ordered. He approached a slight man sitting at the far end of the table and spoke, gesturing at White Blossom. The man nodded to the sentry who returned and took her firmly by the elbow. "Mr. Calwell, an engineer in General Oglethorpe's expedition, will talk with you." With a look of distaste he let go of her elbow and wiped his hand on his pants.

John Calwell was a clean-shaven, man of middle age with a thin mouth and a stern countenance. He wore a powdered wig and was not in uniform.

He held White Blossom with suspicious eyes. "How do I know your story is not a ploy to lead us into a trap, young lady?" he asked, his voice thick with insinuation.

White Blossom swallowed dryly. How could she answer such a question? How could she convince this man that the situation was urgent?

"I can offer you no proof, sir," she finally stammered. "Only the blood on my dress and the fact that I speak English, not Spanish, shows you the truth."

Calwell stared into her eyes, then nodded, apparently satisfied with the honesty he saw reflected there.

"Notify General Oglethorpe that I am dispatching a small rescue party to Fort Mosa," he barked to the guard who stood watching them. "And escort this girl to one of the tents where she can be held until our party returns safely."

"Please sir," Tabitha implored. "I wish to go with you. My mother is among the dead and I want to see to her burial."

"Then at least clean yourself off," he said gruffly. "We will leave as soon as I can assemble a few men." He gave her a half smile. "And help yourself to some coffee and a few corn cakes. You look half starved."

To White Blossom's relief they furnished her with a pony and took the land route back to the fort. They found the Highlander lying in a pool of blood. He was alive, though barely. She heard him addressed as Lieutenant Ian MacDonald and she hurried to his side. Ian's green eyes were unfocused, his red hair matted with blood, his wound bleeding freely. She dropped to her knees beside him, took his hot hand in hers and began to softly chant an old Indian incantation for healing.

He jerked away shooting her a startled look.

White Blossom sank back on her haunches. She did not wish to frighten him. There was a prayer in her Christian Bible, Ezekiel 16:6, that was said to stop bleeding and she began to mouth it instead. She felt an unreasonable urgency for this young man to live. Why had he become so important to her?

One of the soldiers who had accompanied them from the British camp, a burly man also dressed in a kilt, pushed her aside and, speaking soft words of encouragement, held a flask of whiskey to the Lieutenant's mouth. White Blossom saw the flash of recognition in the wounded man's eyes as he ran his tongue around his lips.

"Cory?" he muttered. "Is it really you, mon?"

"Aye, 'tis me."

Lieutenant MacDonald squinted through the blood trickling into his eye. "Cory," she heard him mutter with an oath, "I'll get those red Savages for this!"

The Scotsman nodded with just a hint of a smile. "Hang on, now, Laddie," he said, as he began to swath Ian's head in bandages. "At least ye still have yer scalp, bloody as it is." He turned to one of the soldiers standing nearby and barked, "Get the Lad on a litter and oout of here."

White Blossom watched them carry him out, and although their meeting had been brief, she felt a tug at her heart as she watched him go. She wondered if he would escape the next battle—wondered if she would ever see him again. Probably not. Young as she was she understood that life was like that. Chance encounters can sear indelible memories on your brain, but are seldom revisited.

She looked across the ravaged room and silently mourned the dead around her. Most were British soldiers but a few were women and children who, like her and her mother, had taken refuge in the fort. Against the wall where she sat she saw a baby, clinging to his mother, both of them lifeless and covered with blood.

The soldiers immediately set about the grisly task of burying what was left of their comrade's bodies as quickly as possible.

White Blossom squatted on the floor beside Windwhisper and gently removed the torn blanket from her face. Sightless eyes stared up at her and with a startled gasp she almost dropped the blanket back into place. With trembling fingers she closed the opaque, black eyes then took her mother's hands, callused and work-worn, and folded them across her lifeless chest. Soot and traces of blood caked Windwhisper's face. White Blossom crept to the body of a dead soldier and removed a canteen from his belt, then ripped a piece of cloth from his tunic. She scrambled back to her mother and, after pouring water over the bit of cloth to dampen it, began to wipe her face.

Tenderly she moved the cloth over the broad features, around the small nose and then into the lifelines creasing her mother's cheeks and mouth. White Blossom's tears dripped onto the beloved face and she gave a loud sob, stopping her ministrations until she could gain control of herself.

Finally, she re-covered the body and stood, her back

straight, her chin jutted defiantly. She would ask for water and oil to bathe her mother properly and a clean blanket to wrap her in for burial. They owed her that much!

Later that day White Blossom stood beside her mother's body. The customary preparations for burial had been completed. She had bathed her, painted her face, and sealed her eyes with clay. Tenderly she drew Windwhisper's knees up to her chest, bent her head forward, and wrapped her in a blanket the soldiers had provided. Burial would be at dawn.

The next morning White Blossom stood beside her mother's burial mound brushing away the tears that streaked her own dirty face. From a small leather pouch she removed four kernels of corn and arranged them in a careful pattern on the ground. She began to rock back and forth on her knees and, in a singsong voice, she crooned an old Creek chant,

"From the four corners of the earth, I will
Remember you . . . north, from whence all good
Things come; east, where the sun begins its daily
Journey; west, from whence all darkness of heart
Rest; and south, where memories are born and birds
Soar."

White Blossom stood tall, lifting her face to the sun, her hands outstretched to the heavens. "Oh, Great Spirit of my mother's ancestors . . . and God of the white man . . . bless her in her gentle sleep. Carry her on the wings of morning to her final resting place."

* * *

"How old are you, child?" General Oglethorpe asked White Blossom standing before him with downcast eyes.

"Fourteen, sir."

"And I understand both of your parents are dead. Where is your home, my dear?"

"I have no real home, sir. We last lived at Tustacatty in Georgia but my father was a trader with the Indians and we moved wherever his travels took him."

"No relatives?"

"None that wish to claim me." She looked at him with defiance. "I am a half-breed."

Oglethorpe sighed. "Then we must find a solution to your predicament, young lady."

White Blossom watched him anxiously.

General Oglethorpe was not what one would call a handsome man, but he had a commanding physique, a long aristocratic nose and eyes that showed compassion. He rubbed his chin and gave her a guarded smile. "John Calwell was impressed by your courage and loyalty in seeking aid for Lieutenant MacDonald and has graciously offered to give you a position as an indentured servant in his home. You'll find Mr. Calwell to be a kind man and a fair employer. He has a large house in Georgia at Fort Frederica, three children and several other servants. Frederica is a walled town protected by the fort. You will be safe there."

White Blossom caught her breath. Safe! She had heard that before. At the same time this was her chance to return to her father's people, to the white man's world, although now she would be an indentured servant, no longer free. Could she possibly give up a life that was one with nature, allowing her to roam wherever the seasons took her as she and her parents had done? Did she want a life, bound to a strange family, in a walled town? In any case what choice did she have? She'd learned early on that her life would never be like that of anyone else. To think of traveling by herself to her Indian village over two hundred miles north was foolhardy at best. She choked back her anger, once more caught between two worlds, not welcome in either.

Oglethorpe was watching her, waiting for her answer, an encouraging smile on his lips. She had to make a decision, and quickly. At least haven at Fort Frederica would offer her protection until she could plan her future.

"May I ask how long I would be indentured, sir?"

"Of course," Oglethorpe said with a smile. "Four years, child."

Four years. She would be eighteen then, old enough to wed. She felt her heart flutter. *Was the handsome Highlander garrisoned at Frederica?* Silently she chided herself for such thoughts. Her mother had been buried only yesterday, she was being offered sanctity in an English home, and a chance to establish herself permanently in one place. She should drop down on her knees and thank God for her good fortune and here she was thinking of a soldier she knew nothing about.

White Blossom clasped her hands to keep them from trembling. *Lord*, she prayed, *let me trust that you are guiding me, that this is your will.* Then, with her spine straight and her gaze steady, she looked into the questioning eyes of the tall general. The corners of her mouth lifted in a nervous smile and she said, "You are most kind, sir. I will be happy to serve Mr. Calwell and his family." *And*, she thought with a twinge of regret, *I will cease to be White Blossom and reclaim the name of Tabitha once more.*

Now that her decision had been made Tabitha entered a small, empty tent, where death had so recently claimed its occupants. She sank down on one of the cots and immediately began to appraise her situation.

The first order of business, of course, was to get herself clean. Her clothing was caked with dried, stinking mud from the slimy swamp and her mother's blood stained her dress and leggings. Tabitha eyed a wash basin and a pitcher of water sitting on a collapsible stand along the back wall of the tent. It would never do—the quantity of water was inadequate. She needed to bathe herself from head to foot, wash her hair, and clean her clothing.

Tentatively, she pushed back the tent flap and stepped outside. Several red-coated soldiers squatted by a fire ring holding mugs of coffee. They looked up with curious stares as she approached. One of the soldiers whispered an aside to his companion that caused the man to cast her a suggestive leer.

Tabitha had intended to ask for directions to the nearest river where she could bathe but suddenly thought better of it. One, or *more* of them, might follow her. Instead she veered off to the right as though heading for the officers tent and once out of sight of the watching soldiers she continued to walk toward the forest that encircled the camp.

Tabitha's keen eyes quickly located a faint footpath and she began to follow it through the tangled underbrush. Within minutes the path led her to a small brook running full with fresh water. Dense foliage provided privacy and with a sigh of relief she stepped behind a large hackberry shrub and began to remove her filthy clothing. She placed everything in a pile, then, peering cautiously from behind the bush to make certain she was alone, she walked naked to the edge of the stream.

The brook was not deep enough to completely submerge but she sat down in the rocky stream bed and began to pull handfuls of cold water up over her body. After scrubbing herself clean she reached up, unbraided her hair, and ducked her head into the stream. Tiny bits of dried leaves and twigs floated free as she swished her head back and forth, working her fingers through the long black strands of her hair.

But it was not only the filth of the trip through the marsh that Tabitha needed to wash away. Satisfied that her body was as clean as she could get it, Tabitha climbed out of the frigid water and retrieved her clothes from behind the hackberry. She carried them to the edge of the stream and while the hot sun began to dry her hair and skin she carefully brushed her mother's caked blood from her dress with a small stone and began to douse the garment into the water. As she watched the blood flow from her dress she felt she was watching the last tie with her Indian heritage flow from her in a red cloud. Tabitha's body slumped, her heart aching.

Slowly she rose to her feet. She had not asked permission to leave and did not wish to be missed. She quickly pulled her wet dress over her head and started back along the footpath to whatever waited for her. She was alone now—her life had changed forever.

Among Oglethorpe's forces was a mixed party of Lower Creek, Chickasaw, Cherokee, and Uchee Indians garrisoned at Fort Pupo on the western shore of the St. Johns River. Tabitha was taken there to await their return to Frederica. She had hoped to find other Indian women and perhaps a change of clothing but these were all warriors in General Oglethorpe's service impatiently awaiting the call to launch another raid on the Spaniards.

In addition to Lieutenant MacDonald, several other Highland Rangers had been found at Fort Mosa, badly wounded but alive. They were immediately sent north on the scout boat *Amelia*. Fort Mosa was abandoned, the scene left behind one of total defeat for the British forces. Two thirds of the men of the Highland Company were casualties. The detachment of regulars and the majority of the Yamacraw and Creek were all dead, wounded or captured.

But despite his defeat Oglethorpe remained determined to lay siege to St. Augustine and the fortification of Castillo de San Marcos. The village of St. Augustine consisted of less than three hundred persons and had been established to protect the Spanish colonies further to the south, shield Spanish ships plying the waters between Spain and America, rescue shipwrecked sailors and serve as a missionary base for local Indian tribes. The Castillo, however, was a massive stone structure, heavily fortified, and defiant.

While Oglethorpe waited in his camp along the southern bank of the St. Johns in the hope of occupying the town, the Indians, bored with the lack of activity, threatened to go home. A hurricane-like easterly wind battered the town. The port was firmly blockaded by Spanish ships and his army was demoralized, threatening to desert in a body unless they were returned to Georgia. Reluctantly, Oglethorpe began moving most of the tattered regiment across the St. Johns River to Fort Saint George and by mid-July they began their retreat to

Frederica.

Tabitha marched north along the sea beach with the main body while General Oglethorpe and his officers proceeded on horseback. They set a fast pace and the independently minded Indians and already tired rangers soon dropped behind. The fast march through deep sand under a hot sun was extremely exhausting and Tabitha struggled to keep up. By days end they had reached Amelia Island but two soldiers had died of sunstroke and many others staggered into Fort Prince William too tired to continue.

Tabitha, although blistered by the sun, refused to give up. The next morning they left the beach and picked up an old Indian trail. Tired and hungry, the soldiers pulled the supply carts through thickets and swamps. Tabitha trudged onward, her eyes always looking north, her thoughts scurrying like mice to images of the life that awaited her. Mile after mile, day after day, night after night slipped by until finally they reached the settlement of Brunswick on the Georgia mainland. They made camp for the night and the next day secured passage on a supply boat that carried them across the sound to St. Simons Island.

The boat landed at Fort Simons on the southern tip of the island and after a brief lunch of dried buffalo strips and corn cakes they picked up a trail leading to the larger fort at the northern end of the island. At last, exhausted, dirty, and dehydrated, she walked through the gate protecting the walled town of Frederica.

General Oglethorpe had promised her sanctuary with a family named Calwell and here her new life was to begin.

Chapter Seven

Two Years Later
Frederica Town - June 1742

After her indoor duties were completed, Tabitha set out on her daily errands. Early morning fog had burned off and the sky was a brilliant scoured blue as she walked briskly, skirts swishing, humming a gay little tune. She wore English clothing now and today she was dressed in one of her favorites, a long gown of blue linen with a white collar. She liked the feel of the voluptuous petticoats moving around her ankles. She enjoyed walking but her feet hurt—the new leather shoes she had to wear now were far from comfortable. They were excellent ones, with black buttons and heels but she did miss her soft moccasins.

Still humming she walked up Broad Street pulling her cart with wide wooden wheels and a long handle. At the corner of Barracks Street she entered the market and picked out some succulent-looking salmon, nice and fat, with a rich pink color. She did not trust the boy who brought fish around on a cart. He tended to stretch the truth a little regarding their freshness.

She had just come out of the market and was about to turn south toward the general store to get molasses and several other items, when she saw her friend Anna Meyer. Anna was a pretty girl with a fresh complexion and rosy cheeks that spoke of her German heritage. She was shorter than Tabitha and had light brown hair plaited into two pigtails. Anna was usually cheerful which made her pleasant company, however today she wore a scowl and her face was set in lines of anger.

"Anna!" Tabitha called out.

Anna stopped, and on recognizing her friend, her expression softened and she began to walk toward Tabitha. She nearly bumped into a large woman with a shopping basket in one hand and dragging a bawling child with the other.

"Tabitha!" Anna said with a gasp, the furrows of anxiety ironing out of her face. "I'm so glad to see you." She cut in front of the woman and hurried to Tabitha's side.

"What's the matter?" Tabitha asked, moving closer to the side of the street and pulling Anna out of the way of the woman who was shooting her dour looks. "Is something wrong at home?"

Anna shook her head. "It's that terrible neighbor of ours, Beatre Hawkins." She looked around to make sure that no one was close enough to hear, and then leaned close to Tabitha to whisper, "She is a vile woman. She caught my brother Peter's little dog peeing on one of her rose bushes and she took a pistol and shot the poor little thing." Tears brimmed in Anna's eyes. "Peter is sick with grief. We all are. The dog was such a sweet little thing."

Tabitha felt a sudden twist of anger. This was more than a normal reaction to a domestic accident. The woman was cruel and now she was firing a pistol. "I know you work for her husband in the apothecary shop adjacent to their home," she said, "but Anna I fear for your safety. Can't you leave their employment? You said your father doesn't want you to work anyway."

Anna shook her head. "Nein, I'm trying to put by a little money so John and I can marry sooner." Her eyes searched Tabitha's face for understanding. "I'm just upset for the youngun, is all."

Tabitha inclined her head and gave Anna a tentative smile. "Marry? I know you have been keeping company with John Henney. It is really serious then"?

Anna blushed. "He really hasn't asked me but he hints of it. He thinks this is not the proper time to start a family. He worries the Spanish could come and wipe us all out."

"He is right you know. The threat of a Spanish attack hangs over us all the time."

"Ah, but Tabitha, I would rather be known as Fraulein Henney than Spinster Meyer. Frederica may never be free of danger."

Tabitha laughed. "Well, just be careful in your dealings with Beatre Hawkins."

Anna returned her smile. "I will. Now I must hurry to the bakery before all the fresh bread is sold." She turned into the busy street and they parted, Anna to the bakery and Tabitha to continue her errands.

Tabitha felt no regret for having come to Frederica Town and she was quickly adapting to island life in her role as a servant with the Calwell family. Her chores were many and varied. In the house she helped to spin cloth, knitted socks, mended, churned butter, wove rugs and emptied chamber pots. But she also assisted in the slaughter of pigs, grew herbs and vegetables in the garden and helped to prepare all manner of meat and fish for canning.

More importantly, she had grown to love the beautiful little island of St. Simons. Seven years ago England had established the colony on one of the barrier islands lying off the Georgia coast to stop Spanish expansion from the south, naming both the fort and the town Frederica in honor of Frederick, Prince of Wales, the only son of King George II. It was the southern most bastion against the spread of Spanish rule, lying between Savannah to the north and Saint Augustine to the south. The fort was built on the north-west side of the island where a bend in the river formed a natural vantage point. Thick timber platforms supported cannon directed up and down the Frederica River and a moat edged with sharpened spikes surrounded two storehouses, a powder magazine and a blacksmith shop.

Frederica Town, protected by the adjacent fort, had grown from a village of palmetto-thatched huts to a prosperous town of over a thousand people surrounded on three sides by thick forests and fronted by the winding river. Despite its charm rumors of a Spanish invasion were flying thicker than mosquitoes, reminding Tabitha that Frederica had indeed been created as a military outpost. The town was enclosed with a fence of cedar stakes ten feet high, at the very foot of which was a moat into which water flowed at high tide. It could be entered only by the land gate on the east or the water port on the west. Cannon along the riverbanks were placed to direct fire in either direction and a military road was constructed to connect Fort Frederica on the northern end of the island with Fort Simons on the south.

The streets bustled with activity: British Regulars in their red coats and tri-cornered hats, Highlanders in plaids and tams, Indians in breechclout and moccasins, traders in fringed buckskin, wigged merchants, and townspeople with a sprinkling of women bravely flaunting the ruffles and ribbons of their native England.

Some of the homes were little more than huts of palmetto bowers, however most were built of weathered cypress and tabby—a new form of concrete made of oyster shells, lime and water invented by Heinrich Meyer, the father of her best friend Anna. The houses of some of the wealthy, like that of Master Calwell, possessed window glass and sashes and were of brick brought over from England. Along Broad Street the primal forest had been cleared to make way for rows of orange and mulberry trees and the houses sat on large shaded lots. Public gardens of one acre each were planted outside the protecting stockade walls, the soil hoed, and barley, maize, potatoes, turnips and pumpkins planted. Dates, limes, figs, peaches, plum, and pomegranates were grown in the orchards and horses and cattle were pastured in a large meadow with good hay.

Frederica Town was not the only settlement on the island. Nearby was the New Hampton outpost where a garrison of soldiers and their families lived, and on the southern tip of the island a smaller fort and a settlement of several hundred inhabitants served as a lookout for news of any strange sails that might appear on the horizon. Oglethorpe and several of his officers built substantial homes on acreage close to Fort Frederica, the finest of which was the plantation home of Captain Raymond Demere. In addition to his own fine orchards General Oglethorpe planted six thousand white mulberry trees on the south end of the island planning to use the larva of the North American cecropia moth to produce a high quality silk.

General Oglethorpe, a wealthy English bachelor in his mid-thirties, had been commissioned by the British crown to establish the colony of Georgia both as a haven for imprisoned debtors and as a barrier against Spanish aggression in Florida. However, Frederica Town had become home not only to debtors and indentured servants, but also free families who paid their passage, eager for the Crown's offer of free land. Among the freeholders was the John Calwell family from Temple-Bairn London with whom Tabitha lived.

Now, on this early Wednesday morning Tabitha was headed for Cecil Wainwright's store, near the town gate, instead of marketing at the fort storehouse. The Crown provided rations of meat, bread, cheese, molasses, and flour for new settlers to Frederica for one year until they were established; however the Calwells had been residents of the town since it's founding and were now able to provide for themselves. The weather was unbearably hot, and sand gnats covered her bare arms, nonetheless the river behind her sparkled in sunshine and the air was filled with the scream of gulls.

She pushed open the screened door of the small shop and entered its dark interior. Inside the air was rich with a stew of aromas: coffee beans, cheese, pickles, dried fish, and tobacco together with that of bear grease and sawdust. Ropes of onions and sacks of potatoes hung from hooks on the wooden walls. Bins of hard, white cabbages and other root vegetables lined the walls and on the counter stood glass jars of many different kinds of vinegars, oils and pickles.

"Mornin', Miss Tabitha," Mr. Wainwright greeted her.

"Good morning." She gave him a quick smile and handed him her list. "Mrs. Calwell said she'd like that extra dark molasses if you have it, please."

The storekeeper carefully measured the molasses, rice, sugar, salt, and coffee that were on her list and placed them on the counter. He was the son of the owner, a young, stocky man with a heavy mustache that grew down past the corners of his mouth. As he handed Tabitha each item she placed it in her cart. She noticed his gaze traveling up and down her body. It finally came to rest on her bosom. "I gave 'ya extra measure of the molasses," he said with sly smile, revealing yellow teeth. "Ya know . . . sweets for the sweet."

"Why, thank you, Mr. Wainwright," she said trying to keep revulsion from her voice. She was making small beer tomorrow and the extra molasses would come in handy.

"Me names, Michael. Ya needn't be so formal." He shot her a sly grin. "I been a wonderin' if ya have a beau."

Tabitha thought quickly. She had to discourage his obvious interest in her. "I do," she said pertly. "One of the soldiers at the fort is courting me."

"White or Injun? He asked with a sneer.

Tabitha felt a chill run up her spine. It was always there, just beneath the surface. The ill-disguised prejudice and insensitivity of people who needed to feel that their race was superior.

"I don't see that that is any concern of yours," she snapped as she grabbed the handle of her wagon and stepped away from the counter.

Tabitha left the gloomy store and turned down Broad Street trundling the laden cart behind her. Its wide wheels moved easily over the hard packed shell road making a pleasant crunching sound. She pushed the unpleasant encounter with Michael Wainwright from her mind and once more began to hum. It was a glorious St. Simons day, early morning sunlight filtering through beards of blue-gray moss clinging to massive live oaks, illuminating their leaves and limbs with a special light peculiar to the island. Tabitha loved the beautiful trees, broader than they were high. Their widespread branches swept outward to unbelievable distances, swooping to the ground with gnarled tips for added support. One tree could shade a full half-acre. The ground was littered with leaves, tiny as squirrel's ears, constantly shedding to form a carpet two or three inches deep. Tabitha stopped to finger the fern entwined around the trunk of one of the oaks. The rough, grooved bark of the tree trapped moisture, dust and leaf mold providing fertile territory for seeds of a lovely little fern that grew along its branches. Called "resurrection", because after a rain it was transformed from a shriveled grey to an erect, vibrant green plant. It held a special place in Tabitha's heart. She gave the fat trunk of the tree an extra pat of affection.

As she moved on she looked up into the pale blue sky listening to the silvery sound of soaring skylarks as they dipped and glided with the currents. The air was fresh and sweet with the fragrance of blossoming orange trees that shaded the wide street, and in her heart she thanked God for leading her to this beautiful island. But, the Indian part of her yearned for the quietude of the forest, for a oneness with nature. Life within a walled town, pretty as it was, rankled at times.

Tabitha walked slowly, hugging the shade where she could find it, listening to the sounds of the busy little village: a broad axe felling a tree, a saw ripping a board, a creaky hoist with water splashing from a bucket, fence posts being pounded into the ground, drums beating, soldiers drilling. She passed the homes of Primrose Maxwell, the Wilsons, the double house shared by the constantly feuding Hawkins and Davidson families, and the now empty house of the Perkins family who had returned to England, defeated by the new land.

It was but a short distance to the Calwell house, an impressive three-story dwelling built of a soft grayish-red brick, situated on the north side of Broad where it intersected Barracks Street. She felt very blessed to live in such a fine home but the smile strayed from her face as she thought of her employer. In addition to his duties as surveyor and engineer for Oglethorpe, John Calwell was a merchant, making candles and soap, which his wife sold in a small shop to the rear of their home. While fair with his servants, he was a domineering man and kept his wife constantly in a titter. Tabitha didn't care much for him.

She stopped for a minute to chat with Priscilla Houstoun who was pruning her roses in the yard directly across the street from the Calwell house. Priscilla was a sweet, soft-spoken woman completely unassuming despite the fact that her husband was Conservator of the Peace and a member of a noble English family. She bore the title of Lady Houstoun and she had six towheaded children who were constantly in and out of the Calwell house to play with Henry, Johnnie or Connie.

Tabitha pulled the cart along a pomegranate hedge to the Caldwell's rear door where she unloaded it and carried the supplies down to the basement. It was a huge room with tile flooring and two hearths. All the food was prepared here before being served in the upstairs dining room. It also was used as an informal eating area, both cooler in summer and warmer in winter.

After everything was put away, Tabitha went out to the shop to work with Mrs. Calwell as she always did when her household chores were finished.

Constance was in her usual state of anxiety. "What kept you, Tabitha? The shop has been busy. I needed you."

"This was my morning to shop at Wainwright's," Tabitha reminded her.

"Well, it took you far too long. You must have dawdled along the way. Mr. Calwell will be very upset if he finds customers had to wait." She shoved a clean apron at Tabitha. "Quickly now . . . smooth your hair . . . attend to Mrs. Hawkins." She dropped her voice. "You know how vicious she is. She will waste no time telling everyone how slovenly our help is."

Tabitha smiled sweetly at her harassed mistress. The woman meant well but her demanding husband kept her in a continual state of anxiety lest she not please him. For all that, Tabitha was fond of her. She would never forget the day she'd been presented to Constance, exhausted and clothed in torn Indian garb. Constance had welcomed her and greeted her warmly. Tabitha had been so frightened, thinking that her life was going from freedom to bondage and she never forgot her mistress's compassion.

"I'll tend to her at once," she said as she hurried over to Beatre Hawkins, a thin woman with chiseled features and a constant scowl. Tabitha knew what a vile tongue the woman had.

"How dare you keep me waiting?" Beatre whined. "I've more important things to tend to than dilly-dallying in your shop all morning." She slapped three cakes of rose-water soap on the counter. "Tally my bill, wretched Girl."

"That will be five pence."

"Five pence! That's downright robbery. You can't have figured correctly."

"I did figure correctly. This is our best rose-water soap. If you want to buy it, it will be five pence, Mrs. Hawkins."

Beatre glared at Tabitha, her bosom heaving with rage. "Your employer will know how insolent you are, Girl. She whacked her coins onto the counter, grabbed her purchase, and flounced out the door.

Girl! How Tabitha hated that word. She had a name. It was Tabitha. *Tabitha!* She wanted to fling the words after the sour Mrs. Hawkins.

The shop was busy for the next hour and slowly Tabitha's anger dissipated. She really did love working in the tiny chandlery, illuminated by fat candles burning in clay pots glowing against its rough wooden walls. Dried herbs hung from the rafters and shelves displayed trays of delicately scented soaps and racks of tallow candles. Not just the normal household candles, but also tall, elegant tapers in subtle colors fine enough to export to Pennsylvania and New York.

And she enjoyed chatting with the customers. Mrs. Harding came in with her new baby, a little boy named Isaac, and when she saw Tabitha stretching out her arms she handed him over to be cuddled while she shopped. Tabitha held the baby close and patted his little bottom. Isaac cooed contentedly, his sweet infant scent mingling with that of the shop's beeswax, bayberry, and eucalyptus. She tickled his chin and he laughed reaching up with pudgy hands to pull on her nose. Tabitha smiled. She could not wait for the day she would be free to marry and have a baby of her own.

When the last customer had been served she said goodbye to Constance and began to lock up. She wiped her hands on her apron, then untied it and took it off. Carefully she blew out all of the candles and drew a curtain across the small window before swinging the heavy door shut and slipping the iron-locking bar into place. Then, as she walked down the shell path toward home she stopped to look across the garden. Late afternoon fog shrouded the barracks in the distance, the setting sun tinting the tabby walls with velvety lavender shadows. She sighed. The fortress looked so soft and gentle, belying its military mission in the town.

Then, her gaze settled on a group of Indians carrying baskets of smoked buffalo, venison, and oysters on their way to the Rampart to trade with the soldiers for cloth and trinkets. Watching them she was assailed with troubling memories of her childhood. Tabitha had never really felt a part of the Indian world. She was tall and had blue eyes, traits she inherited from her father and that further set her apart from her mother's people. Muscogee women of the Creek Nation were short with large, black eyes. She remembered her father ridiculing the Indians, calling them child-like as they traded valuable beaver pelts for glass beads and tiny mirrors. She knew he loved her mother, and he treated her people fairly, but she had always sensed that he felt the white man superior. Unknowingly he had made Tabitha feel ashamed of the Creek half of her heritage.

She shook her head and squared her shoulders. She was a part of the white world now and yet she couldn't help wonder if she would ever leave Frederica Town. If so, where would she go? What would she do? She'd like to be a governess but with her mixed-blood and scant training she doubted she'd ever find a respectable position. She'd had no choice in this life dictated to her, defined by loss, shaped by two different cultures. She tried to find beauty in every day, tried to grow in her Christian faith, tried to be grateful for her position with the Calwells, but she was ever mindful of her true status— indentured servant. This troubling thought she pushed to the back of her mind.

A roll of drums from the direction of the fort, calling the soldiers to their evening meal, reminded her of something else she kept locked away. She knew Scots Highlanders, under command of Captain Mackay, were camped at Darien, a short distance to the north. She suspected a certain Lieutenant, Ian MacDonald by name, might be among them. The soldiers from Darien often visited Bennett's Tavern here at Frederica but she had never seen the handsome stranger among them, a stranger whose image had remained vivid in her memory for two years. But then, to her surprise, she admitted that the image of the powerfully built Cherokee in Savannah also returned from time to time to taunt her.

Tabitha shook her head abruptly, refusing to let her thoughts wander in that direction. Shades of evening closed around her. She had better step lively. She would soon be needed in the kitchen to help prepare the evening meal.

Sixteen miles away another evening meal was being prepared, this one for the soldiers at Fort King George in Darien and smoke hung heavy in the air as Ian MacDonald made his way to the tent he shared with Cory. The tent was empty, Cory at the present moment on guard duty.

With relief Ian removed his woolen jacket and hung it neatly on a peg beside his cot. After a full afternoon of close order drills under the hot sky it was damp with perspiration. It smelled like wet wool, or worse, and he wrinkled his nose in disgust at his own odor.

He leaned his flintlock musket against the canvas tent wall and flopped on his cot. There was time for a short . . . a very short . . . nap before supper.

But sleep would not come. The day had been uneasy with tension heightening in the humid air as he walked his sentry post along the palisade. There was a sense of urgency on the Parade Ground and bayonets were added to the drills. Runners told that a Spanish Armada had been spotted south of nearby Cumberland Island. Was a military engagement here at Darien a possibility, or would the Highland Infantry be called out to defend one of the other forts dotting the barrier islands at Cumberland, Jekyll or St. Simons?

Ian scowled. He longed for a good fight. It was pay back time for Oglethorpe's deplorable defeat at Fort Mosa. Besides, it was imperative that the Spanish be contained in Florida. He was proud of his role in the militia and his rank as Lieutenant under Captain Mackay—proud to protect the fledgling colony of Georgia and give the poor of England, seeking refuge from debt and religious persecution, a chance to improve their station in life.

The battle at Fort Mosa had been particularly hard on the Scots at Darien. Only a few Highland soldiers survived the fight and the small town was left with eight young widows and twenty-three fatherless children. He didn't think of himself as exactly noble—after all he had only recently become a Scots Highlander warrior—but there was a side of him drawn to be a protector of the downtrodden. Of course, he had not always been a soldier. In fact, in her letters, Charlotte was openly contemptuous of his role in the military. That was another problem, one he did not wish to address, at least not tonight.

Drums announced dinner and he slid off the cot and donned his damp jacket. He ran his hand through his thick red hair and placed his tam at a rakish angle, then hurried across the parade grounds toward the fort. Tomorrow might bring more of the interminable drills.

Or, war?

The following morning Tabitha threw back her sheet with a groan and hopped from the bed, her bare feet dancing across the rough floorboards. Her room was stuck under the eaves of the third floor, but the tiny haven was like a cozy blanket, offering her the only space of her own that she had ever known. It had a steeply sloping roof and a high, square window. As she looked up she could see a pewter sky promising rain. After pulling a dress of somber gray calico from a peg on the wall she dressed quickly and tied a stark white apron around her waist. With nimble fingers she plaited her long black hair into a thick braid, which she wound around her head and pinned beneath a white mobcap. She looked in a mirror hanging beside the door and gave a small smile. She looked just like a proper English maid.

Tabitha bounded down three flights of stairs to the basement kitchen where Agnes, the Calwell's cook, already had a kettle of porridge bubbling gently over hot embers in the fireplace.

"The others aren't down yet?" she asked in surprise.

"Not a one, mum. The Missus is upstairs. She ordered the table set down here. 'Twill be cooler here, by far," Agnes said.

Tabitha nodded and began to place yellow clay bowls on the round oak table that stood in the middle of the cozy room. The glow of coals from the fireplace reflected on the polished copper of pots hanging from hooks along the wall, the smell of clean linen drifted from the drying rack suspended from the ceiling, and the wooden table and floor were pale from being scrubbed every day. Agnes shuffled to the trammel where a copper pot hung on an S-shaped iron at the hearth. "An' it's to be a wet muggy day. The children will be a han' full, don't you know," she complained, pushing a strand of gray hair from her reddened cheek.

A clatter of footsteps on the stairs announced the arrival of

Henry, Connie and Johnnie. The kitchen soon filled with the children's noise and laughter as they lined up to fill their bowls with porridge and took their place at the table.

Constance and John soon joined the children, and, after everyone's porridge had been eaten, they piled pancakes, corn biscuits and honey on their plates, then began to make plans for the day.

"With this dreary weather I doubt there will be many customers in the shop, and the children will be confined to the house," Constance said as she poured a second cup of acorn coffee into a stoneware mug. "Tabitha, why don't you stay here and keep them entertained?"

John Calwell seemed about to object, and then with a scowl on his face he pushed away from the table and stalked from the room without a word.

Constance's pale hands fluttered to her lips. "Oh, maybe . . ."

Johnnie jumped to his feet. "Please Mamma. I have something I want to make for you. It's your birthday next month. You're gonna be really, really surprised."

"Well, all right. But if I get busy in the shop Tabitha will have to come out."

William Driesler and I are going squirrel hunting," Henry announced with importance. "The weather don't bother us none."

"Doesn't," Constance corrected sternly.

Henry's brows drew together in a scowl like his father's. The oldest of the Calwell children, he was also the hardest to handle. Left in Cork with his grandparents when the Calwells emigrated to America Henry had been hopelessly spoiled. He had joined his parents in America just two years ago, a cocky independent nine-year-old. "Humph, you know what I meant," he mumbled. "Don't . . . doesn't . . . what difference does it make?" He pushed his chair back and bolted from the room.

Agnes quickly cleared the table and Tabitha gathered up her supplies. Armed with scissors, flour paste, needle and thread the children began to make gifts for their mother.

Connie and Tabitha decorated a vase that had been fashioned from clay dug from the bank of the river while Johnnie worked on an elaborate card with hearts and a rather lopsided animal he called a pheasant.

They had been quiet for some time when Johnnie suddenly stopped and directed a quizzical look at Tabitha. "I heard Daddy say you were *mixed-blood.* What does that mean?"

Tabitha froze. The children had always seemed unaware of her Indian background. She wondered what had occasioned Master Calwell to use the words.

"It means that my papa was a white man just like yours and my mamma was an Indian."

"Is that bad?"

Only to me, Tabitha thought with a forced smile. "Of course not, Johnnie. I had a wonderful father and mother and I am proud of both of them. Now Johnnie why don't you put away the card and get to work on that beautiful little horse you are carving for your Mamma."

Chapter Eight

Highland Games were an annual tradition in Scotland and to help ease the tension and threat of impending war the tiny settlement of Darien prepared to duplicate the pageantry of their countrymen with games of their own.

At the roll of drums on Saturday morning Ian sprang from bed, eager for the day ahead. No boring drills or humdrum duties at the fort today! Tomorrow might bring war but today was a day of competition. He had been practicing for months.

Ian pulled on long underwear cut-off above the knee, a military issue black-watch tartan kilt, a shirt of soft homespun and knee socks of red-checkered wool. He pulled his brogues from under the bed and carefully wound the long laces around his sturdy ankles. A snug fit was essential for the hammer throw in which he was participating today. Carefully he slipped his knife into a sheath worn on the outside of his right stocking. Later, after the rigorous games, he would return to the barracks to bathe and don his dress uniform for the parade of clans.

He strutted from the barracks, enjoyed a hearty breakfast, and then hurried from the fort to the field of play where a large crowd of townspeople had already gathered. The area swarmed with activity, Highlanders with bare knees and kilts, the Indians in breechclouts and wearing eagle feathers, all in high spirits and eager to carry on the tradition of the ancient games. More than a thousand years ago the chiefs of Scottish clans used the games to test the agility and strength of candidates for military leadership. Today it was only a festival in which the display of physical prowess played a leading part.

Ian joined a group of men lined up for the hammer toss, the first scheduled game. Cory greeted him with a hearty slap on the back.

"Dinna even think about winnin' this one, laddie," Cory said with a chuckle. "I've got the bloody hang o' the thing."

"Aye, and me as well. We'll see who's the strongest."

Cory chuckled, flexing his muscles. His shoulders were bull like, and his legs as stout as tree limbs. A smattering of freckles across his nose, his quick, infectious smile and appealing boyish look were deceiving. Cory was all man. This game would take full measure of his muscular thighs and calves. The Scottish Hammer Throw requires tremendous discipline and Ian jealously conceded that his friend would probably win. A contestant had to keep both feet firmly planted, with no movement of his legs until the hammer was in the air. Cory had the strength to do it.

Cory was the first to throw and Ian gulped when he saw the distance he reached with all three of his throws. That would be hard to beat.

Ian was last to take his turn at the line, with Cory's throw until now the longest. He stamped his feet to plant them in the sandy soil, then reached down and stuck his knife in the ground beside his right foot to keep it firmly planted. He swung his long arm, sinewy and strong, in a wide arch and with a mighty heave threw the hammer in the air. Each contestant is allowed three throws but he soon realized that neither of his first two was far enough to beat Cory. He had one more try.

With all his strength he threw the hammer forward but his right foot twisted and he lost his balance. He was disqualified.

True to his promise, Cory won.

All morning the competitions continued—the Weight Toss, Rock Throw and Tossing the Sheaf—the contestants all evenly matched. Ian won the Weight Toss and then Putting the Stone by a mere inch but it was the upcoming Tossing the Caber that he was most interested in. He wanted to beat Cory in that match more than any other.

There was a hush in the crowd as two husky men carried a twenty foot long log called a caber and set it on the ground before Ian. It was enormously heavy, weighing well over a hundred pounds, thicker on one end than the other. Ian stepped into place and steadied the pole, thick end in the air, thinner end resting on the ground before him. He stood motionless feeling the balance in the palms of his hands. Very slowly he began to squat, sliding his hands down the length of the caber, careful not to let it tip, until he was crouched on the ground. He sucked in a deep breath gathering his strength, motionless, focusing his mind only on the pole. Then, grasping it in both hands, he stood upright and began to run. With a deep roar he pitched the pole into the air, aiming it at an imaginary mark directly in front of him. The object of the throw was for the pole to arch through the air, end over end, so that it would fall in a straight line directly in front of him. The winner of the competition was the one with the straightest throw.

Ian's was perfect—straight as an arrow.

One of the spectators watching Ian's perfect throw was Tabitha. Mr. Calwell had brought his family to Darien for the games and they had arrived early in the morning full of anticipation. For this day at least they could all forget the threat of war.

Tabitha recognized the red-haired Highlander immediately, although he seemed completely oblivious to the crowd and never once glanced in her direction.

Holding her breath she watched as three more men threw the caber but one never got air borne and the two others fell far afield.

Ian was led to the center of the field for the presentation of the trophy. With her stomach churning Tabitha left the children and hustled over to stand directly behind the judges but Ian's attention was on the trophy not on the crowd and it was obvious that he did not see her.

Disappointed she retreated back to the family.

Mr. Calwell bustled up to Tabitha when the games were over. "The children want to stay for the Parade of Clans," he said. "It will make us too late to return to the island tonight so I have arranged to spend the night at the Martins. Johnnie knows where they live."

"Can we go to the dancing?" Connie asked.

"No. You are too young for such frivolity." He looked at Tabitha with lips set in a straight line. "The Parade of Clans only, is that understood?"

Tabitha felt a surge of frustration at the reminder of her lack of freedom. She had been looking forward to the dances. She tightened her mouth and gazed at the ground. "Yes, sir. Perhaps Connie and I might search for some medicinal herbs along the river, toward evening when it is cooler. Is that all right?"

His brows bunched together, but he nodded. "See you take care. The river bank can be dangerous."

At the conclusion of the games Ian met Cory at the refreshment tent where they quickly gulped down two tankards of ale and heaped a generous slab of haggis on their tin plates.

"Dinna know why I eat this stuff," Cory said with a grimace. "At home it was one of me favorites. Ma made it wi' the lamb's liver, heart and lights and she always used fresh, sweet mutton suet. This tastes like beef and auld fat."

"Aye," Ian said as he dumped his on the ground. "Put some of those meat pies on my plate." He held out his *Quaich*, a deep silver dish from which Scots traditionally supped their porridge and ale. "We've still the parade and all those high stepping dances this afternoon. I need my energy." He smiled and nodded toward a pretty blond-haired girl watching them from the end of the table. "An' I expect you'll need lots of energy to jig with that little widow girl, Sally Cochran."

Cory frowned. "Sally's a bonnie lass, but she's already lost one husband to soldering. She should be looking to one of the farm boys fo' company. I've told her so, told her I'se to stay in the militia. Even so, she does seem to favor me. How about ye, ol' mon? Are ye planning to step out?"

"Aye. But just for a dance or two. I have Charlotte waiting for me in Savannah so I have to be careful not get tangled up with any of these local lassies."

"Charlotte! Ye are a fool, laddie. Ye know her faither will never let you near her again. He already had you shanghaied once. Next time he'll likely finish ye off."

Before Ian could answer, a roll of drums announced the commencement of the fiddling contests and he and Cory took off at a run for the barracks. The dress parade would follow and they had to get out of their sweaty exhibition clothes and prepare to march.

Attired in the red, blue and green tartan of the Clan MacDonald, Ian carried his bagpipe to a clearing in the woods near the Parade Grounds where the pipers were assembling.

His bagpipe had been in the family for several generations, originally belonging to his grandfather, passed on to his father, then passed on to him as the eldest son when his father was imprisoned. The use of the Scottish Highland Bagpipe went back centuries. It was originally developed by his ancestors in the mountainous Gaelic-speaking regions of the Highlands and western islands of Scotland.

Ian placed the bag under his arm and rested the drones against his shoulder. He placed his mouth on the "blow-pipe" and exhaled a mighty lung full of air into the bag. All around him men were running through their scales and the din was incredible. Intended to inspire soldiers in battle, the music of the bagpipe is necessarily loud so that it can be heard for miles.

When all were ready, Ian fell into formation with the MacDonald Clan and stood ready to march.

"Strike up," the leader cried. The bagpipes sounded and,

with their thrilling and jarring tones led the men, stepping in cadence behind the drummers, toward the crowd waiting at the edge of the Parade Grounds.

Slowly they emerged from the shadows, ghostly in a light fog that had swept in from the marsh, pipes skirling, kilts swaying. The plaintive music drifted around their heads like pipe smoke, so emotionally charged that the spectators stood motionless.

Somewhere in the crowd a boy began to sing in a clear, youthful tenor the words to "Scotland the Brave."

> *"Hark, when the night is falling,*
> *Hear; hear the pipes are calling,*
> *Loudly and proudly calling down through the glen.*
> *There where the hills are sleeping*
> *Now feel the blood a-leaping*
> *High as the spirits of the old Highland men."*

What a wonderful heritage we Highlanders have, Ian thought as he strode across the parade grounds, the pipes resting securely in the crook of his arm. A heritage rich in truth and culture. A surge of pride brought tears to his eyes and he shook his head to concentrate on the cadence of the pipes.

Following the Parade of Clans Ian and Cory walked together to the clearing where the dancing was to take place. They looked alike in their Highland kilts, both were the same height, well built with deep tans, but it was there that the similarity ended. Ian had a striking face, broad and square jawed. Cory had a freckled face with high cheekbones and a long chin. Ian had dark red hair while Cory's had more of an orange cast. The clan tartans they wore differed. Shades of red, blue and dark-green predominated in the checkers of the MacDonald plaid whereas the MacGrath plaid had much more scarlet in it. Ian spoke better English, was reserved and quiet with a clear vision of where he was going. Cory retained a heavy brogue, rolled his 'R's, was easy going, prone to take chances where caution was called for and was not afraid to admit he was homesick for Scotland. Despite their differences they were fiercely loyal to one another and each displayed the characteristics of a true Scotsman—shrewdness, easy self-possession and superiority.

Sally was waiting at the edge of the field and Ian noted with amusement the possessive grip Cory placed on her arm as he led her to the spot where they were falling into formation for the Highland Fling. *There's more to this romance than my friend is telling me,* Ian mused with more than a touch of envy.

When the Fling ended Ian joined the men for the all male Highland Sword Dance, a traditional dance first performed by Highland warriors before going into battle. A sword was placed on the floor at the feet of the dancers and a soldier's sure-footed dance around it with no mistakes meant he, and his clan, would come home safely. The music was fast, the sun hot, and Ian gritted his teeth in concentration. The last time he had performed these intricate steps he had been a young lad in Scotland. He was covered with sweat when it finally ended but beamed with pride at his accomplishment.

They then swung into the Shantruse, a dance celebrating the return of the right of Scots to wear the kilt, forbidden for several decades. Cory grinned at Ian as the men mimicked kicking off imaginary trousers, the hated symbol of oppression. His leg aimed the imaginary pants in Ian's direction.

After a short break the fiddlers began a round of Scottish country dancing. Cory claimed Sally and Ian took the hand of a pretty lass who said her name was Libby. She was young and bubbly and Ian realized how much he had missed a woman's company. He felt happier than he had in months.

Cory had to leave for sentry duty in mid-afternoon but Ian and Libby continued dancing until they were exhausted. Ian was slightly drunk and beginning to think of romancing the energetic Libby when a sudden hush fell over the crowd. A harried British Redcoat had rushed into their midst and ordered the drummer to sound a stand to attention.

"Spanish ships are anchored a few miles off the eastern shore of Cumberland Island," he shouted. "Oglethorpe has ordered all militia to Fort Frederica. Be prepared to leave before dawn."

Ian bade Libby a hasty goodbye and ran toward the fort.

Chapter Nine

That same afternoon Connie and Tabitha went to the edge of the forest to look for medicinal herbs. She was hopping to chance upon Guali, used to treat a bilious stomach, which she had been unable to find near Frederica. The girls followed a narrow inlet that ran full with the incoming tide. Under the blazing sun the day was hot but in the shade of the trees that bordered the riverbank they found the shadows dark and mysterious. Somewhere a marsh hen called and nearby a woodpecker worked on a tree. No breath of air stirred the leaves.

With a gasp of delight Tabitha spotted a small cluster of Guali and stepped off the path to enter the trees where it grew. The ground was carpeted with wild ferns and towering clumps of bamboo. Mistletoe hung in thick clumps from the bare branches of a dead cedar and toadstools grew in black humus rotting its way back into the ground.

After gathering the Guali she returned to the path and stopped to look across the river.

And she saw the alligator. He was huge—at least twelve feet long and terrible to look at.

"Tabitha!" Connie cried.

"I see him."

He glided purposely toward them, only his snout and eyes above murky water.

Tabitha hefted the knife she had used to cut the herbs. It

was much too short to do any good if she got that close to the monster. She shuddered.

Slowly he kept coming, the water barely rippling along his massive body, his eyes never leaving her.

She watched with numbed horror as he left the water. His feet were huge, armed with vicious looking claws and he had a long tail which he was throwing back and forth with great strength. He was moving directly toward her. Maybe . . . maybe . . . if she threw something he would turn away. With shaking hands she stooped to pick up a good-sized rock . . . and then she saw the foot.

She froze. It was a foot . . . a human foot. It protruded from a clump of dense cabbage palm along the riverbank and as she watched, it moved.

Parting the fronds she saw the half-naked body of an Indian, mutilated and bloody, his face covered with mud, but alive.

It was the smell of blood that was attracting the gator.

"Help me," the Indian groaned.

Without thinking of her own danger, her face etched in desperation, she grabbed his hand and began to pull him from the brush.

By now Connie had started to scream.

"Run for help!" Tabitha yelled at the hysterical girl.

Connie ran.

The alligator was half out of the water, staring at Tabitha with gleaming red eyes, its massive jaws with rows of dreadful large sharp teeth, big enough to swallow a man, opening and closing, its giant tail swishing back and forth.

"Club," the Indian moaned pointing a bloody hand to a spiked war club that he had apparently hurled at his assailant. The club protruded from muck a few feet away.

Tabitha wrenched it from the ground and with her heart hammering, and yelling at the top of her voice, stormed toward the alligator. It did not move. Its red eyes remained fixed on her charging body. She leapt forward, all of her muscles tensed, and with a mighty heave smashed the club against the beast's head. Her aim was good and it struck hard. The gator snorted and lunged. Tabitha jumped sideways. Her breath came raw in her throat and she gulped air furiously. The gator gave another mighty swish of its tail, then apparently thought better of attacking and backed slowly, reluctantly into the water.

Faint with relief Tabitha licked her dry lips.

From the riverbank there were shouts and running feet. Two brown-clad rangers were the first to reach her and a Scots Highlander in kilt and tartan burst from the woods further along the shore.

"What is it, mum?" one of the rangers asked her.

"A gator . . . and . . . a man. Badly wounded but not dead." She pointed to the Indian half concealed by the brush.

The Highlander, claymore swinging in his hand, skidded to a stop beside her.

"What are you doing with that war club?" he stammered, his gaze darting frantically from her to the bloody Indian.

"An alligator was after him. I hit the beast on the head."

"An alligator?"

"A big one. I hit him good."

Tabitha watched as his look of disbelief turned to one of admiration. A smile flirted with his lips. "Aye, but ye are a bonny lass! Are ye hurt?"

"No, but this man is." She looked at the naked Indian at her feet and gave a gasp of surprise. He had wiped the mud from his face and eyes and Tabitha recognized him at once. It was Broken Arrow, the Cherokee from Savannah.

"Get some help," the Scotsman yelled to one of the men, "and bring a litter. We'll take him to the fort."

"An unknown savage inside our fort?" the ranger protested. "He may be a spy for the Spanish."

"We don't know that. Felled where he is it's more than likely the attack came from the enemy. Till he can talk and we know his allegiance he deserves to live."

Now Tabitha stared intently at the Highlander. She had noticed him at the games earlier that day and he looked vaguely familiar. Then she recognized the voice—he was the Scotsman who had tended Lieutenant MacDonald at Fort Mosa. He had grown a beard and was heavier and deeply tanned but it was the same man. He did not seem to recognize her. But then she had been a child of fourteen, dirty and dressed in Indian garb and all of his attention had been centered on his wounded friend.

She turned her eyes back to the Cherokee brave. He had drifted into unconsciousness and she moved closer to get a better look. Yes, it was definitely him. Whatever was he doing in Darien?

"I know this brave," Tabitha offered. "He came to my aid in Savannah several years ago when rowdies accosted me in the park. He is Cherokee of a clan loyal to the British.

The Highlander nodded. "Weel, we canna leave the mon here. We'll take him back to Fort Frederica. I ken a good surgeon there who can maybe patch up his wounds.

"And I have many healing herbs that may help," she said. She took one final look at the Cherokee's powerful, well built frame. His shoulders were massive, his upper arms bulged. His waist and hips were narrow compared with the corded width of his shoulders, and she averted her eyes suddenly embarrassed to find herself staring at his masculine nakedness.

She would not mind nursing this man at all.

Shortly after her return to Frederica Tabitha walked quickly through a freshly falling rain which, thankfully, provided relief from the insects, the bane of her existence. Even at night one could not escape the black sand gnats and a kind of deerfly that stings like a bee. Smudge pots filled with tar or Spanish moss were kept burning constantly outside under windows. Tabitha didn't know which was worse, the vile, black smoke or the biting insects.

Tabitha was on her way to meet with Pastor Ulrich. She was excited about her work with Ulrich. They were engaged in translating the Lord's Prayer and certain Bible verses into the Creek language. Her employer, Master Calwell, was a pious man and he encouraged her study with the Bible and her time with the Pastor.

Although Tabitha had been converted to Christianity as a young girl she was thrilled to once again be exposed to the faith and the teachings of the fort's chaplain. Tabitha felt a deep assurance in her soul that the Lord intended something good for her life. She had been subjected to mortal danger and survived . . . not once but twice.

Tabitha had found many parallels in John Wesley's Christianity and her own Indian culture. He taught that women in Christ were equal with men and responsible for their own salvation, trusting God for forgiveness. He preached of God's love, reflected in nature and all living creatures and she had found a home in this new faith that helped to heal the bitterness with which she viewed her mixed-blood heritage.

Pastor Ulrich was much like John Wesley, especially with his passion for translation and the call he felt to introduce the Indian to Christianity. He was full of love and good faith and was happy to conduct evening classes for adults and indentured servants who had to work all day. Tabitha knew they were blessed to finally have such a good preacher at Frederica.

There had been quite a succession of ministers to Frederica. First, came Henry Herbert, who stayed only a few weeks, then Samuel Quincy who returned to England sick and dispirited. And, as she had learned at her thirteenth birthday dinner, both of the Wesley brothers, John and Charles, gave up in defeat and returned to England, bewildered and disgusted. It was whispered that William Norris, the next chaplain to come to the fort, had been accused of lewd conduct and of getting his servant pregnant. He fell out with Oglethorpe and was dismissed. The next two ministers died, one on the way to America and the other, a drunkard by all accounts, after being here only a year.

She met Ulrich at the entrance to the fort and they walked

together to his tiny office. He was a small man with long curly hair hanging to his shoulders and wore a black frock coat and knee britches.

"We have a new prisoner at the fort," he said as she settled herself at a scared table that served as his desk. "One I believe you have already met."

"A prisoner?"

"Yes, a Cherokee by the name of Broken Arrow." Ulrich smiled. "I understand he was saved from a hungry alligator by a brave young girl from Frederica Town. The description of the girl sounded remarkably like you. But what were you doing in Darien fighting alligators?"

Tabitha laughed. "I went to the Highland Games with the Calwells. Connie and I were searching for herbs along the riverbank when we found him. I'm surprised he's a prisoner, though. I thought they believed him to be a loyal British scout."

"They're holding him only until they are sure of his story. He claims he was fleeing from the Spanish. I have been thinking that he might be of value to us. We're almost finished with the Creek translations and I would like to begin translating some of the Psalms into Cherokee. You might work with him."

Tabitha pursed her lips. She was not as fluent in Cherokee as Creek and would undoubtedly benefit from his help but from what she had seen of the man he did not seem like a likely candidate to help translate biblical verse.

"Have you talked with him, sir?" she asked.

Ulrich shook his head. "He speaks very little English."

"Then I'll have a word with him when we finish here, sir." She chuckled. "After all, he does owe me something. That was a mighty big alligator."

Later that afternoon Broken Arrow was ushered into the office just as Tabitha was putting away her pen and ink.

She caught her breath at the regal stature of the man. He walked tall and erect with a commanding presence. *One did not fool with this man*, she thought. Today a sleeveless deer-hide vest showed muscled biceps and his short loincloth revealed powerful legs crisscrossed with angry looking lacerations. His head was plucked clean except for a narrow strip across the crown that grew long and was fashioned into a thin pigtail at the back of his head. He stood like a Chieftain with legs widespread and arms crossed. Black eyes filled with fire widened in recognition but he did not smile.

"I recall that you are called Broken Arrow. We met several years ago in Savannah. You may recall that my name is Tabitha." she said.

He looked angry. "Not Indian name."

"My Christian name." She spoke in Creek and he seemed to understand. She continued to interrogate him speaking in halting Cherokee, signing with her hands when she had no words. He said he fought for the British at Cumberland Island but was captured by the Spanish and tortured. He finally escaped and stole away on a sloop bound for Fort King George. After making land he was apparently trailed by a Yemassee as he tried to find refuge but was caught just outside the fort. They engaged in hand-to-hand combat with Broken Arrow the loser. The attacker took him for dead and fled when Tabitha and Connie arrived on the scene.

Broken Arrow had been using his hands to gesture while he spoke and Tabitha cringed when she saw an ugly looking wound on his arm. It was swollen with infection.

"That wound on your arm needs attention," she said. "Has the surgeon been treating it.?"

He merely nodded.

"If you stop by the dispensary tomorrow morning I'll apply some ointment to it. My mother was a Shaman and I have a special herbal preparation that she often used."

"I try," he said.

Parson Ulrich had been listening quietly in the corner and he spoke up now. "Tabitha, you seem to know this man. Had you met him before the incident with the alligator?"

Quickly she told him of their previous encounter in

Savannah.

Ulrich pursed his lips. "Tell him that I will inform Oglethorpe of his allegiance. Ask him if he intends to stay on with our forces as a scout if released."

Tabitha translated and Broken Arrow nodded his head up and down.

Ulrich looked thoughtful. "Say nothing to him about working with us. We will seek him out again once his name has been cleared."

A guard entered the room and, with an apologetic glance at Tabitha, took Broken Arrow by the arm. "Oglethorpe sez he be a wantin' to talk to this Injun."

Tabitha smiled encouragingly at Broken Arrow. "Go then, and tell Oglethorpe the truth. He is a fair man."

She watched him stride from the room with a strange sense of anticipation. It would be good to talk with her kind again.

Or was it more?

Chapter Ten

Under a heavy cloud cover, fifteen piragua riverboats—long, open flat-bottomed ships equipped with oars and two sails—departed the Darien dock bound for Fort Frederica.

Wind and salt spray whipped Ian's heavy hair and peppered his bare knees, lifting the hem of his kilt as he stood with stocky legs widespread for balance against the heavy sea. The lead boat, with fourteen oars and six swivel guns, plowed its way through the strong currents of the channel leading to Altamaha Sound and the northern tip of St. Simons Island.

Sensing a presence behind him he glanced over his shoulder and raised his hand in a mute salute. Cory was staring across the water at the distant shore. "Do you think we're finally on our way to a fight?" Ian shouted against the wind.

Cory nodded, smiling merrily as he moved to Ian's side. "Aye, Oglethorpe willnae be callin' us to the fort at Frederica if he isn't expecting a visit from the Spanish sune. Ye know the Spaniards are determined to wipe out the coastal colonies. Governor Montiano has his cheatry eyes on Charlestown. We Georgians are in his way, a real thorn in his side."

"Weel, we'll give him a welcome he won't soon forget. Montiano may have beaten us at St. Augustine, but we'll be ready for him this time. He'll find out what it's like to come up against a bunch of riled up Highlanders with a score to settle."

"Or a bunch of Toonahowi's Creek Indians wi' blud in their eye," Cory snickered.

"Aye, 'twill be a relief to stop the bloody drills and fire our muskets at something other than the empty sky." Ian fingered the ragged scar that ran from his ear to his hairline. "Two years is a long time to sit in the sun and think of revenge."

The piragua had entered calmer waters and Ian's gaze swept the marsh for signs of the fort guarding Frederica Town. He had visited the walled village before and had spent several memorable evenings at Bennett's Tavern.

A sudden vision of a black-haired Indian girl, floated into his memory. He remembered being told that Oglethorpe indentured her to a family at Frederica. She undoubtedly saved his life at Fort Mosa. What was her name? Tabitha? She was a real beauty, though half-Indian and a child. Maybe he would try to find her. He certainly owed her his thanks, perhaps even his life.

As though reading his thoughts Cory poked him on the shoulder and with a wink and a smile said, "There's many a wee lass in yonder village to warm the cockles of a brave soldier's heart if we've but time to linger, aye?"

Ian's eyes twinkled in merriment. "Not to mention those who keep the beds warm at Bob Patterson's bawdy house!"

"It's not me bed I want warmed," Cory said, his blue eyes shining with pleasure.

The piragua rounded a bend in the river and the Scots Highlanders let out a rousing cheer. Fort Frederica was dead ahead.

After the last evening drill Ian headed back to the barracks where he exchanged his uniform jacket for a loose fitting cotton shirt, grabbed his clay pipe and a pouch of tobacco and headed down a shell lane leading from the barracks to the Frederica River. The water shimmered in the glow of a full moon and he stood for several minutes looking across the river at the vast marsh that lay beyond it. The marshes that surround St. Simons Island fascinated and soothed him. Someday he would like to build a house, facing the western sunset and overlooking one of the marshes.

That is, if he lived that long.

He heaved a deep breath and sank to the ground, settling his back against a towering live oak tree near the North East Bastion and looked back at the twinkling lights of Frederica Town. Two young squirrels, silhouetted against the darkening sky, scampered about darting into grasses along the river edge, pausing with great round eyes and twitching tails to watch him.

A trio of cormorants soared and circled like kites against the sky. Far off a dog barked. A prairie warbler chirped on a nearby bush. Leaves rustled. A hot dry wind swayed the marsh grass and gulls cawed up a fuss where they fought over a morsel of food. Night sounds of birds settling for sleep in the trees by the river were muted. Quiet sounds blended into a rhythm with the river, the fields and the dark shadows of the towering oaks.

With the swift fall of night the pewter sky turned to the deepest blue black. Sand gnats swarmed around his head sinking their microscopic teeth into his skull and Ian brushed them away with a soft curse. He furtively put his hand beneath his kilt and gave a mighty scratch. The gnats had no shame. Some of the Highlanders wore cut off army long drawers to protect their privates but as far as he was concerned it was worse when the vicious little beasts got trapped inside and started to bite.

Ian did not doubt that his Highland Company would soon be thrown into battle against the Spanish forces. He thought back over the events leading to the present hostilities. The cutting off of a man's ear seemed a silly reason to start a war, but then man's fragile ego was usually the real cause of war. That and religion.

The active war here in Georgia had begun last November with the killing of two unarmed Highlanders from Darien garrisoned on Amelia Island near the Florida/Georgia border. Before dawn Yemassee Indians, allied with the Spanish, landed on Amelia and concealed themselves in the brush near the small fort. Two young Scots, John Mackay and Angus MacLeod, were ambushed and killed in a hail of musket fire. They were found beheaded and mutilated, only one more reason for Ian's intense hatred for Indians. When Oglethorpe and the people of Georgia responded, the ill-fated Battle at Fort Mosa was the result.

In Frederica, he could see lamps flicker on one by one as dusk settled over the land. He suddenly felt lost and lonely, thinking of the poverty and political turmoil in far off Scotland. He wondered if he would ever see his home again, the lofty peaks, heaths, glens and dales of his beloved Glencoe. He thought of his father and his brother and his dead mother. His was a sorry story, one he did not often visit, so he forced his thoughts to other, happier times.

What, he wondered, *was Charlotte doing in Savannah at this very minute?*

James Oglethorpe was coming to dinner and Constance Calwell needed eggs for her corn soufflé, so, since this was the season when the huge loggerhead turtles came ashore to deposit their eggs, she ordered Tabitha to go in search of a nest.

That morning as the sky lightened, Tabitha pushed her canoe from the dock and quietly began to paddle upstream. Mist hung heavy on the marsh shrouding trees and grass in gray. A few raccoons stalked the mud flats for crabs and snails among the shallows and an otter slipped quietly down the bank and into the water with barely a splash. The high marsh cord grass grew almost to the edge of the river and although Tabitha couldn't see the creatures it harbored she knew the roots of the grass teemed with aquatic life.

The tide had turned and she directed the canoe from the river into a smaller, tidal creek threading its way through the marsh. As the fog lifted a group of white egrets took on the rosy hue of the dawn sky. A great blue heron stalked a tidal pool for fish. The canoe floated easily as water rose in the narrow creek winding its way to the sea.

The day began to grow warm, the noise of the slough resonant with the loud rattling call of a marsh hen, the tiny clicking of oysters closing their shells and the scurrying rustle of side-dancing fiddler crabs among the marsh grass.

Would she find the turtle eggs she was seeking? It was late in the season, but she suspected nests might be found hidden by sea oats beyond the beach's high-tide mark. More British soldiers were arriving at the fort daily, preparing for the suspected Spanish invasion, and additional food was needed. If she found a nest there would be more than enough eggs for Constance's soufflé and Master Calwell would be pleased if he could present the cooks at the fort with a hatch of the rich turtle eggs.

At a point where the creek spilled out into the ocean Tabitha pushed her canoe ashore and taking a reed basket from under her seat, she began to walk along the beach, littered with a petticoat of jellyfish, moon shells, clams, and angel wings. Her gaze scoured the upper reaches of the sand looking for signs of one of the huge nesting loggerhead turtles that could weigh close to a thousand pounds. She stopped suddenly. Directly in front of her was a faded turtle crawl, a deep groove in the sand with oar-like flipper depressions along the sides and, in the middle, short, pointed marks from its tail where the heavy barnacle-encrusted turtle had pushed her egg-laden body forward.

Cautiously Tabitha followed the trail toward a dense clump of sea oats. She never failed to marvel at God's direction of his creatures. It was usually at this time of the year, early June, when the tide is high in the first half of the night, that instinct drove the turtle to come ashore under cover of darkness to lay her eggs.

Within minutes Tabitha found the telltale depression of a nest about the size of a soup bowl and with her hands she gently scooped the soft white sand away. It was full, with well over a hundred eggs like tiny jewels in the gleaming sand. The turtle was gone. Using her heavy flipper she had packed the sand down hard and smooth, then made tracks away from the nest to deceive predators. Finally, the turtle made her way back to the ocean leaving the eggs to the hatching influence of the sun.

Tabitha smiled with pleasure. One by one she removed the eggs—about the size of a hen's egg with soft, white shells—and carefully placed them in her basket.

Master Calwell would be well pleased and the soldiers at the fort would eat well tomorrow morning.

Broken Arrow sat on his bunk in the stockade patiently waiting for Tabitha's daily visit. He had withdrawn from her at first but she softly talked him into letting her apply salve to the torn flesh on his arm. Now, without admitting it to himself, he looked forward to her coming.

When she appeared in the doorway with a smile on her face he fought to keep his own face stern and impassive. She came directly to his side and took a packet of evil smelling salve from her basket. Broken Arrow grimaced as she eased the blood stained bandage from his arm. Her hand was warm against his skin and he found he enjoyed her touching him.

"It looks much better," she commented as she raised it to her nose to sniff for signs of infection. "The seepage has slowed and the color looks good. I'll apply more ointment and a fresh dressing and I'll look at you again tomorrow."

Broken Arrow never took his eyes from her as she bent over his arm. He liked her dark beauty. Her skin was a dusky rose, her eyes unbelievably blue, framed by thick black lashes. It was obvious to him that the girl who had adopted an English name had also adopted the white man's world surrounding her and was completely unattainable. Despite this, he noticed a soft warmth in her eyes when she looked at him. Maybe it was not as impossible as he thought. In fact he would suffer a thousand wounds if it would bring her to him each day.

He had never forgotten her spunk when he helped her in Savannah. He could remember her words: *I can take care of myself . . . but thank you for coming to my aid.* And then to think she had attacked an alligator to save his life. What a brave girl she was—only an Indian could be so self-assured.

"Let me look at your leg," she said moving her warm hand along his thigh.

He fought to keep his reaction to her touch under control. "It fine," he muttered, jumping to his feet. "Doctor make good."

Tabitha smiled sweetly. "Well, continue to drink the tea I gave you. It will give you strength and help you to heal."

Without a backward glance he limped from the tiny room in the fort that served as hospital and apothecary for the regiment. He tightened his jaw. It was not good for him to think on this girl.

A shadow fell across the patch of garden where Tabitha worked to fill her basket with fresh cut cabbages. Her hand stilled and she snapped her head back to look up at the tall form of an Indian brave standing quietly at her side. For a moment the sun blinded her making his features indistinct but as she raised her hand to shield her eyes her vision cleared and she recognized the piercing black eyes and square jaw of her silent observer.

"Broken Arrow?"

He nodded.

She pointed to a garden bench close to where she worked. "Sit and talk with me. I'm glad the doctor has released you and I hear General Oglethorpe has made you a scout."

He looked disdainfully at the bench, and then hunkered down beside her.

"Toonahowi say you are a Creek from the village of Tustacatty," he said.

"You know Toonahowi?"

"Everyone know Toonahowi. He the general's lead scout and nephew of the great Chief Tomochichi."

"I'm surprised he knows that much about me."

"Toonahowi traded with your father. He recognize you. He say you without mother or father."

Tabitha winced. She felt the old deep familiar tears well in her eyes and reached down to yank a cabbage from its stalk.

"It's true. Both of my parents are gone now. Father first. He planned to build a new trading post near St. Augustine in Spanish Florida. We stopped at Amelia Island for the night and he was ambushed by hostile Yemassee. Rather than start back to Tustacatty on our own, Mother and I were encouraged to wait for Oglethorpe's troops and continue with them to Florida. We took refuge in Fort Mosa where a company of British were patrolling. Spanish scouts attacked the fort and wiped out the entire regiment. A Yemassee arrow found mother. Afterwards General Oglethorpe offered me a post with an English family here at Frederica." Tabitha knew she was babbling and she sucked in her breath fighting for control.

"My father was a great warrior," Broken Arrow said solemnly. "He too was killed by the Spanish. They burned our village."

Tabitha saw the pain that clouded his eyes and the sinews in his forearm tighten.

"Why?"

"We no want them to build fort on Cherokee land."

Tabitha could picture what had happened. All white men seemed greedy for land. Oglethorpe made treaties in good faith, but she knew for a fact that new Scots settlers were pushing their way up the Ogeechee taking Indian land. Many of them married Indian women solely to get possession of their home and land. But she did not voice these thoughts to Broken Arrow.

"I'm sorry," she said instead. "We have all suffered." Her emotions churned as she looked into his solemn face. He represented the part of her mixed-blood she was turning away from, yet she had deeply loved her mother, had loved the honest, simple life of her village, her people's reverence for the land and wildlife. It was all so confusing. A slight frown puckered her forehead. She had a rich heritage she was trying hard to suppress.

Just the same, she had made her choice.

Tabitha had not mentioned the Bible translations to Broken Arrow and she decided not to say anything now—better to gain his confidence first.

He stood and turned as though to walk away, then stopped and with his back to her said, "Toonahowi say you are a slave."

"Not a slave. I'm a bondservant in the home of a family named Calwell. Master Calwell was with the British at St. Augustine and he brought me here. I have two more years to serve, and then I'll be free. But, Broken Arrow, why are you willing to stay at Frederica?"

A strange look passed over his rugged features. "Many of our tribe serve Oglethorpe." He glanced at her over his shoulder. "I go now in sorrow. We talk more later."

With that he slipped away, a dark shadow moving silently into the dark line of forest bordering her garden.

Chapter Eleven

Ian lay down to sleep. The dream was the same as always. The landscape of his homeland.

The high granite outcroppings covered with green ferns, bitter bracken and purple heather, soar to the sky. The sun sparkles over flecks of quartz in the rock like a million stars. Mist swirls and a washed-out sun peaks through. Miles from the road where the MacDonald farm sits, foaming waterfalls stream from clefts in granite rock. Alone and serene, stone walls built by his ancestors, outline pastures where sheep graze in peaceful contentment and wooly cows roam free on the volcanic ridges.

Even in his dream the land was so beautiful he felt his heart would break.

People move slowly through the deep purple valley tending the farm. A man whistles to his dog. He is a big man with the shoulders of a bull, and long black hair. Ian feels special warmth for the man he knows to be his father. A boy sinks his spade into the ground in search of potatoes. He sings as he works and his young voice floats across the valley like birdsong. The soil is stony and a few massive tree stumps serve as a reminder of the backbreaking work required to calm this rugged land.

A figure stands in the doorway of a stone cottage, the house plain, but well built of stones cemented by clay with a low dipping roof of thick turf laid upon unhewn rafters. The figure in the doorway is a woman who beckons to him. She wears her plaid drawn around her head and shoulders.

His mother, long dead.

It is a landscape magnificent but with little mercy. Protected by the Clan and by prayers it has remained in his family for generations, its people hardworking and moral, while the world beyond the valley has become embroiled in struggles for power, in corruption and greed.

Now the dream changes—dark and frightening.

Warriors of the Clan Campbell swoop down on the valley intent on massacring the MacDonalds. He shoves his dirk into his stocking, grabs his claymore and runs, leaping over ice-clad rocks with a blood-curdling scream of rage.

In the village of Glencoe the trusting people seem unaware of their danger. Why don't they run? *he asks himself. A sickening wave of terror wells up from his belly.*

Now the sky becomes dark, the roar of advancing hoards louder and still the villagers seem unaware of their danger. Children play in the snow and he realizes that he must pluck them up and save them from the traitorous Campbells. But suddenly he steps into a moor bog and he cannot move and a choking panic seizes him.

He flails his arms and screams, "The Campbells are betraying you," but they do not hear him. The MacDonalds of Glencoe will perish on this day but he cannot free his feet from the mire to save them. His heart pounds and sheer terror possesses him.

Then he wakes up.

It was a dream Ian had often, a story told often in bitterness by his father whose parents had been killed in the massacre. But, despite the fact that Scotland was under the oppressive heel of Richard II his memory of the valley was of a breathtaking beauty that made his throat ache.

The July heat was sweltering, the temperature near 100 degrees and when early morning drills were over most of the men headed immediately for Bennett's Tavern.

Ian stood just inside the entrance, the smell of beer and sawdust in the air and the rumble of soldier's voices and clinking glasses all around him. His gaze swept the smoke filled room and it was several moments before he saw Cory tucked away in a corner, his red head bent, staring morosely into his tankard of ale.

Ian made his way through the crowd toward his friend and he was almost at his side before Cory looked up and saw him. His face brightened immediately.

"Ian . . . join me," he said rising to his feet.

Ian shook his head. "The day is too grand to spend in this foul room. Let's find the beach, have a lunch of fresh oysters, maybe swim a bit, aye?"

They left the tavern and walked east toward the beach. The tide was out, sandbars jutting far into the sea, the fine white sand hard and clean. Yucca was in full bloom on the dunes and blue morning glories, sea oats and cabbage palm grew in mass profusion along the high tide mark. There was a saying on the island that on St. Simons "the oysters grow on trees," and it was with reason. On the shore was mile after mile of trees, and under them nothing but hills of oysters. At high tide these trees came under water and were covered with oysters that clung to them like mud. During the six hours of low tide the oysters opened their shells and expelled the old water. Ian had learned to eat them raw as they came out of the water and he showed Cory how to grab a handful, squirt the juice of an orange into the open shell and slurp them down with relish.

After filling their bellies they walked down to the water's edge. Seeing a small mound near the surf line with three tiny holes Cory pried a sand dollar from the sand and scooped it up.

"Sally's wee bairn loves to make necklaces from them," he said with an embarrassed grin at Ian's questioning scowl.

"I thought you were reluctant to maintain a relationship with Sally."

Cory looked chagrined. "That's me common sense telling me to lay low. Me heart and manly juices tell me otherwise.

She's a bonny lass, pretty as an Alpine wildflower, and hungry for a man."

"Aye. Hungry for a husband, I expect."

"That too. The lass has an unchancy problem, Ian. Without a husband she's no claim to 'er home. She worries they will put 'er and the wee one out if a mon with a family wants 'er land. That's the bloody English law."

"And are you willing to take on the responsibility of a ready-made family."

"I canna say." Cory frowned as he picked up a broken shell and threw it into the lapping surf. "Funny," he said changing the subject, "how ye don't find many big shells on the beaches here or at Darien. If ye remember, the beaches at Cumberland were littered with huge shells: conchs, whelks and moon snails.

"I've heard it said that there are shoals close to the St. Simons shoreline where the larger shells are deposited."

Cory stood looking at the distant horizon of sea and sky with a wistful look on his face. "I wonder if I'll ever get back t' my real home . . . to Scootlan', I mean. 'Tis true I willnae leave the Highland Company as long as the Spanish are a threat. After that I don't know. I ken Darien is as good a place t' settle down and raise a family as any, but I yearn for dear auld Scootlan'."

Ian thought about what Cory had just said. Love of village, clan or family came first in a Scotsman's life. In the past Highlanders had proven to be a fertile source for military recruitment in Europe although the Georgia recruiters were not there just for soldiers—they wanted families.

"But . . ."

"I know. Yer question still begs an answer. Sally's wee bairn poses no problem but me life as a soldier does. She's already lost one husband t' war." He tilted his head and gave Ian an impish grin. "Besides, I'm half hoping to see that Indian lass I told ye about that hit that gator' over the head. I didn't recognize her at the time . . . she wore an English dress and had her hair covered with a mobcap . . . but I swear 'twas the same lass that brought ye help at Fort Mosa."

"If so, I'd like to see her myself. She was indentured to the John Calwell family and I'm told they live 'bout halfway up Broad Street. When I've time I plan to see to her well-being and thank her properly. Remember though, she's only a servant and a bloody Indian to boot."

"Aye, but a bonny one, if it's the same lassie," Cory said. "Right now I ken we should be thinking of the nearby danger, not of leddies. A big fight is certain." He drew his legs up and locked his arms around his knees. "The sound of the waves always gets me all romantic like," he added wistfully. "I'd like to get me a piece o' land with a couple of those great live oaks and a clear view o' the ocean. Sitting here, looking across the sea and knowing Scootlan' is on the other side makes it seem closer, connected somehow."

"You sound more homesick than romantic."

Cory ran his hand through his hair. "I admit t' being homesick. Ye often tell me o' yer dreams of the Glencoe massacre. Weel, I dream too. But my dreams are o' tumbling waterfalls, o' soaring golden eagles and Loch Alsh all choked with salmon. Aye, Ian, you ken my meaning? Remember the Highland River strath an' the inland lochs? Da used to take me to the sea and we would spend days fishing the firths along the rocky coast. Ye never saw anything so bonny. America has much to offer in the way o' freedom and prosperity but me heart will always be in Scootlan'." His face was dreamy, his brogue thick.

Ian smiled quietly, enjoying Cory's reverie. Funny how the mention of Scotland could bring such a flood of memories washing over him in the space of a few seconds. He could almost smell the peat bogs and hear the laughter of his little brother as they plotted another prank. With a sigh he squatted on the sand to pick up a piece of green glass, worn smooth by the action of the waves and rubbed it between his fingers. "At times I miss it too. Maybe I'll take Charlotte there after we are married." A gull settled on the sand beside him, the breeze ruffling the gray feathers on its back. Ghost shrimp burrowed into the sand leaving tiny holes surrounded by sprinkles of fecal pellets. The water rippled with small whitecaps breaking close to the shore, the tide on its way out. He leaned his head listening to the gentle wash of surf against the hard packed sand with the feeling that this part of the world hadn't changed in the last thousand years. The solitude was comforting and he almost forgot that Cory sat silently beside him.

A little black dog had followed them from Fort Frederica and it trotted over to them with a large stick in its mouth. It looked at them hopefully, and Ian idly scratched it between its ears before throwing the stick into the surf. The dog raced into the water to retrieve it and then swam back to drop the stick near Ian's feet with an excited woof. The game was on with each throw going further and further until finally the dog flopped on the sand, its tongue lolling, the stick ignored.

Ian filled his lungs with salt air, so different from other air, with its own taste and smell. The beach was alive with soundless sanderlings as they scurried on matchstick legs along the tide line, dipping their tiny heads to probe the wet sand for tiny mole crabs, algae and plankton. Ian's gaze swept the restless sea and the horizon. He turned to Cory. "Did you ever notice that no two waves are ever the same," he observed. Nor for that matter any two minutes in our lives,"

"Aye, laddie. Nor grains of sand, nor snowflakes."

"Snowflakes?" I hope I never see them again."

"Then ye will miss one of God's most beautiful creations."

The gull threw back his head and screeched.

Ian rose and brushed sand from his kilt. It was time to return to Frederica. With a lump in his throat his eyes once more swept the horizon. He suspected this might be the last quiet time for him and Cory before the coming battle and as a large pelican flew overhead casting a dark shadow over the sand in front of him he shuddered with a sudden premonition that sorrow laid ahead.

Broken Arrow stood ramrod straight in the tiny storeroom

that served as the Parson's study, his face impassive, his flinty gaze flitting from Ulrich to Tabitha and back again.

"I've been told you are now one of Oglethorpe's trusted scouts," Ulrich said.

Broken Arrow looked puzzled and Tabitha quickly translated.

He nodded yes.

Tabitha gave him a soft smile. "Parson Ulrich and I could use your help."

He merely stared at her.

She continued in his language searching for the right words. "When we spoke the other day I mentioned that I was a Christian. I'm anxious to take the good news about God to all our people. To bring them the same joy I've found," she said, her voice rising in excitement. "We Christians have a book called the Bible. It tells us stories and gives us prayers to say when we need help from our God. We would like to tell these prayers to your people in your language. I know some Cherokee but not enough. I need your help to find the right words. Would you help us?"

"I do not know your God. Your stories will confuse my people."

"The Indians are my people too, Broken Arrow. And I have found great pleasure and comfort in hearing the prayers and stories," Tabitha said softly.

He glanced at the Parson sitting in the corner, then back at her.

His black eyes, sharp as arrow chips, stared into hers. "I talk with you. Not him!" he said.

Tabitha turned to Ulrich and related Broken Arrow's words.

Ulrich looked pained, then nodded his agreement. "Tell him that will be all right. I'll tend to other duties when he is here."

Tabitha quickly translated. "We will tell Oglethorpe that you are helping us. He will be very pleased. I have Wednesday afternoons free and will meet you here" She held up seven fingers. "That will be this many days from now."

"I mark it on my deer hide."

"Wado!" she said, using the Cherokee word for "Thank You."

His eyes, no longer flinty, softened and he smiled, saying, "we friends," as he strode from the room.

Chapter Twelve

Despite the stifling July heat Ian stepped smartly on the North Rampart, his tour of sentry duty almost complete.

He was in full uniform—a tam with a pompon on top, short red jacket, his best black-watch tartan kilt and red plaid wool stockings that came to just below his knees. He ran his hand down the length of tartan that was draped over his broad shoulder, adjusting it at the waist where it was belted, making a skirt-like kilt. The kilt was so comfortable and practical he pitied the poor British soldiers so encumbered by long red coats, knee britches and heavy leather leggings. His tartan left his arms and hands free to handle his musket. In the event of rain the length that was fastened at his shoulder by a broach and hung down his back could be used to cover his head and musket. *Smart we are*, he thought with a grin . . . *very smart.*

On the Parade Grounds the Highland Infantry was running through their drills to the beat of a young drummer. Ian knew the drills by heart. Both here and at Fort King George they had done nothing but drill for months on end. Lulled by the heat and the familiar sound of fifes and drums Ian let his mind wander.

Yesterday, an Indian scout ran the length of the island to report that the Spanish had managed to sail past the fortifications at Fort St. Simons, on the south end, landing at Gascoigne Bluff. Frederica Town swarmed with activity. Eight hundred Redcoats were on duty, ready for action.

Notices were posted on the public wells, cannon rolled into place, and volunteers in town given guns and instruction. They were headed for a real fight for sure.

The jagged red scar on his temple itched and Ian's stomach contracted with anticipation. Someone would pay for his disfigurement and pay well! Just let some Yemassee cross his path. Stinkin' Indians!

The Highlanders were the only company guarding Frederica. Yesterday Oglethorpe had taken the Forty-Second Regiment of Foot, several troops of Independent Rangers, and about thirty Indians to fortify Fort St. Simons. All day the booming cannon had spoken of the battle being fought there.

Ian marched back and forth, slower now, the heat beginning to take its toll. The sun was merciless and driblets of sweat ran down his chest soaking his linen shirt. He yearned for a swim in the secluded creek he had discovered outside Frederica's walls and planned to head there as soon as he was relieved of duty.

His replacement, also in full uniform, suddenly appeared on the rampart and Ian smiled as he recognized Cory.

"Aye, 'tis wi' pleasure I hand over this miserable job," he said to his friend. "The sun is hot enough to bake one's brains."

Cory grinned. "If I haid any brains I doubt I wad ha' left Scotland."

Ian propped his musket against the stone tower and squatted in the meager shade it afforded. "All is quiet," he observed. "Not a ship in sight."

"I doubt they'll come by sea. I expect the land fight ta continue."

Ian withdrew his clay pipe and after smacking it smartly against the palm of his hand tamped tobacco into its bowl and scratched a match on the wall. He drew deeply, his green eyes squinting against the smoke, and let out a soft moan.

"We're vastly outnumbered, you know," he said somberly.

"Aye," Cory replied. "Toonahowi's scout said at least thirty Spanish vessels slipped by our fortifications yesterday afternoon. That means several thousand men to our wee five hundred. Three to one. We canna expect to hold off a force that size."

"Oglethorpe's a wily bugger, though. He'll know how to use these marshes and this miserable jungle to his advantage. He'll fight the Spaniards Indian style."

Cory frowned. "The scout said Oglethorpe plans t' abandon the fort and bring all our lads back t' Frederica. They spent the night putting supplies t' the torch."

"Aye. From the smoke clouding the sky I'd say they burned all they could lay their bloody hands on," Ian added.

"Including blowing up the magazines. I 'bout fell off my cot when the first explosion wakened me. I hope Oglethorpe saved enough for us to fight with. Sounded like he was blowing up the whole darn island."

Ian nodded and raked his fingers through his long hair. "I had my dream about the Campbells and MacDonalds again last night," he said soberly.

"'Tis a bad dream, laddie. One ye should forget."

"I know. Most of the time I remember Scotland with love." He smiled. "Funny thing is I often think of clouds swirling across the top of Highland cliffs and the spring run-off tumbling down their steep ravines. Georgia . . . and Florida . . . are so darn flat."

Cory nodded. "I don't know, Ian, sometimes I think I'll ask to go home when this engagement is over. I'm a man of honor and I'll serve out my enlistment but I long for Scotland wi' all me heart."

"But you know King George has a granite grip around the throat of Scotland. Our country is a breeding ground for plots to overthrow him. It's a dangerous place to be. And what about Sally?"

"Aye, that 'tis a wee problem. But home beckons me. 'Tis the season when the blue heather would be in full bloom and little sheep would be fattening themselves up for the coming winter."

"And I well remember those winters, the winds and snow

of February howling off the bald peaks of Ben Ness."

"Ah, but Ian, think then of the sun a sparklin' on the ice like a thousand diamonds." Cory's blue eyes danced. "An' of a steamin' bowl of Ma's porridge sprinkled with brown sugar."

"I remember. I also remember the half-frozen sheep huddled against dry stone walls, and the numbing cold of those majestic mountains of yours."

"'Tis true, but a dram of good malt whiskey takes the chill from a man's bones. Ye know we make the best in all of Scotland from our little distillery right in Pitlochry. It's the water that's our secret. That same water you remember thundering down the cliff sides."

Ian threw back his head and laughed. "Spoken like a true Scotsman." His face suddenly grew pensive. "Aye, Cory, I make fun but I too remember the beauty of our land. *Tir nam beann, nan gleans, nan gaisgeach.*"

Cory smiled. "Land of the mountains, the glens, and the heroes."

Ian drew on his pipe and leaned against the cool tabby wall blowing smoke at the biting sand gnats.

Cory suddenly cocked his head and fixed Ian with a grin. "Enough talk of battle and memories. Have ye seen the wee lass yet . . . that pretty little Indian girl that cared for ye at Fort Mosa?"

Ian grinned in return. "I've not had the time. You devil, you're always thinking of the lassies, aye?" He swatted at a gnat trying to enter his ear.

"Ye canna tell me ye weren't aware of her beauty. She seemed quite taken with ye, cradling y're head in her lap, bloody as ye were."

"But only a child . . . thirteen or fourteen."

"That was two years ago. The lassie's grown up now and quite an eyeful."

Ian's eyes twinkled. "Aye, and since you think her so bonny maybe you should go with me when I call at the Calwell's. Remember, I'm taken. I've a lass waiting for me in

Savannah"

"But you're still with the roving eye," Cory said with a wink. "What say we amble over to Broad Street after evening reveille and take a look at your wee Indian."

Ian sniffed the acrid, smoke-laden air. "Come evening I doubt we'll be calling on girls. We may be lucky to be alive." He lowered himself from the Parapet, brushing sand from his kilt. "I must go. I've guard duty at the Town Gate."

All during the previous night Oglethorpe, knowing he could not defend Fort St. Simons with his limited force, had his soldiers burn munitions and supplies, drive spikes into the vents of the cannon so they could not be fired, and ruin the wells. By mid-night, anxious to take advantage of darkness, he began to assemble the major part of his regiment for the long, dark trek back to Fort Frederica. The trail north led through dense thickets of palmetto and scrub oak. Thick vines clogged the path making it impossible to accommodate wagon traffic so everything salvageable had to be carried by hand or on pack animals. Oglethorpe stayed behind to bring up the rear and by morning the first of the rangers was approaching Frederica.

In an indirect way the abandoned supplies helped Oglethorpe's forces. The Yemassee Indians, on whom the Spanish counted heavily for scouting forays, found the deserted fort full of intriguing things to loot. Drunk and rich with spoils they had no interest in further exposure to bloody warfare.

The Spanish lost no time claiming the abandoned Fort St. Simons. Just before dawn two companies of Spanish grenadiers took possession of the fort to prevent further destruction of property. They found three seamen, two wounded and one dead, scalped by the Indians. The rest of the day was spent consolidating positions, landing supplies and preparing for battle. Indian scouts were sent out to search for a trail through the forest that would lead them inland to Fort Frederica. Tomorrow they would attack.

* * *

Before reporting to the Town Gate for duty, Ian stopped at the barracks for his weapon, a large, double-edged broadsword called a claymore, and strapped it to his side. After a minute's hesitation he slipped his dirk into its leather holster and reached under the bed to withdraw his sporran, a brass shield intended to protect his privates. Chuckling softly, he fastened it around his hips. This was one area he wanted to take no chances with! He glanced quickly into the sliver of mirror hanging above his bedside table and drew his hands through his long hair. He really needed a haircut. Maybe tomorrow he could visit the barber. Finally he grabbed his musket, slapped his blue tam on his head and was off.

The afternoon was hazy with heat, and sweat dampened his jacket as he walked back and forth before the gate in the palisade that guarded the town. The tide was in and the moat full. Suddenly he spotted a young girl walking along Broad Street toward him. There was something familiar about her, the way she walked, the way she tilted her head in an almost regal manner. He squinted his eyes in concentration. Where had he seen her before?

She was tall, as tall as he, with hair the color of black swamp water worn in a single, thick braid secured by a leather thong. Her blue homespun dress was English with a high neckline and narrow sleeves cuffed at the wrist. A half apron of soft doeskin was tied around her waist. That triggered the memory—soft leather pressed against the wound in his temple. This was the Indian girl who had saved his life at Fort Mosa.

Her eyes sparkled as she reached him and she gave him a warm smile.

"Hello, Lieutenant MacDonald."

"Hello," he stammered. "Tabitha, isn't it?"

"Yes"

"I hardly recognized you. You've grown up."

"I'm sixteen, now."

"And a bonny lass, you are, I must say. I heard you were

here at Frederica. Our regiment just arrived from Darien, but I planned to come by and thank you properly."

"I'm a bondservant in the home of John Calwell." She blushed, lowering her eyes. "I'm happy to see you fully recovered," she said shyly.

Her smile and the flush that came to her cheeks transformed her face and threw him completely off balance. Ian swallowed dryly. Her skin was the color of dark honey and only her eyes, a startling blue that seemed to glow from the inside, spoke of her white parentage.

He touched the scar at his temple. "Recovered except for this daily reminder," he said gruffly.

Tabitha made a move toward the gate and Ian snapped to attention.

"Where are you going, lass?"

"I know these palisades are for our protection, but I feel like a bird in a cage. I need to get outside for just a little while."

"I'm afraid I can't let you leave today. You must know the Spanish are on the island and could be headed our way."

"But it's only for a moment. I won't venture far," she said, her lips pursed, her eyes narrowed. "Only to the burial grounds and a short way up the military road."

Stubborn. "I'm sorry, lass. It's far too dangerous," he said.

Tabitha chewed on her lip. "I heard the noise and saw the smoke from Fort St. Simons last night. I thought all the fighting was taking place there. Do you really think they'll come to Frederica?"

"A scout arrived an hour ago saying that Oglethorpe has abandoned the fort and is on his way here. There will be a battle at Frederica, Tabitha."

"Then, you're right. I'd better hurry home. The Calwell children will be so frightened." Her gaze rested on the musket at his side, then moved up to his face. "You will be in danger, once more, Lieutenant MacDonald."

"Ian," he said, feeling a faint intoxication at the tenderness in her eyes.

"Ian, then. I . . . I pray that God will be with you."

Ian smiled thinly. "I believe both sides will be praying to the same God for victory." He patted the broadsword hanging at his side. "I tend to put most of my trust in my claymore, but thank you, lass." She was glancing away from him now, at something outside the gate. Her dusky face was arresting, the narrow, straight nose, the high cheekbones, and the strong chin. *None of the voluptuousness, here, of Charlotte,* he thought. *There was nothing soft about this girl.*

Tabitha looked back at him and hesitated as though to say more. Then with nothing more than a smile she turned for home.

Ian, confused at his feelings in seeing her leave, found himself watching the sway of her slim hips as she walked away.

As Tabitha retraced her steps to the Calwell house she fought hard to keep from turning to see if he was watching her. Mostly because she wanted to think he was and she did not want to find out that he wasn't. She had no right to feel such a strong attraction for this man of whom she knew nothing. He was a proud Highlander, a warrior by trade and a man of little faith judging from what he had just said. At times she struggled on her own faith journey. She needed no detractors in her life. The man might be married with a family. She shook her head. Thoughts of Lieutenant MacDonald . . . Ian . . . forebode only trouble.

Her footsteps quickened as she pondered the possibility of a coming battle. She must get home and warn Mrs. Calwell if the master had not already done so. Her ears strained for the sound of gunfire but she heard only the distant call of a turkey. With a bleak wintry feeling she looked at the lovely orange trees lining the wide street, the scent of their blossoms heavy in the air despite the cloying smoke coming from the south end of the island. Surely God would not allow war to mar so much beauty.

She was almost at the Calwell gate when she heard the

sound of approaching horses and shouting men. She spun around to see a stream of soldiers filing through the town gate.

As the men marched down Broad Street toward the barracks she could see exhaustion etched on their dirty, scratched faces. Anxious townspeople rushed into the street to call questions but the weary soldiers had no answers. At the end of the long column Oglethorpe appeared with the last of the Forty-Second Regiment of Foot. As he moved among them on his magnificent steed he shouted orders for all citizens to assemble at the Parade Grounds for instructions and Tabitha followed the crowd to listen to his orders.

"All women and children are to be evacuated at once to the mainland," he commanded in a voice ringing with authority. "Every available man in town should secure arms and report for duty. I have pressed into service the crews of several merchant vessels that have moved up the river to escape the Spanish and mounted additional guns on the inner bastion to control the water approaches. We are prepared. Do not panic."

Reassured by the general's leadership that everything possible was being done, Tabitha ran back to the Calwell house to help prepare for the evacuation.

Constance Calwell flitted from room to room in a panic. The elegant home held many antiques and in addition to her silver and rare tapestries she had many pieces of exquisite English porcelain. The townspeople had been told they could take only one valise per person but Constance had Tabitha roll several small vases in petticoats and stuff them into her bag.

Tabitha paused momentarily as she heard John Calwell push the heavy kitchen door back on its leather hinges, then stop in the pantry to use a metal staff to draw off his muddy boots.

"Constance!" he shouted. "Constance! Where are you?"

"We're here . . . in the dining room," she shouted back.

Tabitha was at the china closet wrapping the Calwell crystal goblets in huck towels and watched Constance rush into her husband's arms.

"Oh, John," she cried with a sob. "We're to be evacuated. Everything will be lost."

"Now, now, Constance. Get control of yourself. The fort will hold. Oglethorpe just wants to make certain the women and children are safe."

"And you . . . what about you? Will you stay to fight . . . will you be safe?"

"The men have been asked to stand ready to do what they can."

Constance lifted her head from his shoulder to gaze into his eyes. "Come with us, we need you," she implored.

"You know I can't do that," he snapped. "The boats are for women and children only. Now quit fussing and get your bags ready."

A loud commotion from the street caused them to rush to the open window. Frederica Town was in chaos. People were shouting at one another, livestock and horses were being brought from outlying fields and herded into the protection of the walled town, hogs and cattle ran wild and soldiers were everywhere.

John shook his head. "I need to be out there to help restore order. Get the children ready and pack what you need. You will probably be on the mainland for several days."

"No. I need your help. You must dig up a patch of the garden to bury my porcelain and silver," Constance said.

Tabitha's hands quieted over her work as she watched Mr. Calwell's face flush. He was a stern, domineering man and his allegiance to Oglethorpe was absolute. It was known around the garrison that John Calwell excelled at his work precisely because of these qualities, and he ruled his household and his wife with the same military precision. He did not take orders from his wife.

"Let Tabitha do it, or one of the other servants," he said gruffly.

"All but cook are already gone . . . and I need Tabitha to help with the packing. We've only been given an hour."

"Then let the children do it. It'll keep them busy and give them a purpose. Tell them to dig a ditch beside the parsnips. Where are they by the way?"

"Upstairs packing."

"Well then, I'll be back as soon as I can to carry your bags to the wharf." He saw Constance hand a porcelain figurine to Tabitha. John's ruddy face stretched into a grimace. "For heavens sake, woman, we don't have time to save everything in the house. Families are already boarding the schooner. You must pack quickly. I'll be back in twenty minutes. Everyone must be ready to go. Put your bags on the stoop." He grabbed his boots and slammed out the door.

Constance's hand shook as she took the figurine from Tabitha and placed it beside the silver, and she fought to keep her poise as she issued orders. "Go upstairs and collect the children and their things. Put Henry in charge. Make certain they have packed the necessities. Then send them to me. They can bury these few valuables while we close the house."

Tabitha's eyes widened as she heard the ship's shrill whistle and she fairly flew up the stairs.

When the children were finally dispatched to their mother Tabitha climbed the steps to her bedroom to pack her own valise. Sounds of chaos and the scent of the mimosa tree outside her open window wafted into the room as she hurried to gather her few personal belongings. Lovingly she packed her mother's amulet, a moth-eaten fur cap of her father's, a few beaded headbands and lastly the small Bible given to her by John Wesley when she was baptized.

Two cookies rested on a napkin on a small table by her bed, the smell of anise reminding her that she had had eaten no breakfast and was very hungry. She took a large bite and stuffed the other into her apron pocket. It could very well be the only thing she would have to eat for quite awhile.

To the children it was an unexpected adventure. They

bounded ahead of Tabitha and Constance as they headed for the dock, eager to board one of the sloops waiting to transport them to the mainland. Sad as she was, Tabitha could not help but smile at their exuberance. Only children, in their innocence, have no fear of the unknown.

Teary-eyed women and excited children crowded the rail as the schooner *Safire* pulled away from the Frederica wharf. Constance knew of the great danger to her husband and fought bravely to keep her composure in front of her family. Tabitha ached to put her arms around the trembling woman but it was not her place to do so. Instead, she stood as close to her mistress as she dared and watched the receding shore in somber silence.

Once more she was being dislocated, her safe haven safe no longer. The ship plowed the waters with a brooding menace. If the Spanish were victorious at St. Simons, then the mainland and Georgia's entire coastline would be vulnerable. She thought of Ian and Broken Arrow, both fighting under Oglethorpe's command, and bowed her head in a silent prayer that God would keep them safe. Anxiety roiled in her chest, a low dangerous humming like a hornet's nest under the eaves.

The ship entered a narrow ribbon of water between the island and the mainland. Woods of pine, live oaks and cedar grew close to the banks of the sea-green inlet. To Tabitha's right the quiet marsh grass undulated gracefully before a gentle breeze that bespoke a coming shower.

Almost imperceptibly, a low bank of clouds changed the color of the grass. At times, it was a golden green with a hint of purple in the shadows along the water's edge, at times so dark that the creeks winding through it shone like quicksilver. A Louisiana heron stepped regally across a tidal pool seeking its dinner and several snowy egrets looked up from their feeding to watch the passage of the ship.

To Tabitha's left a glen displayed fig trees hanging full of rich, luscious fruit. She marveled at the wonderful fertility and adaptability of the soil on St. Simons Island. Oranges, lemons, limes, almonds, pecans, bananas, oleanders, crape jasmine and azaleas flourished in a perfect state of harmony with nature.

And then there was man with his war-like ways. Last night cannon had muted the call of the mocking bird, smoke masked the scent of orange trees and today men would face one another with drawn swords and guns. And this fertile ground would run red with blood.

Tabitha was unaware of the tear that dripped from her chin onto the railing.

Chapter Thirteen

While the women and children were being evacuated, Oglethorpe began to assemble his forces. Mary Musgrove sent her Creek Indians, Squirrel King assembled his Chickasaws and Toonahowi his Yamacraws. All told, by days end, Oglethorpe had a force of about seven hundred men to place into battle against close to three thousand well-seasoned Spanish troops.

The assembled soldiers presented a colorful picture. Like their male counterparts in the animal kingdom the men were flamboyant in colorful attire. Men of the Forty-Second Regiment of Foot wore black cocked hats adorned with silver lace, a bright red jacket with green lapels and lining, a red waistcoat, red knee britches and brown spatterdashs to cover their lower legs. Crimson sashes, silver-hilted swords, brass buttons and silver buckles glinted in the sun. The Highland Scots were almost as colorful in their black-watch tartan, blue tams, red jacket and red-checkered stockings.

Meanwhile the Spaniards spent all of Tuesday at the abandoned Fort St. Simons setting up camp, posting guards, and taking possession of the spoils left behind by the retreating British army. There wasn't much of value left and certainly no whiskey. The Indians had seen to that.

The Spanish leader, Florida's Governor Manuel de Montiano, was eager to follow up his advantage and finish the British off, but he still did not know which of several trails led to the fort at Frederica. He waited till morning, and then sent several dozen of his scouts and about forty Yemassee Indians to search once more for the Frederica trail. Within an hour they stumbled onto it and began to follow its torturous path. Although this was the main trail used to travel between forts the jungle like vegetation was constantly encroaching and travel was slow. For four and one-half miles the narrow footpath, infested with snakes and alligators, skirted the savannah marshlands on the eastern side of the island before it turned northwest for another three miles through wooded ground toward the fortifications at Frederica. The Scouts made good progress and by mid-morning they were within a mile and a half of Frederica where they ran headlong into five of Oglethorpe's rangers patrolling the trail.

The Spaniards and Indians dived for cover while the ranger company, still mounted on their steeds, began to fire. One of Oglethorpe's best sharpshooters, William Small, took a lead ball to his leg and fell to the ground. The Indians swarmed over him with their hatchets.

The four remaining rangers raced to Frederica to sound the alarm. They reined their horses, slathered with sweat, to a halt on the Parade Ground where Oglethorpe was drilling the Highlanders.

"The Spaniards have reached Gully Hole Creek. They're almost at the town gate," they shouted.

"How many?" Oglethorpe barked.

"Impossible to tell, sir," a breathless soldier, barely out of his teens, answered in a squeaky voice. "They apparently heard our horses and took cover before we spotted them."

"William Small fell," one of the rangers said. "He's probably dead, sir. The Yemassee were all over him."

Oglethorpe's mind raced. If Montiano's entire army was on the trail and within a mile of the town gate there was no time to lose. His eyes raked the Parade Ground. The Highland Company, under command of Charles Mackay, mustering between thirty and forty men, was the only infantry unit in formation prepared to march. He could not wait to assemble the Forty-Second Regiment or any of his other forces. He had to intercept Montiano on the trail.

"Give me your horse," he ordered the nearest soldier. He vaulted into the saddle and turned to the silent Highlanders watching him with anxious eyes.

"Follow me," he roared as he spurred the horse and led the Highlanders through the town gate and down Military Trail at a dead run.

Salty sweat ran down Ian's forehead burning his eyes. Running a long distance behind a galloping horse during a hot July day in Georgia, dressed in a woolen uniform and carrying twenty-five pounds of weapons and equipment would have defeated lesser men but the Highlanders were a hardy lot. Cory ran at his side and managed a strained smile. "'Tis war, mon," he gasped.

"Aye." Ian felt a stitch in his side and almost staggered, but kept on running, pushing dangling vines out of his face and flailing at the encroaching vegetation. He vaulted over a fallen log landing in mud that almost sucked the shoes from his feet.

Toonahowi, Oglethorpe's lead scout together with a party of Yamacraw and Creek and a party of Squirrel King's Chickasaw had managed to catch up with them and together they raced down the narrow trail. Broken Arrow had joined them and was hurtling along just behind.

Ian drew on all his strength. Demere's rangers were all mounted but somehow he, Cory, and four other Highlanders were keeping up. They had just rounded a slight bend in the wood-enclosed trail when they saw the Spaniards crossing an open marsh headed for the cover of a nearby creek bed.

With a shout, Oglethorpe spurred his horse directly at them. For Indians and Highlanders, all warlike by tradition, the charge represents life at its best. Ian, as all soldiers must if they are to survive, felt a brief moment of fear. Then a surge of adrenalin fired his body and with a whoop to match his Indian comrades he flung himself forward into the mass of Spanish regulars.

It was really no contest. They were evenly matched in number, this was not Montiano's main body, and the Spanish were terrified by the screaming charge. Broken Arrow with blood pouring down his leg aimed his pistol at a Spanish officer, fired, and killed him. With sword drawn Cory chased a soldier into the underbrush, and after several moments of sparring Ian plunged his dirk into the chest of a wild-eyed Spaniard. Soldiers were falling all around him and Gully Hole Creek ran with blood. Then several of the enemy threw down their weapons in surrender and the rest stumbled into the woods and back along the trail.

Oglethorpe regrouped his elated men as quickly as possible and they pursued the fleeing Spaniards. Ian's heart swelled with pride. The Highlanders had fought well. He almost smiled as he remembered the surprised look on the faces of the Spanish when the men came charging out of the woods and they heard the *slaugh ghairm,* the eerie battle cry of the Highlander clans, and the war hoops of the Indians.

Oglethorpe and several rangers rode hard in pursuit of the retreating grenadiers, and then halted at the marsh to wait for the Highlanders to catch up. When they arrived, out of breath but fired with the thrill of battle, Oglethorpe drew them together.

"I have formulated a plan," he said, his voice strong with self-confidence. Montiano will soon send units to counter-attack and I need more men if there is to be a showdown battle. You will block the trail here as best you can while I go back to the fort to assemble the rest of our forces." He looked over the men at his disposal. "Mackay," he barked, "I want your Highlanders on the west side of the trail and Demere's regulars on the east. If any one can delay the advance of the Spanish, you boys can." He turned to the watchful Toonahowi. "Have your braves melt into the woods. Stay hidden until the battle is joined."

As Oglethorpe rode away Ian stood in the thick forest and surveyed the terrain before him with a critical eye. Open marsh perhaps a hundred yards wide lay in front of them.

Charles Mackay strode over to join Ian and together they looked across the marsh.

"They must come this way," Mackay said. "'Tis the only path."

"And wide open," Ian observed.

"Aye. Take your men, Lieutenant, and build a defensive line of fallen logs and limbs in this tree line. I'll tell Captain Demere what we are doing and he can do the same. Then, hide your men well and wait."

Ian immediately went into action. Within an hour several inconspicuous brush piles had been erected, the logs strewn haphazardly so as to appear as natural windfall. Satisfied with the results, he sought out Cory and together they crouched behind a massive log, muskets at the ready. Ian winced as he knelt on the ground. His knees were badly scratched and bleeding. "Times like this I wish we wore britches," he muttered.

Cory fingered a large rent in his kilt. "And this came from a bloody sword a wee bit too close to me liking."

Ian glanced over his shoulder. "At least we're alive and some Indian isn't riding around with our scalp on the end of his pole. Watch your back though, Cory. There must be dozens of lost Spaniards wandering around in these woods looking for the way home." A sudden splat of water hit Ian on the head and he looked up at the darkening sky. "Oh, no! It looks like we're in for a downpour."

Within minutes the sky opened and a steady rain began to fall. Ian loosened the broach at his shoulder and used the length of tartan that hung down his back to wrap his musket. All along the line men bent over their muskets to keep their priming powder dry as they stared across the marsh.

"God may be on our side," Cory said softly. "This rain will make it even harder for the enemy to see us."

Ian looked at Cory in surprise. "First time I ever heard you mention God, unless you were cursing his name."

"Times like this me mind does wander t' its better side."

Just then Ian heard the noise of approaching horses. He

squinted against the rain, peering intently across the marsh. There was definitely movement on the other side. As he and Cory watched a Spanish platoon began to file across a narrow causeway spanning the marsh. Ian readied his musket and held his breath.

Midway across the causeway the column suddenly stopped. Something must have alarmed them. Ian could see an officer talking to several grenadiers and pointing to the pile of logs where the Highlanders hid. The Spaniards consulted for a few minutes then several of their soldiers marched forward to investigate.

The British troops held their fire waiting for them to get within range.

"Ain't that a bloody sight," Cory whispered.

The grenadiers were big men, resplendent in white uniforms and wearing tall hats that made them look all the more formidable. Closer and closer they came until suddenly Mackay shouted the order to fire. Brush and trees on both sides of the trail erupted with the sing of arrows and the blast of smoke from a hundred British muskets. Volley after volley came crashing out of the woods followed by great belches of black smoke that hung low under the rain to settle over the savannah.

Several grenadiers were cut down as they ran to rejoin the halted column, which was hastily retreating to the cover of trees on the south side of the marsh. Once in position the enemy began placing a disciplined fire on the British.

Ian was having trouble seeing. The steady rain held a thick brownish pall of smoke over the forest obscuring the field of battle. The Spaniards were shouting, their drummers loudly beating commands. Ian's stomach clenched. From the volume of noise there appeared to be thousands of men on the other side. And Oglethorpe and his reserves had not arrived from Frederica.

Out of the corner of his eyes he saw a commotion on Captain Demere's side of the trail. Several regulars appeared to have become frightened and turned to flee. Ian watched in disbelief as three whole platoons broke rank and ran with Captain Demere in pursuit.

Real fear now overtook Ian. With Demere's defection only a small company of regulars under the command of John Sutherland remained to hold the left side of the road, his own Highlander Company on the right, and the entire Spanish army in front of them.

"Keep up your fire," Mackay yelled to his men. "They can't see us and they don't know how strong we may be."

Or how few, Ian thought bitterly.

For over an hour the outnumbered rangers, Highlanders and Indians continued firing steadily across the marsh at the Spanish grenadiers. It never occurred to Ian to quit the battle. His blood was on fire, his steely gaze never leaving the marsh in front of him.

"I told ye God called down the rain," Cory said with a twinkle in his eye. "They canna see so they dinna ken that almost half of the British force has fled and the other half hasn't arrived."

About four o'clock the bewildered Spanish formed three companies into marching order and began an orderly retreat.

"It canna be true." Cory sputtered as he watched the grenadiers disappear. He took his tam off and threw it in the air. "We held them," he yelled as he caught Ian around the waist and danced a jig. "We held the bloody devils."

They both turned toward the sound of horses approaching along the trail from Frederica. Oglethorpe rode at the head of a regiment of Marines and the chagrined troops of Captain Demere. The general reined to a halt, his piercing eyes taking in the celebrating soldiers.

The look of disbelief and surprise changed to one of pride and relief. He leaped from his horse and shook the grimy hands of Captains Sutherland and Mackay.

"Good job, men . . . a jolly good job."

Then he looked across the smoky field at the backs of the retreating Spaniards. The marsh ran red with the blood of the fallen soldiers. "I won't be a bit surprised," Oglethorpe said sadly, "if the history books refer to this particular engagement as the Battle of the Bloody Marsh."

Tabitha stood on the deck of the schooner and gazed across the murky water toward the horizon, a glittering margin between sea and sky, broken by golden marshes opening on both sides of the winding river. She stared at the water, felt the warm breeze brush her face and, despite the danger, and like the children, she began to look forward to the adventure ahead of them.

As soon as the boat carrying the evacuees docked at the Darien wharf Tabitha saw to the valises and hustled the children down the ramp behind Mrs. Calwell. With several bags in her hands she stood on the quayside amid the noise and bustle of disembarking women and children. The heat wrapped around her like a damp, muffling blanket. Villagers had gathered to help them, dogs barked and familiar smells assaulted her nose: tar, salt, fish and wood smoke.

Henry, his chest swelling with importance, took Connie and Johnnie by the hand and started along the path leading to Fort King George while the rest of the women and children fell into line behind him.

Hackberry trees, with pale colored leaves and prickly bark, crowded the trail and nearby marsh hens rattled and called. In one arm Tabitha carried Constance's heaviest valise packed with valuable porcelain and in the other her own light satchel. This day, seventh of July, had dawned blurred by a steamy haze and now the sky was threatening rain. Her stomach knotted as she thought about the soldiers and scouts probably fighting for their lives at this very minute on St. Simons Island. Lieutenant MacDonald's face flashed before her eyes and she bit her lip and mumbled a short prayer for his safety. Then she added a small prayer in Cherokee for Broken Arrow.

As they rounded a slight bend in the trail she saw the hulking outline of the fort dead ahead. It was not as large or impressive as the fort at Frederica and, although well fortified with cannon, appeared to be deserted except for a few token sentries. Tabitha assumed that Captain Mackay, with the Highland Infantry, had gone to Oglethorpe's assistance.

As they gathered before the gate several of the soldiers approached and led them across the moat and into the blockhouse and deserted barracks. The women quickly took possession of the beds. Henry and Johnnie claimed a double-decker bunk that stood near the door and Constance and Tabitha took possession of the one beside it. Connie would sleep with her mother.

A hasty meal was thrown together by the fort's overwhelmed cooks to feed the hungry and exhausted evacuees. Tabitha was almost too tired to eat and as soon as the sparse meal was finished they all filed back to the barracks for any sleep they might be able to garner.

Tabitha had just finished tucking the children into bed when Constance hurried to her side.

"The soldiers say we will be moved inland to Fort Argyle if the Spanish capture Frederica. It will offer more protection. They say it is heavily fortified to guard against Indian attacks."

Tabitha flushed. "I know it well. It is on a bluff of the Ogeechee River near Conoochee Creek and my village of Tustacatty."

Constance's lips twitched and she forced a smile. "Yes . . . ah . . . I sometimes forget your origins."

"Well, hopefully the Spanish will be defeated and there will be no need to move us again," Tabitha said in a wooden voice.

"We will pray for that." Constance leaned down to kiss the children goodnight and moved away without a further look in Tabitha's direction.

The next day word was received at Darien that the Spanish had been soundly spanked at St. Simons and withdrawn to the south end of the island to lick their wounds. For now it was safe to return to Frederica and within hours they were homeward bound.

* * *

Several days had passed since their return to Frederica Town and late one evening Tabitha sat before her tiny bedroom window looking across the moonlit lawn toward the Barracks where the soldiers were bivouacked. Her stomach knotted with worry as she wondered if Lieutenant MacDonald had survived the fierce battle she had heard was fought at Gully Hole Creek and the marsh. She could see soldiers moving about the grounds and she was well aware that after taps the Lieutenant could often be seen leaving his lodging to walk past the Calwell home with a fishing pole in his hand.

The July day had been sweltering, the air so hot and heavy you could barely breathe. John Calwell had been in an exceptionally vile mood that had Constance flustered as a hen with a broken egg. Tabitha felt she could not stand the oppressive atmosphere and heat a moment longer so after putting the cranky children to bed she bathed, slipped on a pair of soft moccasins and a loose fitting frock of the thinnest material she could find and left the house by the back door. With a light step she headed down Broad Street toward the river. The fort loomed ahead eerie in the moonlight and Tabitha shivered.

Even so, if there were a chance to catch a hint of breeze from the nearby ocean it would be at the public dock. The fact that Ian might be fishing there did not enter into the equation. At least that's what she told herself.

A hazy moon hung in the sky looking just as woebegone as she felt. The street was deserted, even the normal drunken singing from the taverns was muted and dispirited.

As she drew closer to the river she could smell the faint saltiness of the nearby sea, the damp decaying vegetation of the encroaching forest and a hint of dried beef, fish, and molasses from the fort's storehouse.

Her moccasins made no noise on the shell path. Then her heart leaped as she saw a shadowy form sitting on the dock. It was Ian and he was alone. She sank down beside a live oak, filled with gratitude that he was alive, yet reluctant to disturb his solitude.

Tabitha sat quietly watching his rugged profile in the silvery light of the summer night. She was attracted to Ian, she admitted that, and she thought she had detected a spark of interest from him when they talked. And chance did seem to keep bringing them together. But she did not believe in chance. She had always been of the conviction that if one wanted something to happen one had to make it happen. First, though, she had to find out if he were married.

She cocked her head. Was that music she heard? It seemed to be coming from a tiny piece of metal he held in his mouth and sounded like a stringed instrument, full of curious half-tones.

An owl hooted in a nearby tree and Ian stopped playing to peer in the direction of the noise. He saw her immediately and smiled.

Should she walk over and begin a conversation or wait to see if he would approach her? *Oh, God,* she prayed. *Tell me what to do.*

Neither of them moved. Then a slow smile spread across his face as he removed the musical instrument from his mouth and beckoned to her.

Tabitha's heart thudded in her chest. Ian had the most incredibly masculine features she had ever seen—a strong, square chin, well-defined jaws, and heavy brows over hooded green eyes. He had removed his jacket and a soft homespun shirt clung to his torso, revealing heavily muscled shoulders and arms.

"Tabitha?" he said.

"Yes. I . . . I desperately needed a breath of air. I didn't expect to find anyone here."

"Nor, did I expect to have a pretty lass appear from the shadows to brighten my evening." He patted a place beside him. "Sit down, please. I welcome the company."

Tabitha lowered herself a few paces from him and carefully swung her legs over the edge of the dock, patting her long skirt into place. "Please don't stop playing. I didn't mean to interrupt." She wrinkled her brow. "I have never seen an instrument like that. What's it called?"

"A Jew's harp." He held it out for her to see. It was a small, bow-shaped frame, closed on one end with something that resembled a key. "This one belonged to my father. If it weren't so tarnished you'd see it is made of silver, though most are made of forged iron. See, you hold it against your teeth or lips and pluck this little key with your finger. By holding the closed end in your mouth you can make different pitches and sounds by changing the size and shape of your mouth."

"I've been listening. It's quite amazing."

Ian nodded and placed the Jew's harp to his lips. Music once more tinkled on the night air and Tabitha closed her eyes to drift with the sound. When he finished he gave her a big grin and swung into a lively tune that set her foot to swing back and forth.

She looked at him boldly. "I'm glad to find you survived the battle. From what I hear it was the Highlanders who saved the day."

Even in the faint light of the moon she could see his chest swell with pride. "Aye, our unit did a fine job. As did Sutherland's rangers. He's been promoted to major, you know."

"There were Creek warriors, too, weren't there?"

"Yes, and they scared the hel . . . heck out of the Spaniards with their bloodcurdling yells."

"Do you think the Spanish will return?"

"Oglethorpe suspects they will. In fact he has ordered a company of us to scout Fort St. Simons and Gascoigne Bluff to see what they are up to. We leave at dawn."

"I hope you find them loading their ships to return to Florida."

"If they do retreat there is a rumor Oglethorpe will make another raid on St. Augustine."

"Oh, dear. Is there always to be war and bloodshed for possession of this beautiful land God has given us?"

Ian gave her a rueful smile. "I guess so. Everyone wants the American soil—if not the sneaking Indians, then the French hotheads and the land thirsty Spanish. I, for one, have a score to settle in Florida." He fingered the angry scar at his temple. "I lost many of my best friends at Fort Mosa. I'm itching for revenge . . . literally."

Tabitha cringed. The disdain in Ian's voice when he said the word "Indians" was quite obvious. She felt her temper begin to boil. Did he not know that the land Britain and Spain were fighting over rightly belonged to the Indians? That the desire to wrest it away from them came from his own kind. She bit her tongue to keep from retorting.

Silence descended on them as Tabitha searched for something light-hearted to say. Several piraguas, with sails furled, bobbed on the black water. A large fish jumped for an insect, the moon washing its fins with silver, as it landed with a loud splash.

Ian chuckled as he watched the ripples spread in a large circle. "And me without a pole. I figured the water too warm tonight for the fishing to be worthwhile."

"I love to fish . . . as a child I begged my father to take me with him." Frown lines puckered her forehead. "In the white man's world it isn't considered lady-like for a woman to fish with the men. I imagine Master Calwell would have apoplexy if he caught me."

Ian looked at her intently. "Was your father Indian, or was it your mother?"

"My mother. My father was a white fur trader."

"You speak excellent English."

"When hostilities broke out between the Creeks and the French, my father sent me to Savannah for the summer to live with my grandparents. I was tutored in English and introduced to Christianity. I loved Savannah. I miss it."

"My fiancée lives there."

Tabitha blinked with surprise. His fiancée! She fingered a crease in her skirt with trembling fingers, feeling the blood drain from her face. "Will you be wed soon?" she asked fighting to control the hitch in her voice.

Ian did not answer immediately. In his characteristic way, when searching for a thought, he removed a pipe and tobacco from his leather sporran and prepared it for smoking. Still not speaking, he struck a match on the rough wood of the dock and took a deep draw, his forehead knotted in thought. "There are complications. Her father does not think me a proper suitor for her hand."

"Because of your profession as a soldier?"

"No, although I'm sure that will present another obstacle." A thin spiral of smoke encircled his head as he drew deeply on his pipe. "It's a long story if you've the inclination to listen."

Tabitha merely nodded her head.

"By blood I am a Highlander of the Clan MacDonald from Glencoe. My mother died of milk fever after the birth of William, my youngest brother, and my father was imprisoned during the Jacobite rebellion. During his imprisonment we were cared for by an elderly uncle, Randolph MacDonald. When Da was released we returned to our farm and barely eked out a living. One day, my friend and I attended a rally in Inverness and listened to the promises of a Georgia recruiter about a better life in America. We decided to emigrate." He hesitated, then with a wry grin continued. "I won't go into the details but I had a turn of bad luck while waiting to sail and was forced to seek indentured service. But I was lucky in a way. Gustav Bruner, a well-known clockmaker in Savannah purchased me as an apprentice.

"Mr. Bruner was a hard taskmaster, but he taught me well. Unfortunately, my temperament is not that of a clockmaker and I'm afraid he recognized my rebellious nature with increasing concern."

Ian chuckled and drew deeply on his pipe. "To my dismay, he also recognized that where I lacked enthusiasm for the clock making trade I made up for it with an interest in his beautiful daughter, Charlotte. Despite his displeasure Charlotte and I fell deeply in love. Mr. Bruner made it clear that he had no intention of letting his daughter marry an indentured tradesman. She has a social position in Savannah and was to be presented at last year's cotillion. With her beauty and sizeable dowry she could have the pick of any number of wealthy young bachelors. He forbade Charlotte to see me.

"I'm afraid his displeasure fell on deaf ears. We sought every opportunity to be together and one night he caught us together in an embrace. I guess he decided drastic measures had to be taken."

Ian fell silent and Tabitha, who had forced herself to remain quiet and not interrupt the flow of his story, finally said, "What happened?"

"He had me shanghaied."

Tabitha gasped.

"I went to the local tavern the next evening to have a pint and think about my situation. Apparently he paid someone to powder my ale because when I woke up the next morning I found myself on a ship with a regiment of Scots Highlanders bound for the Georgia port of Darien."

"Could you not have escaped? I mean you were still in the colonies."

"Yes, but I'll admit I was intrigued by the Highlander Company. I felt like I had come home, that I was among my own. Without knowing it I was bored by life in Savannah and craved something more exciting. My best friend was here and full of enthusiasm for the life of a Scots Highlander soldier. Now I've learned to know myself. I'm a leader not a follower. Besides, it's obvious that Mr. Bruner is not going to take me back into his home and business and is certainly not going to give his approval for me to marry his daughter."

"But you have been in touch with her? She still waits for you?"

Ian nodded. "We correspond through one of her friends. She loves me and says she will wait until she is old enough to wed without her father's approval. When this present bout of hostilities is over I plan to ask for a time of leave and go to

Savannah to see her." Ian's voice became wooden, distant. "I don't know what will happen. Charlotte writes that she waits for me, but she is a beautiful, wealthy girl and I suspect many are in pursuit of her."

"Does she know her father is responsible for what happened to you?"

"Aye, that is how I know I was not shanghaied by accident. She wrote that she overheard him talking to her mother. She was furious, of course, but there was nothing she could do. The deed had already been done."

Tabitha's pulse raced and she forced herself to study him. Until now she had denied to herself how deeply attracted she was to this man. Now that she knew he was in love with another could she bury these feelings and maintain a simple friendship? He apparently liked her and enjoyed talking to her. Loneliness, like a heavy blanket, smothered her and she shuddered.

Ian had twisted to watch her with a strange look on his face. Did he sense her distress? Forcing a smile to her lips she said, "She is a lucky girl to have someone so committed."

"Sometimes I feel guilty, though. Her father has unintentionally led me to my true vocation. I was born to be a member of the Highlander Company, not a clockmaker. Charlotte was born to a life of wealth, to having anything she wanted. I wonder how she will adapt to military life."

A thousand answers flew into Tabitha's mind but she dared not give voice to any of them. After all she did not know this girl and she did not want to sound like a jealous shrew.

Instead she said. "You must love her very much."

"I do," he said gravely and looked away. A muscle throbbed in his jaw. "But I have chosen a dangerous profession."

His words saddened her. "I pray God will keep you safe from Spanish eyes tomorrow. Do be careful."

"To quote a Scottish poet, 'I care not for risk, my blood runs free and kens no protection but the cross o' the sword.'" His voice swaggered as he mouthed the words.

"Do you not believe in the protection of the Lord?"

"Of course I do. My family always attended the Presbyterian kirk in our valley and my mother was quite devout while she lived. But I can't help wonder where God was when she died young, my father was falsely imprisoned and old man Bruner's thugs drugged me and dumped me on a ship."

"God was with you. Didn't you say you have found your true vocation? We cannot know His plan for our lives. But we must trust Him to know what is best for us."

"God? I thought you Indians only believed in a Spirit of some kind."

Tabitha winced. Whatever else the Lieutenant was he was no diplomat. "I am a Christian," she retorted hotly.

"And a spunky one from what I hear. Cory told me about your fight with the alligator."

"Cory?"

"My best friend. He was the Highlander who came to your aid at Darien. He didn't realize you were the same girl who had saved my life at Fort Mosa until later. You were a child then." A tiny smile flickered over his mouth. She could not tell if it was admiration or only amusement. He smacked his pipe on the palm of his hand. "Cory was quite impressed by your bravery when you saved that Indian from the gator'. He has been pushing me for an introduction."

"Then why haven't you . . . introduced me, that is? As I remember he was quite handsome and quite compassionate toward the brave who was injured."

Ian seemed disconcerted by her answer. His sea-green eyes seared her with intensity.

Tabitha found herself blushing, something she seldom did. It annoyed her because she had no wish for Lieutenant MacDonald to get ideas that she had feelings for him.

"I will," he finally said. "Next time we see you. But I warn you he's quite the ladies man. You are far safer sitting here talking to me."

"I'll remember that . . . now, I must get back," she said,

making a move to lift herself from the dock. Ian held out his hand and helped her rise. It was warm and firm and she brushed against him as she rose to her feet. Did she imagine it or did she detect a sharp intake of his breath and a tightening of his hand.

"Thank you for listening," he said softly. "I don't often open up to people this way. I hope you will come again." He chuckled. "I might even bring an extra pole the next time I feel an urge to fish."

He was still holding her hand and Tabitha gently pulled it away. "It helps to talk." With that she walked away, careful not to turn around and look at him one last time.

As Tabitha headed back to Frederica, Ian stood with his hands on his hips, looking after her. It was crazy, he knew that, but he couldn't shake the feelings this girl stirred in him. He had felt the warmth of her body as she brushed against him and he was fervently thankful for the darkness that hid his unexpected reaction. It must have been talk of Charlotte that stirred his emotions. This girl was an Indian, he reminded himself, and truth be told he hated Indians.

He remembered listening to Charlotte's father who had no respect or tolerance for the Indians who could often be seen, noisy and intoxicated, on the streets of Savannah. He had impressed upon Ian that Indians were a morally corrupt race since it was well known that their young unmarried women cohabitated with numerous young men before marriage. He often recounted tales told to him by his good friend, Major Regor, who insisted that the Creek way of making war was cowardly. A warrior could choose to join or not join a war party, and even after joining he could quit and return home at any time. If a war party was overwhelmed they often turned and ran to save face.

Mr. Bruner painted vivid pictures of things Major Regor had seen, of Creek warriors displaying mutilated scalps atop their war poles and burning their prisoners alive.

Ian had listened intently to these tales. Mr. Bruner's

contempt and hatred for Indians did not fall on deaf ears and gradually he adopted his employer's prejudices as his own.

Other incidents came quickly to mind—one, a grisly tale told by the survivors of Fort Mosa. After celebrating their victory the Yemassee had taken prisoners, including Captain Mackintosh and about a dozen men of the Highland Independent Company. The Indians stripped them, bound their hands behind their backs, and began marching them to Saint Augustine. Two prisoners who were too badly wounded to walk were killed and their heads chopped off. One of the severed, dripping heads was sadistically rubbed in the face of Edward Lying, a soldier of the Highland Company.

Ian never got over his revulsion for the vicious act.

He sat back down on the dock and put the Jew's harp to his mouth once more. As the music drifted on the motionless air his soul quieted and his thoughts turned back to Charlotte. He had to talk to Captain Mackay. He needed to ask for some leave time to return to Savannah. Despite her assurances he could not expect Charlotte to wait forever without some physical contact.

Physical! He chuckled. The way he was feeling tonight it was a good thing she was far away in Savannah.

Chapter Fourteen

Tabitha sat on a rocker under the slopping roof of her tiny room, a mug of coffee freshly brewed from roasted grains of corn in her hands. A southwest gale was blowing. The chandlery was closed because of the storm and she had a rare afternoon of free time. She had tried to read her Bible but her favorite passages in Proverbs failed to sooth her. She was furious with herself for letting her thoughts dwell on the Highlander.

Outside of her window lightning flickered and anvil clouds seethed and merged. She had always had an unnatural fear of lightning. She set the coffee on the small table beside her chair and rose to pull the curtains across the window. Suddenly, there was a searing flash of white light followed by a hellish crack. Through the window she saw a tree at the end of the street explode with a low roar. Her fingers clutched the curtain and she stood paralyzed, watching sparks fly into the air, showering the thatched roof of the hut next to the tree. Within minutes puffs of smoke and fingers of orange flame began to appear in a dozen places among the thatching. As Tabitha strained to see through the rain-streaked window her lips formed a silent O. It was the home of Willie Driesler, Henry's young friend. Tabitha felt a chill run up her spine. Henry had announced before the storm that he was going over to the Driesler's where he and Willie planned to clean their squirrel rifles. Johnnie went with him.

Tabitha tore out of the room and clattered down the stairs screaming for her mistress.

A wide-eyed Mrs. Calwell met her at the bottom of the staircase.

"The Driesler home is on fire," Tabitha gasped. "Henry and Johnnie are there."

Constance's face turned ashen.

Outside alarm bells had begun to clang and Tabitha grabbed Constance's arm pulling her to the door. "We must go to them," Tabitha cried as she practically pushed the stricken woman out into the storm.

The rain seemed to shock Constance into consciousness. She gathered her skirts in her hands and began to run wildly down the street toward the hut where by now the roof was engulfed in flames.

Excited voices rose above the wild storm as lightning streaked across the angry sky and people streamed from all directions toward the fire. Tabitha could make out the tall, red-haired figure of Ian MacDonald at the head of a bucket brigade shouting orders to his soldiers as they passed buckets of sloshing water along the line that snaked up from the river. He was stripped to the waist and was directing a wide circle of men ringing the burning hut which was now completely aflame. Each man grabbed a slopping bucket from the line, dousing the ground in a frantic attempt to keep the fire from spreading.

Despite their efforts the flames shot higher, licking across the dry grass, and water hissed loudly, raising clouds of steam as it hit hot embers. The acrid smoke from the burning building left the men gagging and gasping for breath.

"Keep water coming," Tabitha heard Ian shout as he stomped his feet viciously on a patch of burning grass. "It's getting away from us." Suddenly, he threw down his bucket and raced toward the fort waving his arms frantically. "Form another line. Keep the powder magazine wet."

Tabitha had finally caught up with Constance and together they raced into the yard of the burning home. Her legs trembled, her nose burned, her throat was raw, and she shook with terror at the thought that the children were trapped inside. She and Constance had to get them out.

Seeing their intention several soldiers threw down their buckets and ran toward them. A burly soldier locked Tabitha firmly in his arms and another struggled to grab Constance by the shoulders to pull her back.

Constance let out a strangled cry. "Let me go! My children are in there." She wrenched herself free from a restraining hand, ripping the sleeve from her dress, and catapulted herself toward the smoldering door of the hut.

Ian had returned to the house fire and as he saw what was happening he made a diving lunge at Constance pulling her to the ground. "Everyone is out," he gasped, trying to quiet her squirming body. "Everyone is out . . . the children are safe."

Tabitha rushed to Constance's side and helped Ian pull her to her feet and away from the searing heat of the burning hut. Tabitha smelled hair burning as sparks showered down on their heads and arms.

"—over there by the shed," Ian was yelling as he pointed to a cluster of people huddled together. "A woman with two little girls and three boys." Tabitha and Constance turned as one to peer into the direction he pointed. Dense smoke and clouds, low and black, obscured their vision but as they strained to identify the children two of them broke loose and began to run toward them. Constance opened her arms and Henry and Johnnie flew into them.

Tears of relief streamed down Tabitha's face and she brushed sweat-soaked hair off her forehead. She placed a trembling hand on Constance's bare arm. "Take them home, ma'am," she said. "I'll see if I can help Mrs. Driesler."

Just then a huge boom shook the ground and everyone froze. The burning hut was at the end of Broad Street, next to the fort, and the fire had jumped to mounted cannon where several bombs were stored. As the bombs exploded it sounded as though Heaven itself was crashing down.

"Wow," Henry shrieked, as he stared saucer-eyed at the

fireworks erupting around him. "Ain't that somethin'?"

Johnnie hid his face in his mother's skirts and began to cry and Constance looked like she might faint as another explosion rent the sky.

"Everyone protect the magazine," Ian barked at the soldiers as he tore across the yard. "Continue to direct your water there. The hut is gone."

The fort's powder magazine, holding several hundred balls and bombs full of powder, sat nearby. If it too caught fire there would be a disaster of unbelievable consequence. They would have nothing left with which to defend themselves.

By now several other houses were burning and the noise of fire, and storm was deafening. Tabitha feared the strong wind would set the entire town aflame.

Mr. Calwell, who had been supervising several workers at General Oglethorpe's farm located outside Frederica's walls, suddenly appeared out of the gloom and rushed to Constance's side.

Henry, his words tumbling over one another in his excitement and haste to get them said, told his father of everyone's escape from the burning building. "I smelled the smoke first and told Mrs. Driesler the house was on fire," he said. "She didn't believe me, so me and Willie we ran outside and looked up an' sure enough the roof was burning. I ran back in and tole 'em all to get out."

"Then you are a real hero," Mr. Calwell said as he put his arm around his son. "Now come. We must all get home." He looked at his wife, taking in her torn dress and soot-blackened face. "Are you hurt, dear?" he asked, visibly shaken.

"No, I don't think so." She began to cry.

Mr. Calwell took her in his arms and then drew Henry and Johnnie into his embrace. With head bowed he said a short prayer before leading them away.

Tabitha had been standing beside the children the entire time and she noticed that he did not even glance in her direction. She also was covered with black soot, her eyebrows singed, and a large hole was burned in her skirt. Of course, it was only natural that his concern should be with his family, but it brought home to her the realization that she was only a bonded servant in the Calwell household.

She walked toward Mrs. Driesler who knelt beside her children silently weeping. The poor woman's husband had been one of the fatalities at Ft. Mosa and now her hut, humble as it was, and all of their belongings were gone. But before she could reach the forlorn woman, Pastor Ulrich strode up and knelt down beside her. Tabitha was glad he was there. He would have better words of comfort than she. Sometimes explanations of God's actions eluded her and she found her faith waver. Still, some things were not for man to understand.

Tabitha looked up into the heavens. The black clouds had disappeared giving way to a sky the color of gunmetal streaked with yellow. Clouds of ashy smoke and steam rose from three smoldering buildings, but the fire seemed to have been confined to an area around the Driesler home, and the flames were slowly flickering out. There was a lot to be grateful for. The wind had died down and the fires appeared to be contained. They had not spread to the powder magazine where the town's weapons of protection were stored, nor to the Pastor's office nearby which served as school and church.

As Tabitha looked around she wondered what would happen next. After two years of peace and quiet this was turning out to be quite an eventful Frederica summer.

Broken Arrow had reluctantly agreed to help with the bible translations. Tabitha suspected it was more to be with her than from any real desire on his part to adopt an understanding of her God. On the other hand one never knew what good might come from exposure to the Word.

He patiently taught her the Cherokee syllabary, a script used for writing the Cherokee language. It had been devised by a half-Cherokee named Sequoyah and its use had spread rapidly.

Last week they had finished working on the Lord's Prayer

and today Tabitha had chosen several verses from Psalms. She noticed that Broken Arrow was unusually quiet.

"Is something bothering you?" she finally asked, laying her hand on his arm.

He flinched. "General want me to stop work here. Need me as a scout."

"Oh, well maybe I can talk to him. I'll tell him how important you are to our project."

"No! I scout. Not sit here with you."

"But you are doing much more. You are—"

"No!" He practically snarled the word. "I go now."

Tabitha watched in amazement as he bolted from the room. Then she remembered his reaction to her touch on his arm.

She smiled.

Ian sat at his usual spot on the wooden dock, his long legs dangling over the side, a bamboo rod in his hand. He tried to keep his eyes on the tip of the pole but found his gaze wandering sideways to the trail where the Indian girl usually approached the landing. He relived what he could remember of their last meeting. Over the course of several evenings he had pretty much poured out his life story to her. Somehow a routine had been established. Each night after the Calwell children were asleep, Tabitha slipped down to the river where he waited. He found himself looking forward to her company with more than a normal amount of anticipation.

There was a welcome breeze this evening, the air fresh and clean. His fingers idly stroked the smooth surface of the cane pole. A sudden vision of home flashed across his memory: he could almost feel the wind whipping through his long hair as he rode his Highland sheltie across mountain glens. Ian drew a deep breath. He was a wee bit homesick tonight.

He turned at the sound of footsteps crunching on the grit of the shell path and felt his pulse quicken. It was Tabitha.

She walked tentatively toward him and he motioned for her to sit beside him.

"Come join me lass . . . 'tis a fine evening," he said.

"I fear it will rain again before morning."

"Better at night than during the day when we must drill. 'Tis a fact I don't relish another storm like yesterday." He looked at her and chuckled. "You do look rather odd with only one eyebrow."

Tabitha's hand flew to her face and her face turned a dusky rose.

Ian laughed. "Never mind. It gives you a rather rakish look. Seriously, though, I never saw such weather as you Georgians have. It rains, then the sun shines, then it rains and the sun shines again. Me uniform never dries out."

"At least your uniforms are cooler than those of the poor Redcoats with their woolen jackets and britches."

"A bonny thing the wearing of the kilt is. We Scottish have always been more practical than the British, though it would be considered heresy for them to hear me say so." Suddenly he whipped his arm into the air at a mighty tug on his line and for the next few minutes his attention was focused on landing a large sea trout. Gently, so as not to tear its mouth, he removed the hook and held it up for Tabitha to admire. Brown-black spots covered the fish's back and its gills, even in the pale moonlight, were a bright crimson. It probably weighed out at four or five pounds.

"Would you like to take it home for your supper tomorrow night," he asked.

"Yes . . . ah, on second thought . . . no. I'd have to explain where I got it. The truth might not sit too well with Master Calwell."

"Just tell him a passing soldier gave it to you."

"But that would be a lie."

Ian looked at her in surprise. The girl continued to intrigue him. She had integrity as well as a great deal of spunk. The flopping fish tried to free itself from his hand and he looked it in the eye. "Back ye go, then," he said as he lowered it into the river. "The lass has given you a second life." He laid the pole aside and turned to Tabitha with a troubled look. "One of our scouts was speaking of rising trouble between the Creeks and Cherokees. Are they not allies?"

"My people and the Cherokee have never gotten along. They are always fighting one another. They speak of peace then use any excuse to wage war. It's so sad. We are all one people but we cannot live in harmony."

"The same is true everywhere, Tabitha. In Scotland one of the worst massacres ever to take place happened when the Clan Campbell feigned friendship to the Clan MacDonald, and then destroyed them."

"Clan MacDonald? Is that not your name? Did it involve you?"

"Indirectly. Would you like to hear the story? I'm afraid it's a long one."

"Please. I love to hear you speak . . . I love your Scottish brogue."

He beamed at her. "I'll try to keep it under control so you can understand me. It does tend to get a little thick when I get emotional. Nonetheless, some fifty years ago the Campbell clan violated one of Scotland's most hallowed standards of conduct—that of extending hospitality to all who call at your door.

"It all started in 1691 when William of Orange demanded that the Jacobite chiefs take an oath of allegiance to the Crown before the first of the New Year. Lacham MacIain, Chief of Clan MacDonald, lived in my village of Glencoe and he was hampered by misfortune and severe winter weather on his trip to Inverary where the oath had to be given. He was six days late in getting there.

"Well, the greedy King jumped on this tardiness. It was a chance to seize the entire county of Lochaber, home of the Glencoe MacDonalds, and incidentally my grandparents. Before January's end a Captain Campbell arrived in Glencoe with one hundred twenty Redcoats of the Earl of Argyle's regiment, proclaiming that they were only there for a stopover of a week or so. MacIain welcomed Campbell into his home.

"After enjoying MacIain's hospitality for two weeks Campbell received the orders he had been waiting for. All mountain passes out of Glencoe were to be secured and its inhabitants murdered.

"At five the next morning MacIain was shot at his door and died at his wife's feet. She was wounded and died the next day." Ian stopped and took a deep breath to regain control of his feelings. He thought it unmanly to allow them to show so nakedly to this girl. He continued, "Thirty-eight members of our clan were put to death and more perished in flight over the snow bound mountain ridges."

"And your family?" Tabitha asked in a whisper."

"My grandparents froze to death in one of the passes."

"And what of your parents?"

"My father was one of the survivors. He was just a child. But that wasn't the end of it. The entire glen was decimated—all of the homes burned, cattle, horses and sheep stolen—the one surviving MacDonald, an old man of eighty, murdered." Ian's square jaw quivered in anger. "It was a crime of greed, a crime by a Scotsman against his fellow Scots."

Tabitha shook her head. "Greed is behind most of mankind's ills. Proverbs says, 'Greed and death are alike in this: neither is ever satisfied.' But, Ian, we must put anger behind us, it can only fester and destroy us. Think instead on the pleasant memories of your homeland. Were your people farmers?"

"Not really. The soil in the Highlands is very rocky and poorly drained. We were primarily sheepherders. What little farming we did is in what are called strip-fields."

"Strip-fields?" Tabitha asked.

"Aye. Well, the thin soil of the glen is worked in strips, the first overturned onto the next, which has been mucked with animal dung. The seed is thrown into this second strip where it produces a meager crop . . . only enough to serve our own tables and that poorly."

"Do your father and brother live on the farm?"

"Aye, they run cattle and sheep and are quite content." He chuckled. "You would laugh to see Scottish cattle. They have long hair and are quite wooly, but pretty beasts with large brown eyes that peer at you through bangs of fur."

"My mother's people, the White Sticks, are farming people."

Ian laughed. "White Sticks?"

"In the Creek Nation our villages are divided into Red towns and White towns. Red towns are home to the warriors who hold ceremonies such as war dances and launch raids for war and revenge. Peacemakers live in White towns, such as our little section of Tustacatty, and keep track of alliances, sign treaties and offer safety to refugees. Our braves are called White Sticks."

"What a strange form of government. You mean you have two different towns in one village?"

"Yes"

"Odd," he mused.

Tabitha looked at him and said nothing.

Ian pulled his pipe from his pocket and took a moment to prime it. They sat quietly looking across the river at the marsh, its tall dark grasses shimmering in the moonlight. Finally, Ian spoke. "I find it hard to think of you as being Indian. With your blue eyes and American dress you look white and speak better English than I do. How do you think of yourself . . . as Indian or White?"

"With confusion," she admitted. "Because my father wanted me to speak English and become a Christian the Indians of our village resented him and consequently me. I am tall whereas Creek women are very short and except for my black hair and dark-toned skin I do not resemble them very much. But I admire their way of life, Ian. Their simplicity and honesty, and their respect for nature and the land are qualities I find hard to discern in most white people. I loved my mother very much and I have never been ashamed of her. But I also love the refinement of the white world, the opportunity to learn and grow. I would like to know more about art and music. Most of all, I guess, it is only as a white person that I have the opportunity to be a Christian." She looked at Ian, her blue eyes dark with intensity. "People of mixed blood find they are never really accepted by either race, so it makes little difference how I think of myself."

Ian noticed a tear glistening on Tabitha's cheek and felt a stab of remorse. He had been a clumsy oaf to bring up the subject. He jumped to his feet uncertain what to say next.

"I must get back to the barracks before they sound taps," he finally stammered.

"I think I'll sit here for a little while. It's a lovely evening."

"I don't like to leave you alone."

She frowned. "Why?"

"The soldiers on this fort aren't to be trusted," he said.

Tabitha stared at him for a moment and then they both burst out laughing.

"Come on, lass," he said fondly. "I'll walk you home."

A week had passed since the bloody battle at the marsh. Oglethorpe rested his troops, strengthening his defenses in preparation for another attack. However, Montiano, the Spanish commander, was in a quandary, convinced that another advance up the military road would be disastrous. Thus far, his Indian scouts were unable to find an alternative route through the dense forests. Oglethorpe had destroyed the wells, their water was in short supply, plus Montiano worried that the British naval flotilla stationed at Charlestown could be on its way to Oglethorpe's aid. More importantly, each day carried them deeper into hurricane season.

Montiano made a final attempt to avoid the disastrous land route to Fort Frederica and land his forces via the river passage, but the British held him off with vicious gunfire. In defeat, the Spanish withdrew once more to their encampment at Gascoigne Bluff.

Broken Arrow had become one of Oglethorpe's best scouts and he was able to infiltrate the Spanish camp and pick up information about their plans. He reported back to Oglethorpe that they were thoroughly dispirited and disorganized. It appeared that the time might be ripe for an attack on the Spanish camp. Accordingly, just a little over a week after the battle at the marsh, Oglethorpe assembled a four hundred man raiding force and under cover of darkness led them to within a mile of Fort St. Simons.

Ian, Cory, three rangers, and four Indians were sent forward to reconnoiter the area around the Spanish garrison at the Bluff. The Indians went first, following a faint deer trail through tangled underbrush until they were close enough to see canvas tents glimmering in the moonlight. They huddled together planning their strategy. Ian was in charge, deciding they should fan out in two directions to estimate the strength of Montiano's force and pinpoint the sentry posts.

Suddenly, the night's silence was shattered by the discharge of a musket. The sound was coming from their troops to the rear. Cursing, Ian flung himself on the ground. *What in the devil was going on? Oglethorpe wasn't to attack until he received their report.*

He lay on the ground for several seconds and then cautiously raised his head to look toward the Spanish camp. Half-clad soldiers spilled out of tents shouting frenzied orders. Drums beat the alarm and dogs barked furiously.

Ian's lips pursed with suppressed fury as he crept over to where Cory lay on the ground. "Some trigger-happy fool from our company has given the whole attack away."

"Aye, Laddie. We'd better get our butts out o' here. We—" Cory stopped in mid-sentence and stared in disbelief as a figure, dressed in a merchant seaman's uniform came crashing through the woods. The man shot them a terrified glance then continued running toward the alerted camp. "What the bloody . . .?" Cory sputtered.

"Must be the fool from our company who fired his musket," Ian said wryly. "Whether it was a mistake or not he knows Oglethorpe will have his tail for giving us away so he's heading for the protection of the Spanish camp."

"Where he'll probably spill his guts and tell Montiano the full strength of our forces."

"Then we better turn back. This game is over."

* * *

Ian approached the general with a report on what he had seen. Oglethorpe nodded his head. "With the element of surprise gone, an attack against such superior numbers will be fruitless. We will, however, rattle Montiano's nerves a bit," he said smiling slyly. "Have the drummers taunt him with as loud and lengthy a rendition of the "Grenadier's March" as they can muster. And, Lieutenant, I want you and Sergeant MacGrath to stay here after we leave. Keep half a dozen Highlanders and Broken Arrow with four of his scouts. I want to know what that wily Spaniard will do next. Spend the night and report back to me at Fort Frederica tomorrow morning."

Ian saluted. "Aye, sir."

The enemy came suddenly, slipping soundlessly from the primal forest, five Spanish grenadiers and six Indian scouts. Within minutes Ian and his men were surrounded, the attackers running from tree to tree to conceal themselves, exchanging fire with Ian's men from behind whatever cover they could find.

The Yemassee led the attack, screaming their blood-curdling war cry "Occaneechee," as they charged directly at Ian and his men. Ian fired and saw the bullet strike an Indian. The Indian's step barely faltered. He kept coming and despite the desperation of the moment Ian felt awe at the man's courage. The Indian came on and Ian, without time to reload his musket, threw it on the ground and fired his pistol. The man staggered but kept coming, his spear in his wavering hand.

Ian drew his dagger and plunged it deep into the man's chest, killing him instantly.

Quickly he recharged his musket and pistol and sank his knife hilt-deep in the sandy soil to clean it of blood. Directly in front of him another Indian was coming at him with a spear, but he parried the thrust with his musket barrel and darted sideways. Grasping his gun with two hands he swung the butt of the rifle into the Indians face. The man took the full force of it and with blood spurting from his nose went down. Ian finished him off with his knife.

There was fierce fighting on both sides—men darting from tree to tree for protection, bullets whining. Suddenly, Broken Arrow and his scouts charged from the woods, arrows singing through the hot air, taking the attackers on the flank. Their presence was a total surprise, and the Spanish attackers broke and began to retreat. Ian aimed his pistol and shot another Yemassee as they fled into the trees.

After leading his men from the woods, Ian surveyed the faces of the Highlanders who had survived the attack. Argus, George, William and then further along, Colin and John. Anxiously he counted them off as they arrived. Michael Cochran was the last to stagger in, pressing his hand against a bleeding wound to his thigh. Cory was not present.

Ian's brows bunched in a deep pucker. "Cory MacGrath?" he asked of the men gathered before him. "Where is he?"

"I saw him fall," Michael said. "An Indian got him in the back."

A muscle throbbed in Ian's jaw, the bad news striking like hammer blows. "No . . . no . . . not Cory!"

"Aye," Argus said and there was an odd look in his eyes that Ian did not like. "We dinna have a chance to help 'im. The bloody Indians were everywhere."

A cold hard ball formed in the pit of Ian's stomach. "Come with me," he said to Michael and Argus. "We need to find him at once. He may only be wounded."

He did not miss the look that passed between the two men, yet deep in his heart he felt Cory must be alive. His friend was a survivor, too vibrant and full of life to let death claim him.

They went back to the copse of woods where the fight had taken place. Ian's legs felt like wood as he trod over bodies and searched behind bushes for his fallen friend. Surely Cory's red hair would be easy to find.

Suddenly Argus shouted at him and pointed to a kilted figure lying in a clump of cabbage palm. Ian ran and dropped to his knees. Cory was lying on his back, his arms outstretched, his face split open by a tomahawk. There was no red hair. No hair at all. His scalp was gone!

Ian was so sickened by the sight of the savagery he was unable to move, then a huge spasm of nausea rose in his belly and he vomited on the ground. Argus and Michael stood silently, unsure how to help their commander handle his grief. Each had lost friends in battle and, officer or not, the Lieutenant was human and his loss personal.

Ian fought for control of himself. After a moment he reached down and tenderly loosened the bloody broach holding Cory's tartan at his shoulder. Slowly, with a lump the size of an oyster in his throat and fighting back tears, he pulled the plaid from beneath Cory's body and placed it over the mutilated face.

Broken Arrow came to stand beside him. "He your friend . . . I sorry." He reached out his hand as though to place it on Ian's shoulder. Ian recoiled and pierced him with a look of pure hatred. "Keep your heathen hands off me." He spat on the ground. "All Indians are savages. I want nothing to do with any of you."

Broken Arrow backed away, his hands balled into tight fists, a wounded look on his face. He started to say something, then shook his head and walked away.

Ian watched him go. Loathing welled like bile in his stomach. In his estimation there were no good Indians, however loyal they pretended to be to the British cause.

His face twisted in anguish he knelt and picked his friend up in his arms, tucking the corner of Cory's tartan around his bloody head. With a dull, empty ache in his chest he carried him from the woods.

They buried Cory deep in the earth, within sight of the sea. Ian took the time to plant an acorn from a live oak tree beside the grave so that in time its branches would shade him where he lay, facing east toward his beloved Scotland.

Later that night Ian stood in the light of a full moon

watching the ghostly sails of the Spanish armada slip quietly out of St. Simons Sound heading south. He was overwhelmed with grief, mourning for his best friend. He knew, although the Spanish were retreating, that the war was far from over. But for now, at least, the colonies were safe.

Chapter Fifteen

Tabitha had been instructed to deliver eggs to Nevil Smith, the town baker. She walked light-heartedly down the length of Barracks Street swinging her basket, her skirts swishing, her eyes searching the Parade Ground where plumes of smoke hung in the air from musket practice.

Early morning shadows danced where great live oaks spread black patterns of shade over a path covered with leaves. Tabitha stopped to watch an armadillo, dressed in its medieval armor, root in sandy soil with his long snout, looking for ants.

She was turning in to the bakery when she glanced to her right and saw him. He was some distance away but she was certain it was him . . . Ian. There was no mistaking his hair. He was heading up Broad Street toward the town gate. His head was lowered dejectedly, and he walked slowly—not with his usual purposeful stride—along the shell street.

She quickly deposited her eggs with Mr. Smith, jamming his pay in her apron pocket, and, with a smile of apology for her hastiness, hurried out the door and back up Barracks Street.

Ian was leaning against the upper palisade that formed a firing wall, gazing at a group of soldiers trading with some Indians on the rampart. She approached slowly, uncertain of his mood.

"Ian," she said as he shifted his gaze and looked at her with eyes cold as ice.

"I . . . I thought it was you. I'm surprised though . . . I thought you to be on a foray to Fort St. Simons."

He gave her a withering look.

Tabitha felt as though she had been hit in the face with a pan of cold water.

"Wha . . . What's wrong," she stammered.

"We were unable to complete our mission."

Ian's voice was raspy, his eyes bloodshot, as though he had been a long time without sleep. Or had he been crying? Tabitha didn't know what to say. She had a sudden fierce urge to take him in her arms and soothe away the trouble.

A muscle twitched in his jaw. "Cory is dead . . . scalped by your heathen Indians." He watched her with contempt. "Savages—that's what your people are." He flung a curse at her and she cringed. Ian had never said a foul word in front of her.

Tabitha clenched her fists, heat flooding her face. "Don't you dare swear at me or address me as a *Savage*." Her voice trembled with anger. "I'm sorry you lost your friend. Very sorry. But such is war."

"And scalping—is that a part of war, too?"

"It's a practice I abhor and am ashamed of, but let's not forget it was introduced to our people by the white man. That's a piece of your history you white people choose to forget. There was a time when a bounty was offered for every Indian scalp presented to the Crown. So, who are the savages? When the Indian scalps an enemy it is a form of revenge as well as show of strength . . . not as exchange for money. Aside from that, Lieutenant, I am not responsible for what my people did to your friend."

He stared at her. She saw the fierceness in his eyes, the uncompromising set of his jaw. "Your people," he spat. "I had almost forgotten who you really are." He began to move away.

"You cannot separate what happened from me?" she pleaded.

"No."

"Or forgive?"

"Never!"

His contempt was almost more than she could bear. With her spine straight and her chin raised, Tabitha turned away. Whatever life brought next she refused to be defeated or ashamed of who she was or where she came from.

After finishing her evening chores Tabitha walked across the street to the Hawkins's house in search of Anna's company. Neither of them received much free time from their employers and Tabitha had not seen her friend since the boats turned back to Frederica after the brief battle at the marsh.

She walked quietly, her breathing slowed under the sodden heat of a Georgia summer. Johnny Houstoun squatted in the grass playing marbles, and two women talked across their garden wall, waving fans of palmetto fronds to fend off the mosquitoes. She jumped as a female painted bunting, its plumage olive-green-and-yellow, swooped directly in front of her face. The little bird's mate, his body a gaudy red with a yellowish back and a purple head, set up a noisy fuss in the yard.

Tabitha picked up a clump of the moss and rolled it in her hands. It had a wonderful salty smell that would cling to her hands for hours. She turned at the sound of water splashing from a bucket and waved to Elizabeth Harrison, the public midwife. In a small garden, across the street, white-haired John Welsh pulled a hoe through his peas while his wife stooped to pull away the weeds. Tabitha, lost in her thoughts, almost missed the garden gate that led to the Meyer house.

Anna was in the kitchen washing dishes from the evening meal. Loose hair escaping from her mobcap was twisting into a soft curl from the steam of the hot water. She was so pretty, small and dainty. Tabitha felt awkward next to her.

She grabbed a linen towel and began to dry the dishes. "It'll go faster," she said when Anna gave her a puzzled look. "I need to talk to you."

When the last dish had been put away Anna took off her apron and hung it on a peg behind the door. "Let's sit out in the garden, it's a mite cooler there than in this steamy kitchen," she said.

Anna and Tabitha crossed the lawn bordered with flowers open in all their glory, fragrant roses, purple iris, and daisies big as pancakes. They settled themselves on a bench made from a thick slab of cypress placed across two blocks of tabby.

Anna reached out to take one of Tabitha's hands. "You seem troubled. Is something wrong?"

The concern in Anna's voice brought a lump to Tabitha's throat. It was not in her nature to confide her personal feelings to anyone; acceptance of life's hardships without question was the pattern of her Indian people. Even so, she felt she would burst if she could not vent the emotions whirling inside her chest. "I can't help myself, she said with a sob. "I've fallen in love with Ian MacDonald. And it's hopeless . . . hopeless. He's engaged to a girl in Savannah and he is terribly prejudiced against Indians. Despite all of that we were becoming friends. But now his friend, Cory MacGrath, has been killed—scalped in fact—and he blames me."

"Why you?"

"Well, not really me. When he found Cory had been scalped it reminded him that I am part Indian. We exchanged very bitter words at our last meeting."

"He shouldn't be angry at you for that. I know the Highlanders have fierce loyalty to their friends but this Cory was a soldier after all and death is a part of war." Anna pursed her lips. "I am surprised, though. You seem to be pursuing a man who you say is promised to another."

"I'm not pursuing him. I just want to be his friend, and . . ."

"And?"

Tabitha felt heat flood her face. *And,* indeed. If the truth be told she wanted much more than friendship.

"You're blushing, Tabitha. How far has this gone?"

"Aside from our encounter at Fort Mosa, I've only talked

with him a few times. But just last week we talked for the longest time and he told me practically his entire life story. We were very comfortable together. That's when he told me about his fiancée in Savannah."

"Does he plan to marry soon?"

"He said there are complications. Her father doesn't approve of him. Oh, Anna, I know it is wrong of me but I can't help hoping she will find someone else before this war is over." Tabitha twisted her hands in her lap. "I intend to remain his friend and keep hoping."

"What about your spat? And what if the Highlanders are ordered back to Darien?"

Tabitha bit her lip. "It is hopeless, isn't it?"

"It does seem that way."

They sat quietly as the evening wrapped its arms around them. Children, unmindful of the heat, called to one another as they played on the roads, rolling hoops, throwing a ball to and fro, playing tag.

"What about you, Anna?" Tabitha finally asked. "Has William asked for your hand yet?"

"He's very devoted and quite possessive but he really hasn't made a commitment. He doesn't feel he's well enough established as a cooper to take on a wife. And he worries about the Spanish threat."

"At least you're a free servant and could marry if he asks you," Tabitha said with a wry smile.

"Free, but I work for a man with the most disagreeable wife in the entire colony of Georgia. Only last week Beatre broke a bottle over the constable's head."

"Good Heavens."

"Honestly, Tabitha, you can't imagine anyone having such a vile temper. She seems to hate children and screams at them anytime they get near our house. I don't know, maybe it's because she's been unable to have children of her own. Both she and Dr. Hawkins seem to be such unhappy people and they take it out on their neighbors. I . . . I admit I'm afraid of her."

"I guess everyone has their own problems. But that doesn't help us with ours, does it?"

"It wouldn't hurt to pray."

Yes, Tabitha thought. *And where would that get me?* Today God's presence seemed like a distant shadow she could no longer see. All her Christian life, even in her darkest hours, she'd been comforted by the knowledge that He was looking over her. Now she felt all-alone.

"Your prayers are more easily answered than mine, Anna. As long as you truly love William and are not looking at marriage as simply a means of escape from the Hawkins."

Anna face flushed with anger. "What a terrible thing to say. Of course, I love him."

"Oh dear, I'm sorry. I didn't mean it the way it sounded. I'm just so upset over Ian's rejection that I don't know what I'm saying. I envy you, Anna. I don't know if I'll ever find love with a man. Why did I have to become so enamored with one who is completely out of reach for me?"

Anna grinned. "Well there's always Cecil Wainwright at the store. He says you're the prettiest girl in town . . . says he can't look away from your sparkling blue eyes."

"Humph. It's my bosom he can't look away from."

"Then there's always that Indian, Broken Arrow. I see the way he watches you."

Tabitha strove to keep her face impassive. As good a friend as Anna was she used the phrase *that Indian* as though being Indian were inferior. "Broken Arrow and I have a lot in common," she said testily, "and I will admit he's a handsome devil."

Anna looked away. "Ya, of course." She cleared her throat. "I think . . . I believe we're on delicate subjects this evening. Maybe we should switch to a safer topic."

"But I can't seem to think of anything except Lieutenant MacDonald," Tabitha said with a soft moan.

"I think it's those fantastic legs of his sticking out from under that kilt that have you bewitched." Her face grew red and she whispered. "I've often wondered what they wear underneath."

"Anna!"

"Well, haven't you?"

"Sometimes," Tabitha admitted with a giggle. She felt a strange warmth creeping down her belly. When she was around Ian she was aware of sensations she had never experienced before, a longing for she knew not what. She felt far out of her depth, awakened to a part of herself that spoke of being a woman.

"Tabitha, dear, I must be getting back," Anna said, glancing over at her. Her eyes crinkled mirthfully. "You look all flushed. I think this is a dangerous conversation."

"I think you're right," Tabitha said shakily as she rose to her feet. Ian MacDonald was her private fantasy—nothing more. She should have kept her problems to herself. If she had learned anything in life it was that she could not afford to indulge herself in dreams.

After Anna went back across the lawn to her home Tabitha continued down to the river. She had some serious thinking to do and settled herself on the bank next to the dock.

Movement caught her eye and Broken Arrow strode from a nearby thicket to stand on the red clay riverbank. Tabitha's eyes studied him. He stood straight as an arrow, gazing across the golden marsh at the sun sinking below the horizon. He was immobile, his profile etched in bronze, oblivious to Tabitha's gaze. He brought back all the old memories of her childhood, of her mother and father, of her torn loyalty between her Indian and her English culture, and she was filled with longing.

Broken Arrow started to chant, his arms outstretched, his eyes closed. Seeing him praying to his God stirred Tabitha strangely. Since her baptism, her own prayers were to the Christian God. She turned slightly to see him better and her skirt dislodged a small stone that splashed into the water. Startled, he turned and saw her watching him.

He walked toward her. "Dangerous for girl alone. Many

woman-hungry soldiers here." He spoke in Cherokee, hunkering down beside her.

Tabitha wrinkled her nose at his strong scent but she smiled up at him dismissing his admonition with a wave. "As I told you before, I am able to take care of myself."

Broken Arrow nodded but said nothing. The moon cast a glow over the slow-moving water outlining the low-slung oaks and the silvery trunks of cypress trees lining its bank. The view was soothing, ageless in beauty.

"I sorry you choose to be called Tabitha and not White Blossom," he said. "Sorry that you follow English ways."

Tabitha groaned in despair. There it was again—the constant reminder of her two worlds. She still felt pride in her Indian heritage, she understood their ways and wished to remain a part of their culture, but instinct told her that her future lay with the white man. Besides, she had accepted Christianity and it was becoming an increasingly important part of her life. How could she explain to Broken Arrow in a way that he would understand?

When she did not answer immediately Broken Arrow, encouraged, continued in rapid Cherokee. "I want you to come back with me, back to my village. I do not want you to be a slave."

"But I told you I am not a slave. I'm an indentured servant."

"Same thing. I take you back to our people." His black eyes glittered with intensity as he watched her. "I am a good man with many horses. I will ask you to share my blanket."

Tabitha's jaw dropped open.

"The English will not come after you," he continued. "They are afraid the Spanish will return. I have a canoe waiting in the marsh. Clouds cover the moon and the tide is right."

It was a long speech for Broken Arrow and Tabitha felt herself surprisingly intrigued with the idea of running away under cover of the dark night, of returning to her Indian roots and sharing her life with this grave, steady man. There was no future with Ian MacDonald; her last meeting with him was proof of that. And John Calwell was becoming more and more intolerable to work for as his position in the colony grew in importance. His control over poor Constance was such that she was constantly changing the household routine, fearful that she would do something wrong and bring down his wrath.

"And would your Cherokee family treat me as one of them? There is no love lost between Creek and Cherokee and I am of mixed-blood," she said slowly.

He frowned. "Do white friends treat you as one of them?"

Tabitha did not respond. The answer to that she well knew.

He moved closer, his black eyes staring into hers. "Here you have no people. You not free."

Tabitha's chin lifted defiantly. "My indenture will be satisfied in two years and Mrs. Calwell treats me like family. I even eat at the table with them."

"They not blood."

"No, but I respect my debt to them." She swallowed hard. "John Calwell is a very controlling person. He would not stand for a servant to run away and upset his household. He would surely send scouts to bring me back."

"Frederica still on alert, afraid Spanish will return with much hatred. Your General Oglethorpe not spare men to look for runaway servant."

What he said was true enough. Escape would probably be easy. She shook her head. She couldn't believe she was seriously thinking about this. Still . . .

"Broken Arrow," she said, not looking at him, "let me pray about this. I will come here tomorrow night with my answer."

He scowled, his lips a tight line. Then he grunted and without another word slipped into the darkening woods.

Later, alone in her tiny room, Tabitha sank to her knees beside her bed and folded her hands in prayer. What was right for her in this world? If she stayed she would only pine for a man promised to another. But if she left, she would be disobeying God's commandment to honor her debts. She put aside Broken Arrow's offer to share his blanket. That was out of the question. Her quandary was whether to leave Frederica and her obligations to the Calwells to return to her Indian culture.

All night Tabitha tossed and turned and when the rising sun began to lighten the sky she had not reached a decision. With a groan she rose and went to the open window, drawing the curtains aside to gaze across at the soldier's barracks. Silently, she prayed for an answer and as she did, her gaze was drawn to the shadowy form of Parson Ulrich, his long frock coat flapping about his knees, a Bible clutched in his hand, as he hurried to his office. And suddenly she knew that the Parson would have no trouble with the dilemma facing her—the right or wrong of running from her responsibilities—and neither should she. It was wrong. It was as simple as that.

She would find Broken Arrow and tell him she could not go.

Chapter Sixteen

Ian picked his way through the tangled underbrush that separated the small village of Darien from the fortifications at Fort King George. He had been dreading this visit to Sally Cochran since Cory's death, but it was one he knew he had to make. Friendship demands the unpleasant as well as the pleasant.

Sally's small house was hardly more than a hut, typical of those hastily erected by settlers on land provided by the Crown until a more substantial dwelling could be erected. She was one of the one hundred seventy residents recruited from Inverness in Scotland and brought to America to settle Darien. Cory had told him that she married a young Highland soldier garrisoned at the fort but he had been killed at Fort Mosa before he could build a proper home for her and their little girl.

Ian removed his tam and clutched it in his hand. He knocked on the door and waited.

Sally slowly opened the door and stood looking at him with swollen eyes. Her face was pale and she twisted a rumpled handkerchief in her hand. "If you've come to tell me of Cory's death, I already know," she said, her lower lip trembling.

"How . . . who told you?"

"Toonahowi."

Ian's eyebrows lifted.

"He and his scouts brought word to Captain Mackenzie, yesterday."

"I'm sorry, Sally. Terribly sorry. Cory cared very much for you. If it's any comfort our last conversation was about you."

Tears began to trickle down her cheeks and Ian stepped forward to gather her trembling body in his arms. She buried her head on his shoulder and he let her cry.

Finally she pulled away dabbing the handkerchief at her eyes. "How . . . how . . . ?"

"It was quick. He was struck from behind and knew no fear."

"He did not suffer then?" she asked, her voice breaking.

Ian fought for control to block the horrible memory— Cory's bloody body, mutilated and scalped. He had to offer what comfort he could to this grieving girl.

"No, he did not suffer. We buried him on a bluff overlooking the sea. I'll take you there some day if you like."

She nodded. "I would like that. We talked of marriage, you know, but he was afraid this might happen."

"I know. You and your little girl have had more than your share of grief."

Sally gave him a watery smile. "You must think me completely without manners. Won't you come in for a cup of tea?"

Ian swallowed. He did not think he could sit and make idle conversation about his friend. His own grief was too raw, his anger too deep. "I'm sorry, I'd like to but I must get back. Perhaps when our regiment is recalled to Darien I can come and we'll talk."

"Please do." She rose on her tiptoes and planted a chaste kiss on his cheek. "Thank you, Lieutenant, for caring enough to come. I know how deep your friendship ran and I know you grieve for Cory too. And thank you for giving him a decent burial. He would like being by the sea."

Ian turned quickly and strode away before she could see the moisture in his own eyes.

* * *

After leaving Sally, Ian walked back to Fort King George to give a full report on the withdrawal of Spanish troops from St. Simons. He ate a hasty lunch then dejectedly boarded the Darien boat for the trip back to Frederica.

The morning fog had burned off and the sky was a brilliant blue. Lulled by the rhythmic dip of the oars and with a warm breeze washing his face, Ian let his mind drift. He tried to concentrate on memories of Charlotte but his thought kept scurrying away, like nervous mice, to a honey skinned Indian girl named Tabitha. He had been cruel to her, he knew that, and regretted the words spoken out of anger and grief. He had begun to look forward to seeing her appear on the dock where he took his evening smoke. There was honesty about the girl, a strength and depth he'd never encountered in his casual contacts with other women. He thought of her amazing blue eyes, her modesty and quietness. And he had to admit she stirred desires in him, desires difficult to ignore.

He was no fool. She was as attracted to him as he was to her, but he suspected she was blinded by her naiveté to the danger of her feelings. These feeling had to cease. In the future he would have to avoid Tabitha.

He was promised to Charlotte and they had pledged to be faithful to one another until they could wed. He could never seriously consider a liaison with a half-breed unless it was to simply satisfy his sexual tensions, but some unspoken trust existed between him and Tabitha, a trust he would not break simply to appease his lust.

Screeching gulls searching for food followed the boat's wake as it turned into the Frederica River. Ian walked to the bow of the piragua to watch the distant outline of the fort draw near. Perhaps he would walk down to the dock this evening and if Tabitha happened to be there he would offer his apology. He owed her that much.

Then he would avoid future meetings with her.

When Ian arrived back at the barracks a letter from Charlotte was waiting for him. He tucked it into his pocket, waiting to savor it until he was alone. After the evening meal he walked quickly to his favorite spot along the river and settled himself on the dock.

With eager fingers he tore open the envelope and unfolded a single sheet of scented stationary. He pressed it to his nose, the smell of lavender impressing Charlotte's essence in his brain and he imagined her in his arms, his hands tangled in her silken hair, his lips exploring hers. The image was almost more than he could bear.

With mounting anticipation he began to read.

Dearest Ian,

It is with a heavy heart that I take pen to paper and write you this letter. On Saturday last, dear Poppa collapsed in his shop and within the hour the Lord called him home. It was his heart and mercifully he went quickly and did not suffer.

St. Andrews Church could hardly accommodate all of the mourners, he was so well known and loved. He was buried at Bonaventure.

Mother is prostrate with grief and hardly moves from her room. All of the details of the funeral fell into my hands and now I have the added burden of running the business and planning our future. Without the assistance of our able solicitor, Mr. Martin, I do not know how I could possibly cope.

Dear Ian, there is one bright spot in the tragedy that has befallen me. With Poppa gone you are free to return to Savannah. And I hope you will do so at once. We have many decisions to make. I feel certain you won't mind leaving that dreadful army to take your rightful place by my side.

This letter is of necessity short as I have many business matters to attend to. Let me know when I can expect you. I love you.
Your betrothed,
Charlotte

Ian read the letter a second time, then a third, his brows bunched in thought. The news of Mr. Bruner's death was not unwelcome. It removed all obstacles to marriage with Charlotte, but there was something about the tone of her letter that bothered him. She was summoning him like she might her pet dog. She assumed he could just walk away from his military obligations and into her arms. Well, he couldn't, nor did he want to. The war with Spain was far from over and he suspected that Oglethorpe was already planning a spring offensive against St. Augustine. The militia had become his vocation, one he did not wish to change.

Light had faded to dusk and a sliver of moon floated on a raft of clouds. A strong breeze rippled the surface of the river as it pushed its way to the sea and the air was heavy from Frederica's tar pots, burning to repel the clouds of mosquitoes. Ian's hand crept up to finger the raised welt on his temple. With the immediate threat of attack over, and the Spanish on their way back to Florida, it would be a good time to ask for a leave to go to Savannah.

He and Charlotte did indeed have many decisions to make.

Ian lay on his bunk staring at the slats of the bed above him.

Cory's bunk.

Empty!

At times he questioned the futility of what he was doing. Spain and England were old enemies who shared a common dislike stemming from religious differences and imperial clashes. Now they had brought this animosity to the Colonies and continued to fight for dominance over land that Ian reluctantly admitted belonged to the Indian. Neither England, France, nor Spain discovered this country. The Indians were already here.

He wondered how things would all turn out in the end.

James Oglethorpe was an unlikely leader. He had been sent to Georgia as a trustee, a thirty-seven year old wealthy English bachelor with limited military training. His task was to colonize, to build forts and lay out towns, not to lead troops in battle against the Spanish. Not that Ian didn't respect him. Oglethorpe served them well with an overpowering self-confidence.

Take for instance the battle just fought. That the British defeated the vastly superior Spanish force was nothing short of a miracle. Had it not rained, keeping the musket smoke close to the ground and blinding the enemy, would the British have won? Was it chance or God's will? He shook his head. His mother had always seen to it that he attended the kirk in their village but since coming here he had lost sight of his Presbyterian upbringing. Lately, though, he had been feeling disquieted, as though something was missing in his life. He thought of Tabitha strong in her quiet faith. Strangely, it brought her a peace he did not seem to have.

Ian closed his eyes. He remembered Tabitha telling him that they held chapel services here at the fort. Sunday he would go. He would say a prayer for Cory's soul.

And for his own, as well.

Chapter Seventeen

General Oglethorpe supplied the townsmen with a nightly pint of beer after a day's work but Master Caldwell preferred to make his own in the Indian fashion and it always fell to Tabitha to prepare it when their stock ran low. Tuesday morning found her in the basement stirring a caldron of the small beer he liked. It was a hot, smelly job and one she did not favor.

She frowned as she dropped a fistful of roasted Indian corn into an iron pot and added water and sassafras root. While it came to a boil she busied herself sweeping the brick floor and putting the kitchen to order. Agnes was sick from an infected mosquito bite and Tabitha had already prepared breakfast and gotten the family under way. Her cleanup chores finished, she lowered the trammel in the fireplace and removed the lid from the pot of bubbling small beer. The corn was soft so she added a quart of molasses and recovered it to let it simmer. The smell was nauseous.

Suddenly Henry came clumping down the stairs, his cheeks flushed with excitement.

"Tabitha . . . Tabitha . . . Oglethorpe is in the parlor and he wants to see you."

"Me? You must be mistaken. The general does not know me."

"No. It's you he wants to see. Papa is with him, looking all stern and important. They said to bring you up right quick."

Tabitha's stomach gave an alarming lurch. Had Oglethorpe somehow found out about her conversations with Broken Arrow? If so, she was in much trouble. She laid aside the long paddle she was using to stir the brew and swung the pot on its crane away from the fire. With trembling fingers she wiped her hands on her apron and followed Henry up the stairs.

Unsure of herself she waited in the doorway of the parlor until the two men, deep in conversation, noticed her. Her employer waved her in and she stood anxiously in front of them.

"General Oglethorpe would like to speak to you, Tabitha."

"How may I serve you, sir?" she said, acknowledging Oglethorpe's nod with a curtsy.

He stood motionless and, tall as she was, he towered over her. His blue eyes observed her thoughtfully.

John Calwell cleared his throat importantly. "The general has suggested that you may be able to offer him some assistance with a problem that has arisen."

Puzzled and frightened, Tabitha looked from one man to another.

"Tabitha," Oglethorpe said, "I have a need for an Indian interpreter."

She felt weak with relief. It had nothing to do with her secret meetings with Broken Arrow. Struggling to keep her face impassive she looked squarely at him. "Does not Mary Musgrove serve as your interpreter, sir?"

"She does and an excellent liaison and diplomat she is. Only, she is Widow Matthews now. John Musgrove died some time ago and Jacob Matthews just last month."

Tabitha was surprised at the pain reflected in Oglethorpe's gray eyes. Was there more to the relationship between the general and his interpreter than was openly acknowledged?

"Of course" she said. "I did know that, sir. We are just used to calling her Mary Musgrove."

"Unfortunately, important business matters have necessitated her return to her trading post at New Venture and she is unavailable to serve us just now." Oglethorpe smiled and motioned toward a chair. "Please have a seat and let me explain my needs."

With a wary glance at her employer, Tabitha perched on the edge of the proffered wing-backed chair. Calwell sat down opposite her but Oglethorpe remained standing, his intense eyes watching her carefully.

"It has been brought to my attention that a Lutheran visionary by the name of Christian Prieber, went amongst the Cherokee Indians in Carolina and proposed that they form an Indian commonwealth to protect them from what he claimed to be white encroachment. This is in spite of the Cherokee Treaty with the English. Prieber has won their admiration by dressing as an Indian and learning their language. He is accused of attempting to incite them to begin a war by killing all those who traded amongst them.

"The British authorities in Charleston are demanding his arrest but the Cherokees refuse to extradite him. I feel it prudent to visit their chief and reason with him before real trouble breaks out and treaties are broken.

"You may consider this a problem of the Carolinians, Tabitha, but the war with Spain is far from over and we need the loyalty of all of the Indian tribes. The Crown feels it imperative that I meet with the Cherokee representative, Chief Walking Stick, to resolve the matter and, of course, I need a trusted interpreter."

"Where sir, is Chief Walking Stick's village?"

"Far to the north. But because of the war he has agreed to meet me half way between Augusta and Savannah at the village of Singing Spring."

"Singing Spring is near my village of Tustacatty," Tabitha said brightly.

"So I understand."

"It is Creek land. The Creeks and Cherokee don't like one another."

Oglethorpe did not answer and Tabitha turned her eyes toward Mr. Calwell who as yet hadn't spoken. "Sir . . .?"

"You have my permission to go with the general if he

needs your voice to speak with the Indians." He puffed out his chest. "It is the least we can do to help the cause."

"And Mrs. Calwell, sir?"

"Oh, she will moan and cry but she will just have to make do. Now, what do you say, child? General Oglethorpe is a busy man. He can't wait forever for your reply."

Oglethorpe looked at him with annoyance then turned to Tabitha with a smile. "Are you willing to accompany me?"

"Yes, sir. I will be pleased to help the cause."

"Good. Where did you learn to speak such excellent English?"

"In Savannah at the home of my grandfather. He wanted me to be as fluent in my father's tongue as I was in my mother's. Reverend John Wesley later tutored me during his brief stay in that town. Now I study with Pastor Ulrich."

"And I'm told you speak many Indian dialects."

"Yes, sir. I know five tongues of other tribes," she said proudly.

"Do you still retain Indian dress?"

"Yes, some."

"Wear it then. Mary Musgrove Matthews has found it beneficial to dress in deerskin when addressing her people, rather than in English clothing. We will be gone for several weeks, traveling overland by horse. I will take several Indian scouts from here and leave on the morrow. Pack sparingly, Tabitha, we must be quick. Captain Mackay will take charge while I am gone." He hesitated then smiled. "You will be amply rewarded, of course, when our mission is accomplished."

"Thank you, sir," she said with genuine humility, eyes down and with a slight curtsy.

Tabitha rose, confident and proud of Oglethorpe's trust in her ability. She hesitated, and then spoke boldly, "The Indian recently rescued at Darien and now serving as your scout is here at Frederica. He would make an excellent envoy, he is Cherokee and he knows many Chiefs. I will be happy to ask him to accompany us if you wish."

She heard the sudden intake of Calwell's breath and Oglethorpe looked surprised, then his eyes crinkled in amusement. "Of course . . . you refer to Broken Arrow?"

Tabitha nodded.

"He has served me well. And I understand it was you that saved this man from the jaws of an alligator by hitting it over the head with a club." He extended his hand. "I think we shall get along fine as a team, Tabitha. You and your Indian friend be at the dock at dawn."

As the sun sank to an orange strip at the edge of the marsh, Tabitha met Broken Arrow on the riverbank as prearranged. She carefully told him of Oglethorpe's request for an interpreter and his promise of a reward for her time. With rising excitement she told him of the idea that had been forming in her mind all afternoon. If she asked Oglethorpe to purchase the remaining time on her indenture as her reward it would free her without breaking the white man's law and making her a criminal.

Broken Arrow seemed hesitant at first but finally agreed with her plan and promised to act as a guide. He would meet her in the morning at the dock.

Tabitha had one last task before she left. That was to say good-by to Anna.

She found her at the cooperage with William. Because of the daytime heat he was working late by the light of several oil lamps to fill an order he had received from the fort's storehouse. The little shed was stacked from floor to ceiling with completed and partially finished barrels. Wood shavings covered the earthen floor and bundles of staves lined the walls. William was bent over a bench vise using a drawknife to shape a stave. He was a burly man, blond, clean-shaven, and dressed in britches and a loose-fitting shirt with rolled sleeves that revealed bulging biceps. Anna was sitting on a finished barrel watching him with adoring eyes.

They both looked up in surprise when Tabitha entered the

shed.

"I've come to say good-by," she said without preamble.

"Good-by?" they both coursed.

"Yes," Tabitha said brightly. "I've been asked to act as an interpreter and accompany General Oglethorpe to a Cherokee village northwest of Savannah."

"Goodness," Anna said. "Sit down and tell us all about it. William, bring that stool over for Tabitha to sit on."

William brushed dust from the seat of a tall stool and looked at Tabitha from raised brows. "I thought Mary Musgrove Matthews was his interpreter."

"She is, but she is away just now and he needs someone quickly."

"How long will you be gone?" Anna asked.

Tabitha fidgeted on her seat. Anna was her dearest friend and if they were alone she would have confided in her but she dare not reveal to William that she planned to ask for her freedom and might not return to Frederica. "It is uncertain," she said not meeting Anna's inquisitive eyes.

"Is it dangerous . . . is it an Indian uprising?" William asked.

"Please, Tabitha," Anna implored. "Tell us all about it."

For the next few minutes Tabitha explained what little she knew about the upcoming trip.

Anna watched her with amazement. "Yah, Tabitha, you are the bravest girl I've ever known. I can't imagine agreeing to do such a thing."

"It's for the safety of the colonies," Tabitha said modestly.

William, who had stopped working to listen, moved once more to his vise. "You are to be commended," he said gruffly drawing his knife across a stave, "but I for one prefer a woman to stay in the home and care for her duties there."

Anna blushed and gave Tabitha an uneasy smile. "William and I have news of our own," she said. "He is going to ask Poppa for my hand in marriage."

"Oh, Anna that is wonderful," Tabitha cried as she rushed to put her arms around her friend. "Have you set a date?"

"Not really. We think maybe in the fall."

Tabitha knew it was sinful to feel envy, but as she looked at Anna's glowing face and William's proud smile she wished desperately that she could be the recipient of that type of love. Her best girlfriend would soon be a bride and quite possibly Ian would soon take Charlotte to be his wife. What was there for her? She needed to feel love too. Everyone needs to feel love. She fought to keep a smile on her face as she walked over to William and shook his hand.

She struggled to maintain her composure as she hugged Anna once more, said good-by and hurried out into the darkening night.

Before preparing for bed Tabitha packed her few meager possessions into a canvas bag: her folding tin candlesticks, a pouch containing her amulet, a priming horn, and her sewing kit of needles, threads and sinew along with bags of tiny beads to make repairs to shirts and leggings. She added a change of clothing and several beaded headbands and gently placed her Bible on top of everything.

Of late she hadn't been sleeping well and she suspected tonight would be no exception. She pulled her Bible from her nightstand and, sitting in a rocker beside the oil lamp at her window, she thumbed to Jeremiah 29:11 and began to read.

> *For I know the thoughts that I think toward you,*
> *saith the LORD, thoughts of peace, and not of evil,*
> *to give you an expected end. . . .*
> *And ye shall seek me, and find me,*
> *when ye shall search for me with all your heart.*

She sought other verses, praying for guidance, but her prayers drifted into worry. She looked out the window toward the barracks, its rough tabby walls shadowed rose and purple in the gathering twilight. *Was Ian there?* Or was he sitting at the dock where they had so often talked in friendship? Was he still bitter toward her, toward what her mixed blood represented?

Although her experience was limited, she suspected that Ian was unlike other men. Though he was usually kind to her she knew he could be cynical and prejudiced. The Highland Scots were reputed to be fierce warriors and she sensed that Ian could be a cold-blooded killer when he needed to be. Nonetheless there was also a challenging vulnerability about him.

Tabitha knew that Ian professed love for another woman. Rashly, she found herself wishing he would forget Charlotte and love her instead. *What would it be like to have Ian MacDonald reach out to her—to hold her in his strong arms and kiss her?* She almost swooned at the thought.

Then she shook her head in disgust. Such thoughts were draining. He was taken and she was at this very minute plotting to leave Frederica to return to her native village. Even knowing this, she struggled against a hunger to search him out one last time, to hear his voice, to look into his green eyes. Why was that so wrong?

Her back straightened with purpose. She had to say goodbye. She owed him that didn't she? She yanked a shawl from the peg by her door and threw it over her shoulders. If he was at the pier then God meant it to be.

And if he was still angry and would not talk to her, then God meant that to be, too.

Tabitha made the short trek to the dock with determined steps and was rewarded when she saw the shadowy form of the man she sought. Her face flushed when Ian looked up at her with a tentative smile. His eyes had an intensity that made her breath quicken and her pulse race. Ian's eyes had always fascinated her, sea-green and large, supremely confidant eyes that never wavered. Several days ago he had acted as though he hated her. She believed it then, but now she was not so sure.

His steady gaze made her body warm.

"I'm sorry about my language the other day," he finally said. "I was angry and upset. Cory was the most loyal friend

I'd ever had." His large hands clenched into a fist. "I loved him like a brother."

"I feel your heartache, Ian," she said softly. "I didn't know Cory well, but I sensed his goodness."

"He was only twenty-two." Ian's mouth curved bitterly. "He had his whole life ahead of him."

Tabitha's hand fussed with a pleat in her skirt and she kept her head lowered. She searched for words that wouldn't sound trite or insincere. She knew only too well the hollow emptiness of losing someone that you loved. She always hated it when a well-intentioned friend said, "I know how you feel . . . I lost someone too." Each person feels grief differently and deals with it differently. Ian had lashed out in anger.

"You're very quiet, Tabitha. What's wrong . . . are you angry with me?"

There was gentleness in his voice that made her heart beat faster. She lifted her head and forced herself to look into his eyes.

"I . . . I have come to say goodbye," she said, striving to keep the tremor from her voice.

"Goodbye? But I haven't said anything about going—" He stopped in mid-sentence, his eyes squinting in bewilderment. "Ah . . . I've received no orders to return to Darien."

"Not you . . . me. I have been asked to accompany Oglethorpe to a meeting with the Cherokee as an interpreter. We leave for North Georgia in the morning."

"Oh, well," he said with a soft curve of his lips. "You will be back."

Tabitha hesitated. She cared deeply for this man. She wanted to be honest with him, but she dared not reveal her plans.

"I will be gone for some time," she said forcing a smile.

Tabitha watched the display of emotions that crossed his rugged face: disappointment, regret, and something else that caused her to wonder.

"I will miss our talks," he said finally.

"Me, too," she said softly, lowering her eyes.

They sat quietly, each lost in their own thoughts. Twice he cleared his throat as though about to say something but each time he remained silent. Only the sound of frogs setting up a clamor from the river shallows and the summer night music of katydids broke the quiet of the evening.

Finally he turned toward her. "I've received a letter from Charlotte. Her father is dead."

Tabitha's stomach churned. "Then you are free to wed?"

"Aye. I have asked Oglethorpe for leave to go to Savannah to talk with her. I don't know, Tabitha, I love her, but we have been apart for a long time. There are many issues between us that must be resolved before we marry."

Tabitha did not trust herself to speak. It was settled then. He had just said he loved this other girl. Ian would go his own way and she would go hers. They were still friends but that was all it was or could ever be. She moved as though to rise. "I must go," she said shakily. "We leave before dawn."

As he helped her to her feet his fingers brushed hers lightly sending a warm tingle up her arm. She knew the touch was casual but she suspected he felt the pull too. With her spine straight and her chin raised she walked away. Whatever life brought next, she would neither be broken nor bowed. A line from the Book of Mark came to mind. *Be not afraid, only believe.* She had to believe it would all work out somehow. That God was indeed watching over her. That He had his plan.

Chapter Eighteen

The next morning Tabitha, garbed in her old familiar deerskin dress and soft moccasins, with a canteen at her waist and a canvas bag packed with a hunting knife and one change of clothing, left the Calwell house for the river dock where she joined Oglethorpe. With him was a unit of ten rangers, two packhorse men, Broken Arrow and three other Indian scouts.

Their packhorses were loaded on one of two flat-bottomed piraguas. The general handed Tabitha into the other boat where the men already manned the oars. As they pushed off, heat rose in shimmering waves across the golden marsh, clouds of gnats encircled them and mosquitoes whined around their ears. The men strained at the oars moving the boat swiftly through tranquil water the color of gull's wings. The vegetation changed from dark magnolia leaves to pale marsh grass and the river widened, then darkened. High walls of cypress and live oaks draped with Spanish moss banked the swampy waters smelling of mud and decaying vegetation. The heat and the dip of oars in the slow moving river were hypnotic and as the day wore on Tabitha often found herself dozing. They moved along the banks sometimes in the shade of overhanging branches, sometimes in the brightness of the lazy sun. Several times deer swam across the river, turtles could be seen sunning themselves on fallen logs, and she saw alligators lazily dozing on riverbanks.

The Inland Passage led them to Savannah where they paused for Oglethorpe to consult briefly with the local authorities and pick up an additional map. Tabitha could not help wondering if Ian was here, at this very moment, claiming Charlotte as his wife.

The next morning they continued north on the Savannah River to an Uchee Indian town three miles west of Pachacola Garrison where they replenished their supplies and picked up additional gifts to be presented to the Cherokee chiefs. After spending the night in the small village they loaded everything onto packhorses. The rivers, which had always served as major transportation arteries for the Indian tribes, would no longer be of help to them. The rest of the trip would be an overland march to Singing Spring and Tabitha was given a sweet tempered Palomino pony. There was no saddle, only a woven blanket on the pony's back but she did not mind; she was a good rider.

Just before sunset they stopped and made camp near a stream. Horses were allowed to wander in the vicinity of the camp with a leather hobble tied between their forelegs to keep them from straying too far. Guards were posted and meat and other food were divided among the party. After eating, the men lay down to sleep with their weapons nearby, using their saddles for pillows. Tabitha was too tired to erect her sleeping tent so she, too, wrapped herself in a thin blanket and slept under the stars.

Before dawn the Indian scouts set out to hunt deer and turkey for the group's food supply. On their return, a quick breakfast was prepared, the horses rounded up, and the party headed northwest toward the land of the Cherokee. The going was slow, the trail faint and narrow with tree branches closing in on the riders from all sides. Every inch of the ground on either side was taken up with weeds and vines and grasses. Almost every creek bed was a swamp where the riders were forced to dismount and wade through the stinking mud. It brought back to Tabitha many vivid memories of her journey through the swamp at Fort Mosa two years before.

They stopped before noon for two or three hours in order to rest and to skin the wild animals the Indians had killed during their morning hunt. Their bounty was good, three turkeys and two rabbits. That night, after preparing the meat over an open fire, they ate well.

The first major river crossing was the Ogeechee. Broken Arrow found an abandoned raft and the general, Tabitha, and the rangers crowded aboard and paddled across while their horses were made to swim alongside. The scouts floated the supplies across in a skin boat, a small collapsible craft carried in one of the horses packs and easily assembled by stretching a leather cover over its wooden frame.

They had been on the trail two days before Oglethorpe brought his horse forward to cantor beside Tabitha.

She watched him with awe. He was a fine looking man, his eyes clear blue under level brows. A powdered wig failed to hide the fact that his hair was red and of remarkable fullness.

"How long has it been since you lived among your people, Tabitha?" he asked.

"Several years, sir." She glanced at him. "As you know, my mother was killed at Fort Mosa."

"Fort Mosa was a very unfortunate incident. After successfully taking the fort I ordered the rangers to change camp each night but they chose to disregard those orders. Instead they returned to the fort each night. The Spanish caught on quickly and, as you know, they attacked while all were sleeping."

"I'm sorry, sir. I wasn't blaming you. But not only my mother and almost all of your Highlanders died, many Indian warriors met their death, too."

"It is I who am sorry, Tabitha. But such is war. Orders are misunderstood and innocent people die. Now let's not talk of such sad events. Tell me about your people that I may understand them when we meet."

For the next hour they talked as they rode side by side and, when the general finally pulled away, Tabitha felt that they had forged an unlikely friendship.

* * *

The next evening, as the group stopped to make camp for the night, Tabitha sought the company of Broken Arrow. They had been traveling together for over a week but had little opportunity to talk. As he hobbled the ponies, Tabitha pitched her sleeping hut near the campfire and prepared her bed for the night by piling leaves over freshly cut limbs. She poured two tins of steaming acorn coffee and invited Broken Arrow to sit by her side.

"Our progress has been slower than I expected," she said as he hunkered down by her side. "How much longer do you think?" She spoke in Cherokee, practicing the flow of it off her tongue.

"Three days . . . maybe more." He turned his piercing black eyes on her. "I see you talk much with general. Have you bartered for freedom?"

"No. I want to wait until our negotiations with Chief Walking Stick are successful. Then Oglethorpe will be more in my debt."

"You plenty sure talks will be good."

"With God's help they will be. The colonies can't survive if an Indian war between the Cherokee and British breaks out, what with the French threatening the Carolinas and Spain threatening another attempt against Georgia."

"God! Humph. Better ask Great Spirit."

"I've asked both," Tabitha said softly.

Broken Arrow poked the fire and fell silent. The campfire hissed and crackled, the blue flames casting shadows on his broad face. He had not spoken again of his offer to share his blanket . . . of marriage . . . but she saw the way he looked at her, the way he protected her. In the darkness, beyond the camp, forest animals scurried and watched the human intruders with luminous eyes. Tabitha took a deep gulp of coffee, grimacing at its bitter taste, and thought of her unhappiness. Several days ago when they passed through Savannah she spotted a tall soldier in Scottish garb. For a moment she thought it was Ian, but, of course, it wasn't.

Nonetheless, the brief glance at the stranger had gone through her like a knife. *Would he return to Frederica with a bride? If so, she didn't want to be a witness to his happiness.* The thought was almost more than she could bear.

Broken Arrow flung the dregs of his coffee into the fire and rose. "I go now. Sleep tonight near ponies. Marauding Yemassee have been spotted. Your red-headed Oglethorpe's scalp much in demand."

The night passed uneventfully, but the next day was a struggle of endurance for both men and animals as the packhorses were forced to ford the alligator infested Ogeechee River.

Each day, as the Indians hacked their way through the tangled weeds and vines of the inhospitable forest, Tabitha steeled herself to brave the added danger of snakes and biting mosquitoes. Then at night there were the ants to contend with, velvet ants, red pepper ants, carpenter ants, small black ants and big brown ants.

Their party was on meager rations and everyone was hungry and completely exhausted. It was hostile territory and twice they spotted Indians wearing war paint. If the Indians decided to attack they could not expect rangers to come marching to their aid, or Highlanders with claymores swinging, and if any one of them should fall on the rocky path and suffer a broken bone there would be no doctor to tend their needs.

By week's end, Broken Arrow found an old buffalo trail that was relatively clear and led to within several miles of Singing Spring.

Tabitha prayed that they were not too late to persuade the Cherokees to remain loyal to their treaty with the white man.

The Indian braves sat in a ring. In their middle sat Broken Arrow, Chief Walking Stick, General Oglethorpe, Tabitha and John Gray, a resident fur trader whom the general had persuaded to record notes of the meeting. After Broken Arrow introduced Oglethorpe to the assembled chiefs they began to parlay. Oglethorpe sat on the grass in the council circle on a bearskin rug, Tabitha beside him. A northeast gale was blowing. One of the scouts had rigged a sailcloth windbreak, but red dust blew into their eyes and the painted skins of the chiefs were taking on a rust-like patina.

Tabitha sat ramrod straight carefully translating the important words passing between Oglethorpe and the assembled heads of the Cherokee tribes. She had been surprised to find that Chief Walking Stick was accompanied by many other chiefs of the Cherokee nation. This was an important meeting indeed.

Point by point the Indian grievances were addressed. Oglethorpe promised that the English would observe the land boundaries established by an earlier treaty and encroach no further on Indian lands. The Cherokees reaffirmed their allegiance to King George II, but they would not turn the man they considered their friend, Christian Prieber, over to British authorities. On this issue they stood firm.

Chief Walking Stick rose from the grass and stood to face Oglethorpe. Staring directly into his eyes he began to speak. "My brothers and my friends who are before me today, The Great Spirit has made us all, and He is here to hear what I have to say to you today. The Great Spirit has made us both. He gave us land, and he gave you land. You came here and we received you as brothers. When the Spirit you call God made you, he made you white and clothed you. When he made us, he made us with red skin and poor. When you first came we were very many and you were few.

"We are good, and not bad. The reports that you get about us are all on one side. You hear of us only as murderers and thieves. We are not so. We think of ourselves as civilized, we live in log houses, we tend animals and we farm the land.

"The Great Spirit made us poor and ignorant of your ways. He made you rich and wise and skillful in things which we know nothing about. You bring papers that we cannot read. Now a good man, Christian Prieber, has come among us to help us with these things we do not understand and you wish to take him away. Before the white man came to our land we were a free people. They make their own laws and govern themselves, as it seems good to them. Your ministers tell us that we live wickedly. We live as we were taught it was right. Shall we be punished for this? I am not sure what these people tell me is true. Prieber helps us find the truth.

"The Great Father that made us both wishes peace to be kept. We want to keep peace. We ask that you help us do it. We do not want riches but we do want to train our children right. Riches would do us no good. We could not take them with us to the other world. We do not want riches, we want peace and love.

"Shadows are long and dark before me. I am old and shall soon lie down to rise no more. While my spirit is with my body the smoke of my breath shall be toward the Sun for he knows all things and knows that I am true to him."

With that the Chief crossed his arms in front of him and closed his eyes. He stood silently for a moment then walked back to his place in the council circle.

Cups of strong black tea made from cassina leaves were passed back and forth as the two parties stared at each other in stony silence. Finally, Oglethorpe nodded a weary assent to Tabitha. "Tell them we honor their decision. We wish their friendship and want peace between our nations. We trust in the honor of their chiefs to abide by the old treaties. We will leave Christian Prieber, but plead that they not listen to the words of one man who travels a path that can only lead to war and bloodshed."

Tabitha breathed an inward sigh of relief. Oglethorpe was wise to realize the value of quelling a major uprising by conceding this one point. If she were any judge of reading faces she suspected that Oglethorpe had secret plans for dealing with Prieber. Best she didn't think on that subject. She wished to trust the word of the tall general.

With a beaming smile Chief Walking Stick had pipes and rum brought and all joined hands drinking and smoking in friendship. Chief Walking Stick presented Oglethorpe with a buffalo skin and the general was generous with his gifts. Brotherly relations had been reached, all rejoicing in the return of friendly dealings. They began to ladle cups of foskey, a bitter black medicine drink, and pass it among the people. The braves began to celebrate, beating little drums made of kettles covered with deer skins as they sang. Outside of the ring others danced, naked to their waists, with many trinkets brought by Oglethorpe tied around their middle. Their faces and bodies were painted and feathers adorned their hair. In one hand they shook a rattle and in the other held the feather of an eagle. One of the chief warriors sang of the many wars he had been in and how he had vanquished the enemy and the general won the hearts of the Indians by shouting his approval.

Tabitha realized her job was complete. She rose silently, leaving Oglethorpe to smoke the calumet pipe of peace contentedly with the chiefs.

That evening after the new peace treaty had been signed a noisy celebration began. A boar was roasted, dried pork and venison simmered in soot blackened kettles. Oiled warriors, reeking of buffalo grease, danced to the wild beat of drums, drunk on rum mixed with sagamité and the air was heavy with the smoke of the sweetgrass and the kinnikinnick they smoked. Women swayed and chanted and children joined hands dancing in imitation of their elders.

Tabitha saw Broken Arrow standing tall beside a roaring campfire watching her. He was resplendent in a red deer hide vest and wore earrings of silver, a silver ring in his nose, and a necklace of alligator teeth. A roach headpiece of deer hair, painted red, with gray porcupine quills was fastened to the back of his partially shaved head by pulling a pigtail of hair through a hole in the middle of the roach and securing it with a bone. His face was painted, the powders made from the dry rot of heart pine mixed with iron oxide, yellow-clay taken from the bluff of the river and dried blue delphinium flowers mixed with bear grease. Four black stripes ran from his eyes to his jaw, his muscular arms were bare and painted with circles and lines, the time honored fashion of her people.

Tabitha felt her blood sing. How much freer her Indian people were in expressing their almost childlike joy than the staid, white-faced Englishmen she dwelt with at Frederica. *Why had she denied her heritage for so long?*

By first daybreak, following the night of dancing and feasting, Oglethorpe's troops folded their tents and began the homeward trek.

They had been on the trail for about an hour when the general once more pulled his stallion alongside Tabitha. "You were a great help, my girl," he said. "In addition to your aid with the translation it was obvious the Cherokee liked and trusted you."

"I'm sorry you did not obtain all the conditions you desired."

"Make no mistake, Tabitha. Prieber will be silenced."

Tabitha shot him a look of dismay.

Oglethorpe smiled ruefully. "At times the white man is not nearly as honorable as the Indian." He spurred his horse and began to pull away. "Now let's not permit those thoughts to mar our beautiful day. Forget my hasty words. We have put our problems with the Cherokee Confederacy to rest and can concentrate our efforts on containing our real enemy—the Spanish aggressors."

"General . . .!"

He reined his horse and looked back.

"Yes?"

Tabitha clutched her bridle with white knuckled fingers. She was nervous and so afraid of what she was about to ask that her stomach was fluttering. She had to breathe in and out deeply and speak her words carefully in order not to stumble. "Sir, I believe I have served you well. You promised that I would be amply compensated at the end of our trip. Do you stand by that offer?"

"I do. Is there something special you wish?"

"I would like to ask for my freedom, sir. I have two more years to serve on my indenture."

He stared at her in surprise. *Had she been too brazen in her approach,* she wondered? Well, he had made the offer of compensation. She had not asked for it. She set her mouth and returned his stare.

He rubbed his chin and looked at her with a twinkle in his eye. "I think your request is fair. When we return to Frederica I will settle your indenture with Mr. Calwell. I assume you will want to stay in his service as a paid servant."

"No, sir. That is why I ask you now. I wish to return with Broken Arrow to my village. It is nearby. I want to stay with my people."

Oglethorpe looked at her intently. "You are certain that this is what you want? There are many more opportunities for you in the white man's world. You are an intelligent girl . . . lovely as well. You could marry and take your rightful place in society."

"I will always be a *mixed-blood*."

"Times are changing. Indians are not all thought of as savages—they are recognized as worthy of our respect."

Tabitha shook her head. "I appreciate your words, General Oglethorpe. But much prejudice still exists. The Indians accept me better than the white man. Besides Broken Arrow has asked me to wed."

"I see."

Chapter Nineteen

Midmorning sun slanted through the trees and flashed through Tabitha's long black hair. The sweet scent of an early morning rain mingled with the aroma of a nearby stand of loblolly pine. She and Broken Arrow moved through the forest, their moccasins making no sound on the damp leaves underfoot. For half a mile the trail grew faint and treacherous. Thick vines of strangler fig intertwined with sparkleberry and Virginia Creeper embraced many of the trees and, where lightning had scared their trunks, brightly colored mushrooms clung to the wounds. The air in the forest was silent, muted by great festoons of blue-gray Spanish moss. Ever so often, deep in the woods, turkeys clattered and called.

They had been on the trail to Tustacatty for two days and now as they reached the edge of the great forest the land opened before them into a long shallow valley sliced by the serpentine Oconee River. Far beyond it, to the west, they glimpsed the outline of a mountain range. They stopped and stood in silence, gathering their breath and taking in the view. The immensity of the valley, dappled with cloud shadows of deep purple was enough to lift the human spirit. At least it was for Tabitha.

A hawk rose in lazy circles on the warm air currents, its shadow sliding across the valley floor. It swooped suddenly toward the earth, skimming close to the ground for a mere second, and then arched again into the sky, its search for food unsuccessful. Undaunted, the dark bird glided in a widening circle until it once more spotted a potential dinner and dove toward its prey.

"Tabitha, look," Broken Arrow said, pointing ahead and staring intently into the distance. "There is smoke of village."

Tabitha caught her breath. "Tustacatty?" she asked.

Broken Arrow nodded. "Perhaps a half days ride. If we hurry we can reach it before nightfall."

They set off at once, making good time, but as twilight approached they decided to stop and make camp, feeling it would be better to approach the village in the fullness of a new day.

While Broken Arrow went to a nearby stream to fish for their supper Tabitha hurried to gather branches from the pine forest and carry them back to the clearing they had made for their evening campfire.

They built the fire but didn't light it. Instead they sat on a fallen log and watched the sun sink, vast and golden through the vast sky and into the trees. Tabitha watched the twilight strike the wilderness, thick and wild, as one by one the stars appeared and the ghost of a moon floated in the indigo sky.

With the darkness came a chorus of wild animals, panthers and wolves, bear and wildcats, inhabiting the nearby woods.

Tabitha shivered "We had better get the fire going,"

"It time," Broken Arrow agreed. Using a drill of cedar wood he worked it in a circular motion until a spark appeared over the tinder. The wood was dry and caught immediately. They stood back, watching the flames dance. The fire snapped and crackled, sending sparks spiraling into the black sky. When it had settled, Tabitha spitted the fish that Broken Arrow had caught earlier and together they ate it with relish.

The meal ended, she poured mugs of steaming acorn coffee and they sat cross-legged beside the fire staring into the flames that rose tall and comforting into the windless night. Both were silent, both lost in their thoughts. In the distance the sudden nickering of a wild pony was answered by the powerful "hoo, hoo, hoo" of a great horned owl.

"It good to be back in forest away from towns and walls," Broken Arrow finally said.

"Yes," Tabitha agreed. "I couldn't believe it when I saw how Savannah has grown. It's twice as big and busy as when I visited my grandparents."

Broken Arrow nodded. "The white man's wants are different from those of the Indian. They tear up our mother the earth and build their big houses. They break the cycle of life for everything. Our sisters the plants, our brothers the animals, they're all dead or washed away.

"The Great Spirit made us and gave us this land we live in. He gave us the buffalo, the antelope and the deer for food and clothing. No one puts bounds on us and unlike the white man we take only what we need."

He spoke in English and Tabitha looked at him in amazement. She had often suspected that Broken Arrow was more intelligent and versed in English than he let on. Indians on the whole had a good ear for the English language and picked it up easily.

"You have been playing possum with me," she teased. "Your English is quite good."

He looked abashed then a smile lifted the corners of his mouth. Come to think of it she had never seen him smile either.

"There are many things about me you not know," he said.

"I know you are steady and kind. That you think things through before you speak. That you have dignity and pride."

His face sobered and the firelight cast dancing flickers of gold across his high cheekbones. "Do you know that I make good husband for you?" he asked softly.

Tabitha looked away from his steady gaze. She was not ready to make that commitment. She hesitated then said, "I do know that. And I thank you for your offer. But I need time. Time to return to my village, time to get to know my people again." Her lip trembled. "It is a big step for me, Broken Arrow, to return to Indian life. I will always be half-white. And I will always be a Christian."

He poked the fire and did not answer, then threw the dregs of his coffee on the ground and rose to place more wood on the glowing coals. As sparks danced in the air he turned to face her. "I think the Great Spirit and your God much alike. Do you not believe in the three Beloved Things that live with him? The Clouds . . . the Sun . . . the Clear Sky?"

"Yes, but as a Christian I do not worship them. I believe God made the Beloved Things and I worship only God."

Broken Arrow replied in his own tongue. "The Beloved Clouds saved my life when the Spanish came upon us at Cumberland Island. Much rain and sometimes hail came upon the enemy and that on a very hot day. And the ground made a noise under them, and the Beloved Ones in the air made noise behind them. And the Spanish were afraid and went away, and left their meat and drink and their guns. I tell no lie. I think and talk to the Beloved Ones always—in my home, in my village and in war, before and after I fight."

"Then," Tabitha said, "I would interpret that to mean that God—the one you call your Beloved One that lives in the Sky—has often saved your life."

"He has. Many bullets have gone on this side and many on that side, but He would not let them hurt me."

"The book we Christians call the Bible tells us many things of God, our Beloved One above and his Son. Would you like me to tell you one of the stories?"

"Not now. Soon I must return to Oglethorpe to fight war. If we ever at peace I should be glad to know what you have to say."

Tabitha nodded and made a move to rise and Broken Arrow extended his hand and drew her to her feet. Her eyes were almost level with his and as she looked into their black depths she saw tenderness and longing. Her breath quickened as he drew her toward him. She was close against him, aware there were only the breechclout and the evidence of his desire between them. Tentatively their lips touched, then parted, then gently touched again. His mouth grew warm but he held her gently as though afraid he would scare her away.

Tabitha had never been kissed by a man. Except for a few unpracticed advances by young boys her experience with the opposite sex was quite limited. She felt herself responding in a way that amazed and confused her. She dared to trail her hands down to squeeze the corded muscles of his arms and then to clasp the sinewy hardness of his chest. "Oh," she whispered, her voice trembling.

Suddenly Broken Arrow twisted his head and raised his hand as though to silence her. She saw he was gazing intently into the dark beyond the fire. He took her hand and made a small gesture with his chin and Tabitha turned and looked where he was staring. Her eyes strained to adjust to the dark. Then she saw it. Some twenty yards away, at the edge of the clearing, a mountain lion stood staring back at them with gleaming yellow eyes.

He was a young male. By the pale light of the moon Tabitha could see that his coat was sleek and his shoulders well muscled. His manner was regal as he studied them both intently, swishing his tail from side to side. Time seemed suspended, as they stood motionless, scarcely breathing.

Broken Arrow made no move. Instead he fastened the cat with a steely gaze and began to speak to it in the Cherokee language.

The great cat growled, then became quiet as it surveyed them warily.

A sudden swirling gust of wind touched the dying embers of the fire sending a shower of sparks into the indigo night. The startled lion looked up and with an annoying swish of its tail turned and made its stately way back toward the shelter of the primal forest.

At the edge of the woods he stopped, turned and stared one more time. And then he walked away and was gone.

Tabitha had not realized how tightly she was clutching Broken Arrow's hand until he squeezed it hard before releasing it.

"See," he whispered, "Fire Spirit, sent by the Beloved One in the Clouds, came to help us. The night is still. There was no wind to stir the coals."

"Yes, Tabitha said with a shaky smile, "God was surely with us."

They settled once more by the fire, not saying much, just watching the glowing embers. Broken Arrow finally rose to build up the fire for the night and the flames rose clean and steady. Tabitha worried over their sleeping arrangements. Things were somehow different now. She had a small sleeping tent and he offered to put it up for her. But Tabitha said she loved the freedom of sleeping in the open and on a night like this she wanted to go to sleep watching the star-washed sky. So, she spread sweet smelling pine boughs on each side of the fire and he walked into the woods to give her some privacy as she prepared for the night.

Settled on her makeshift bed she looked across the fire to where he lay watching her. As she looked up at the polished disk of a moon she asked him about his family. He told her about his father and what a great warrior he had been and about his four brothers and two sisters whom she hadn't seen for many moons.

"It sounds as though you loved your father very much."

"I want only to be like him."

"And that means being a warrior?"

"Yes."

They fell silent again. Strange, Tabitha thought, how both of the men in her life wanted to be warriors. *Because*, she realized, *there are now two men*. And as different as Broken Arrow and Ian were, so were the feelings they stirred in her.

Night wrapped about her and the moon slipped in and out of clouds. She rolled over and drew her legs to her side as slowly she relaxed and drifted off to sleep.

Tabitha woke before dawn, lying comfortably on her bed of fresh cut pine, the sky a dark indigo blue with thousands of sparkling stars.

She thought of the day before and the emotions it had stirred in her: fear, yet awe at the majesty of the mountain lion, the comforting presence of the Holy One, the feeling of once more being one with the land, the stirrings of womanhood in her body. She glanced at the sleeping form of Broken Arrow. The rise and fall of his breathing was steady and his face slackened in sleep had a softness that touched her.

She looked back at the sky, watching the blue lighten as the first morning glow lit the eastern sky. Dawn was coming. And so was the decision as to the course her life would take.

Slipping quietly from her bedroll, she walked to the edge of the small clearing. The night chill enveloped her bare skin, and clothed her with gooseflesh. Shivering, she walked through the deep grass toward a small creek. As she walked she watched the sky continue to lighten from a pale gray to a pastel blue. Already there was a subtle change in the colors of earth and sky foretelling the changing of seasons. It would soon be fall, the winter more pronounced here in central Georgia than on the island she was leaving.

By the time she reached the little stream of clear water the morning chill had burned off. She slipped out of her deerskin dress, took off her amulet, and stepped into the shallow pool to wash. When she was through she pushed the water from her skin with one hand and then the other. It was a shame she had to don the same dirty dress, but she had no other. It was not lost on Tabitha that caring for her personal hygiene was crude in comparison to life in the white world. A frown creased her brow as she hung the amulet around her neck and she pursed her lips. It would not do to dwell on such thoughts. She lifted her chin and hurried back to camp.

Broken Arrow was tying a length of sinew around their rolled-up sleeping furs when she stepped into the clearing. He looked at her carefully and gave her a decidedly wicked grin.

"You very pretty with hair wet and dress stuck to skin. Maybe I too quick to tie up bedrolls."

Tabitha felt the blood rush to her cheeks. It had been growing harder and harder to ignore the growing feeling of intimacy between them as they traveled together. Broken Arrow was deeply attracted to her, she knew, and she felt he had showed admirable constraint in waiting for her to show that she would welcome his advances. Last night there had been no further talk of his offer to share his blanket with her but she saw the look of desire in his eyes each time he looked at her.

Ignoring his comment she laughed nervously and knelt down to add some dry tinder to the coals of their campfire. "I should not have taken the time to bathe, but, oh, the water looked so enticing. I'll make us a quick breakfast and then we can be on our way."

Broken Arrow looked at her intently his expression growing tight. "Soon, little one, we must talk of future."

He walked away before she could form an answer. Sudden tears welled in her eyes. And how would she answer him when the time came? She still loved Ian, would always love him and thought of him every day. Only he was out of her life now and she must move on with hers. Resolutely she wiped a tear from her cheek. Tonight she would take it to the Lord in prayer. She would trust Him to guide her in the right direction.

After a quick breakfast of corn gruel and acorn coffee it took little time for them to rinse their cooking utensils in the stream, shoulder their bundles and head north on the final leg of their journey. As they followed the well-worn trail Tabitha was flooded with memories of having been here before. She was returning to a world she never should have left. Everything seemed so familiar: the slash pines, the plants, and the red Georgia soil. They would soon be at the confluence of the Oconee, the Ocmulgee and the Altamaha rivers and her village of Tustacatty. The more landmarks she recognized the greater the excitement grew inside her. She had loved it once, before being sent to her white grandparents in Savannah. Could she learn to love it once more? And what about her Muskogee relatives? Would they accept her back into tribe after she made it clear that she was choosing them, or still treat her as different. Not quite white but not quite Indian either.

The area was familiar to Broken Arrow too. He had visited the Tustacatty Trading Post several times in the past and when he came to a fork in the trail he took the one west without hesitation.

They were well in view of the village when they heard a horse approaching fast. They stopped and held each others hand as the horse was pulled up and its rider leaped to the ground.

Tabitha saw a tall youth, almost a man, who stood gaping at them in surprise. She looked again. It was her cousin.

"Aluste? Aluste, is it you? It's me, White Blossom. White Blossom of the Otter Clan."

"White Blossom? What are you doing here? We heard you had been killed in the Florida war," Aluste said in amazement.

They rushed forward and threw their arms around each other then the youth backed off as though embarrassed by his show of emotion. Aluste was, after all, nearly a man now. Hugs of greeting were one thing, but such a display of affection, even though they had been playmates of the same hearth at one time was something else.

Tabitha saw her cousin looking from her to the Indian brave standing silently behind her. "I think I had better introduce you to my . . . friend," Tabitha said. "Aluste of the Otter Clan of the Muskogee Tribe of the Creek Nation, this is Broken Arrow of the Antelope Clan of the Cherokee Confederacy."

Broken Arrow moved toward the boy with both hands outstretched and Aluste grasped them firmly.

"I am Aluste, cousin to White Blossom. I welcome you, Broken Arrow of the Cherokee."

The introduction complete Tabitha's cousin turned somber black eyes on Tabitha. "Your mother and father—they also live?"

"No, both are dead. It is a long story, one I will tell you later. What about your parents, Bald Eagle and Wilimico?

Are they in good health?"

"Yes," Aluste said proudly. "Father is a great warrior and a man of great wealth. He runs the Trading Post now." He gathered the reins of his pony in his hands. "I'll walk to the village with you so no one will think you mean them harm."

"Thank you, Aluste," Tabitha said warmly. "Let's hurry. I can't wait to see the rest of my family."

The trail was well used and wide enough for Aluste, leading his pony, and Tabitha to walk side by side, although Broken Arrow was forced to walk behind. They had left the protecting trees and small brush and the land appeared harsher than Tabitha remembered. Green grass struggled to grow in sparse patches on the barren red earth that surrounded the village.

People began to materialize out of the dusty air eyeing them cautiously. Several men carried spears aimed directly at them and as the procession approached Tabitha saw apprehension on every face.

"Aluste! Whom are you bringing here?" a man's voice called out.

"We are family. I am White Blossom," she answered, greeting her people in their language. Apprehension turned to surprise as the villagers began to crowd around her.

"White Blossom? It can't be. White Blossom is dead," a woman cried as she hurried forward to stare intently into Tabitha's face.

Tabitha recognized her at once. It was Wilimico, her Mother's sister, a short, plump woman with dry, wrinkled skin and several missing teeth. A long black hair grew from a mole on her chin.

"But it is me, Auntie," Tabitha said with a warm smile. "I survived."

"And your mother?" Wilimico asked hopefully.

Tabitha looked at the ground and shook her head. "Only I live," she said her eyes speaking her despair.

"You left many moons ago to travel with your white father. He always thought you too good to be one with us, teaching you English ways. What are you doing here now?"

Aunt Wilimico hadn't changed a bit. She was just as blunt and direct as always.

"I have decided to come home. To claim my heritage as a Creek."

Her aunt pursed her lips and squinted, her black eyes, snorting derisively. Then her face softened as Tabitha stood resolutely before her, offering a tentative smile. Slowly Wilimico stretched out her hands and Tabitha stepped forward to grasp them.

When Tabitha finally freed herself from the offer of acceptance she turned to Broken Arrow who had been standing quietly on the sidelines. "Broken Arrow of the Antelope Clan of the Cherokee Nation, meet Wilimico, of the Otter Clan of the Muskogee Tribe of the Creek Confederacy."

The perceptive woman looked at him carefully. "I welcome you, Broken Arrow, but I wonder at your reason to return White Blossom to her people. We talk later." She turned to Aluste. "Put his things in the Ceremonial Lodge. White Blossom will stay with us."

The rest of the assembled villagers greeted Broken Arrow with reserved acceptance, but much curiosity. Their greeting to her was more open. Most remembered her and she was shyly welcomed home.

When the crowd finally dispersed Aluste led Broken Arrow across the village square toward the Ceremonial Lodge. It was a circular town house, with clay walls and a cone-shaped bark roof, used to shelter the old and homeless as well as visiting guests. It would serve as his quarters for as long as he stayed at Tustacatty.

Paths led away from the village center, like the spokes of a wagon wheel, leading to individual clusters of four houses each, rectangular, pole-framed structures with mud-packed walls and bark-covered, gabled roofs. Tabitha followed Wilimico walking along a well-trodden path, keenly aware that they were passing the Trading Post and her childhood home. Tabitha stared at the long, log building blinking back tears as memories of her father washed over her.

"Your uncle, Bald Eagle, has Trading Post now," her aunt said proudly. "Very good business."

They walked on in silence. Naked and half-naked children played in the dirt. Chickens ran free and dogs were everywhere.

Her uncle's home was at the edge of the village, surrounded by cultivated fields that spoke of his standing in the community. His property consisted of a winter lodge and kitchen, a summerhouse, a storage hut and a large warehouse open on all four sides like a Seminole chickee.

Tabitha followed her aunt to the summerhouse. Wilimico pushed back a door covering of soft leather and held it up for her to enter. Inside thin cracks of daylight could be seen between some of the wooden siding, but deerskins lined the walls to ward off drafts and created a soft cozy feeling. There was a small fireplace near the front of the building with a hole, protected by a rain cover, cut into the roof above it.

Curtains of soft yellow leather separated three small sleeping areas and Wilimico led Tabitha to an area in the corner where a bed, not much more than a wide wooden shelf, was fastened to the wall, covered by stuffed leather padding and furs. Tabitha placed her knapsack on the bed and squinted in the dim light at the outline of the room. This, then, would be her home. A faint smell of charred wood and the strong odor of bear fat used in the lamps permeated the enclosure. Unbidden memories of her cozy little room under the eaves at Frederica crowded into her mind, the smell of rosewood and beeswax in the chandlery, the tang of salt air on the evening breeze. She shook her head. She would not allow her mind to go there. Those were material things only. Here was family and freedom. Still . . .

Wilimico was giving commands to several women who had crowded into the longhouse. There would be a feast tonight in honor of White Blossom's return. It would be the last feast before preparations for the annual Green Corn Festival began. She began to rummage through a large willow basket in the corner until she found a clean deerskin dress, adorned with beads and feathers. Wilimico pulled it from the basket and shoved it at Tabitha.

"You will want to look pretty to meet your clan," she said curtly.

Tabitha could tell the dress was too big but she accepted it gratefully. At least it was clean. She would have to begin work on a new dress for herself as soon as possible.

That evening, after a lavish feast of roasted wild boar, people gathered around the fire with cups of tea or lightly fermented dandelion wine. It was time to tell stories, recount adventures and, especially, to learn more about their visitors, Broken Arrow and White Blossom.

The entire village of Tustacatty had come together to pass judgment on the new arrivals. Most of them thought of Tabitha as somewhat of an outsider, she was kin only through her mother, and they had always been disdainful of her white blood. Tabitha knew the story well. When her mother fell in love with the white man who ran the Trading Post and married him he had tried to become one of them. They had lived here as a family and he had learned the Creek ways, but he had never gone through any ritual joining in his own right. He had tried—he loved his wife—but in his heart he was a white man and he could not make the decision to settle with them permanently.

However, Tabitha was of the Otter Clan and the questions began naturally enough with inquiries about her mother.

"How did our daughter, Windwhisper, of the Otter Clan meet her death?" a woman asked.

As painful as it was to talk about, Tabitha began her story of the missing years ending with the massacre at Fort Mosa and the fatal Yemassee arrow that had found her mother.

There was silence, then a young brave spoke out. "And this Cherokee—this Broken Arrow—how did you meet him?"

Tabitha looked at Broken Arrow. It would be better if he told his own story but he was clearly uncomfortable speaking at length in the Creek language and uneasy at the number of stares being directed at him. One brave in particular scowled at him from the edge of the clearing. The Indian was hollow-cheeked and bare-chested, having a scalp lock and wearing a breechcloth. Tabitha recognized him at once as her uncle, Bald Eagle. He had not greeted her.

Tabitha looked back at the expectant faces watching her. Briefly she recounted the story of the alligator and Broken Arrow's gratitude to her for saving his life. Then she spoke of his loyalty to the British and General Oglethorpe by acting as guide and interpreter to the peace talks at Singing Spring, and his promise to Tabitha to return her to her people after Oglethorpe gave her freedom. She did not mention his offer to take her to wife. According to Creek tradition he must first speak to her uncle before any formal announcement could be made. Then, if they did marry, tradition required that he become a member of his wife's Clan, the Otter Clan of the Muskogee Tribe. He would no longer be a member of the Cherokee Nation. It was a big step for such a proud man and one they had not discussed.

Tabitha paused and took another sip of her tea. The hostile stares had disappeared during her narrative. The men nodded in admiration at Broken Arrow's brave actions.

Her uncle stepped forward and placed both hands on her shoulders. "You are welcome to my hearth, White Blossom." He directed a stony stare in Broken Arrow's direction. "Your friend must prove himself if he wishes to stay."

Well, Tabitha thought, *at least this is a start. It will take time, but time is what I need.*

Within the week, feverish preparations began for the annual autumn day of rejoicing. The Green Corn Festival, the most important of all the Creek rituals, takes place near the end of the summer when the last corn crop has ripened. It was a time of renewal for the village, marking the beginning of their new year, and would last for an entire week.

The village buzzed with activity. Men made repairs to all of the communal buildings while the women cleaned the inside of their houses. Wilimico tackled her cleaning like a demon and Tabitha was assigned the task of scrupulously cleaning the cooking utensils and taking all of the bedding outside to be aired, beaten, or washed. Old or worn possessions were discarded. When the inside of the longhouse met with her aunt's approval the hearth fire was extinguished. It would be rekindled only from the Sacred Fire to be lit in the village square as a part of the renewal ritual.

The most important men of the village, including chiefs and shamans plus elders and warriors, had been fasting for days while Tabitha helped the women prepare huge amounts of corn and other delicacies for today's feast. Tonight they would gather in the square for the first of the Green Corn Dances, to break their fast and light the Sacred Fire.

Tabitha dressed carefully for the evening festivities. She had managed to alter the deerskin dress supplied by Wilimico and it clung softly to her slender body. She braided her freshly washed hair and wound it around her head securing it in the back with a bone barrette adorned with feathers and a headband of bright blue beads, the color of her eyes. *Oh*, she thought wistfully, *what I wouldn't do for a looking glass to see myself.* But nothing that would show her reflection was available so with a final pat to her hair she left the longhouse and headed for the Corn Dance.

Broken Arrow, excluded from participation because he was a Cherokee, waited for her at the edge of the town square.

His eyes softened as his gaze traveled up and down her body. "You very pretty. I like new dress," he observed quietly.

Tabitha's mouth quirked in a smile. His eyes said he was admiring more than the dress.

"Thank you," she said demurely.

Together they climbed the sloping bank encircling the square and lowered themselves to the hard packed earth from which they would be able to observe the dancing.

Broken Arrow's stomach growled and she glanced at him

in surprise.

"Cherokee also observe Green Corn Festival," he said wryly. "I join your Creek brothers. I fast and drink your Black Drink to purify my body."

Tabitha shuddered. *Better you than me.* The Black Drink was a ceremonial tea made from a poisonous shrub called *Illex vomitoria,* tobacco and other herbs. It induced vomiting and repeated emptying of the bowls to clean the body of evil spirits.

A gusty, fitful wind swirled red dust around them causing Tabitha's eyes to tear. She looked at Broken Arrow. A light film of powdery dust coated the oiled shoulders of the tall warrior but it did not detract from the beauty of his bare, heavily muscled chest and biceps. His head was freshly shaved with a narrow ridge of black hair standing straight up in the middle and his face and arms were painted in stripes and circles of vermilion and black.

One by one the villagers joined in the dancing and soon Tabitha found her heart pounding and her body swaying to the primal beat of the tribal drums. At the conclusion of that dance the villagers lit the Sacred Fire and then resumed their dancing, which increased in noise and frenzy lasting well into the night.

The next day coals were taken from the Sacred Fire and each home's hearth fire rekindled. All day the women cooked food for an even greater feast, this time of deer meat. That night games, such as stick-and-ball and archery contests, were held. There was more dancing and feasting, and then everyone closed the ceremony with a communal bath in the river for purification.

Everyone, that is except Tabitha. She retained too many of her Christian virtues to uncover her body for all to see. She saw the hostile looks directed at her as she hid herself in her modesty. She was not giving herself wholly to their Indian ways and she saw resentment on their faces. Other examples of relaxed morality bothered her as well. She had not failed to observe the nightly excursion of braves and young girls into the woods nor had she failed to see the confusion in Broken Arrow's eyes when she held herself aloof.

At the end of the week the festival was over, the entire village ready for a fresh start of the New Year and Broken Arrow let it be known that he was tired of waiting.

He strode up to her as she was sitting in the shade of a sweet gum tree weaving a new willow basket and hunkered down beside her. "I wish to make my intentions known to your uncle, Bald Eagle, tomorrow," he said briskly. "To ask to mate with you. Do you want this, White Blossom? I hope you do. If not, then I will be on my way."

White Blossom could not speak. She had anticipated the proposal but could not find the voice to respond.

It was the decision she had refused to face. It was on her mind constantly, but until now she had been able to push it aside, not wanting to acknowledge that she was going to have to make a choice. Now the question was asked, out in the open, and waiting for an answer.

And what was her answer? Yes, she would marry him, spend the rest of her life with him, but she was not sure she loved him because of her feelings for Ian.

Which should she choose—the white world and a love denied, or her Indian heritage and a love promised?

"I wait answer," he prompted

"Tomorrow," she whispered. "I need to look into my heart to be sure. I will give you my answer before the sun goes down tomorrow."

Chapter Twenty

Just before Ian left for Savannah a letter came to him from his brother, William, in Scotland. It was an answer to the letter he wrote ten months before telling William of his love for Charlotte, his banishment from Savannah and his present day service as a Scots Highlander in the King's Army. His letter had painted a realistic picture of his life in America and then he asked William to send news of those he loved in the old country. Now this letter, so long in reaching him, brought the dreaded news that their father had died shortly after Ian's letter arrived. He was buried next to their mother and grandparents at the farm in Glencoe.

William wrote that the farm was doing well. He had increased the flock and built several new sheep pens. Ian realized there must be times when William feared his return to Scotland. As the eldest son the land was Ian's birthright if he wished to claim it.

William wrote that he had married Sarah Petrie and they had one son. Sarah was expecting again and he hoped for another boy because the sheep croft was growing and a man needed sons to help. His letter ended, *Do you think of coming home?*

Ian could feel the tension in William's final question.

The next day he sought the services of the local magistrate and signed over the land holding to his younger brother. That night he sat down to pen a letter to ease William's fears. He wouldn't return to Scotland, he wrote, unless someday on a visit. He praised William for keeping to the land and sent his love to his new sister-in-law. He was enclosing a legal document signing over his rights to the farm. It was clear that the MacDonald farm would be in the proper ownership.

When he finished the letter he set out for a leisurely walk. A week ago his Highland Company had returned to Fort King George and he decided to take the river path that followed the Altamaha into the village of Darien. He knew he would never leave here. Georgia had captured him despite its bugs and humidity and the threat of destructive hurricanes. He loved the smell of salt air, the gentle ocean breezes, and the golden dappled light filtering through the majestic oaks. This land was where he wanted to build a home and raise a family.

He debated about stopping to see Sally but decided against it. Hopefully, she was getting on with her life and seeing him would only remind her of Cory. He did stop for a moment in Darien before a small park where someone had planted several azalea bushes and placed stones on the grass in the form of a cross. Somehow it reminded him of Tabitha and her quiet faith. The thought unsettled him and he moved on quickly.

As he started back toward the Fort, Ian left the path to stroll to an abandoned homestead that sat high on a bluff overlooking the broadest part of the mighty Altamaha River. It was a perfect place to build a substantial house and had far better farmland than the keeping in Scotland, free of rocks with deeper loam, and fatter grass. He reached down to pick up a clod of dirt and crumbled it in his fingers, standing quietly, letting the essence of the place seep into his soul. He had lingered here many times and was beginning feel a kinship, a sense of belonging. He knew it could be claimed for a reasonable price, its owners having returned to England. He even had a name for the property—it would be called MacGrath Bluff in honor of his friend Cory.

Resolutely he turned back to the path. He had been granted a two-week furlough and Monday he would leave for

Savannah. Now all he had to do was convince Charlotte to leave her opulent house and make her home here as the wife of a soldier.

And somehow he didn't think that was going to be easy.

The Inland Passage between the coast and sea islands is a beautiful one. Ian hugged the rail of the Bonnie Bride, contentedly smoking his pipe, letting his gaze rest on the expanse of quiet, level marsh stretching out before him. The marshes had always intrigued him, a shimmering gold during the summer months, filled now with tidal pools and teeming with life.

At the edge of the marsh, as the schooner glided into a wide shining channel, he could see the blue outline of the mainland. The bay sparkled in sunlight, the deep tang of sea wrack filled his nostrils and white gulls soared overhead filling the air with their screeching calls.

Ian crossed to the other side of the boat to look across at the misty island of Sapalo, lying between him and the great Atlantic booming on its outer beach.

Over one hundred miles of serpentine river wound past the sea islands of St. Catherine's, Ossabaw and Skidaway, which the Spaniards called the Golden Isles. From the earliest times, when the Creek Indians used them as hunting islands, through the century of Spanish occupation, when missions were founded and chapels were built upon them, to the present settlement by the English under Oglethorpe, their history has been romantic and interesting. Ian was almost sorry when the Bonnie Bride docked at Savannah and the short journey was over.

He disembarked and bounded up the steep ballast stones that connected the wharf to Bay Street. New buildings were going up everywhere. The town had surely doubled in size since he left it four years ago, but thanks to Oglethorpe's foresight it was a beautiful town, laid out in spacious squares with natural parks every two blocks. By three o'clock Ian was standing in front of Charlotte's stately home, elegant in its simplicity, with wrought iron gates as delicate as lace.

When he saw Charlotte's house he almost broke into a run, he was so eager to see her. Her home was on a corner, facing another square, a two story brick with a curved double stairway leading to the front door. Bruner's Clockworks sat beside it, back from the street, reached by the familiar winding brick path.

He paused, his heart pounding. It had been four years. How much had Charlotte changed? He had not had time to write to her so his arrival would be a surprise, one he hoped she would welcome. He straightened his plaid and adjusted his tam to just the right angle, then bounded up the stairs and pulled the bell.

After what seemed an eternity Elsie, the Bruner's maid, pushed open the door and stood on the threshold looking at him in amazement.

"Bless my stars, you can't be young Ian," she stammered.

"The same, an' all grown up now," he said with a broad grin. "And hoping to find Miss Bruner at home to accept a caller."

"Oh, too glad I am to see you. Come in . . . come in. I'll call the mistress."

Elsie guided him through the foyer and opened the door to the Bruner's bright, airy withdrawing room with windows overlooking the garden. "Wait here . . . I'll see to Miss Charlotte."

Ian entered the small, elegantly appointed chamber. Floor-to-ceiling arched windows with leaded glass gleamed with the last rays of sunlight. A crystal bowl of white magnolias sat on a round mahogany table filling the room with their cloying scent. He was too nervous to sit so he walked over to examine a large oil painting of Charlotte that he had never seen before.

His heart gave a lurch. He had forgotten how beautiful she was!

He turned away, staring at the gilt-edged mirror on the far wall, its beveled glass reflecting the leaves of the magnolias in the deepening dusk.

He heard a sudden swish of skirts and turned to see her running across the room with a look of happy amazement. She stopped a few feet from him and stood motionless, her eyes raking his body, her breath coming in little gasps. With a cry he stepped forward and gathered her in his arms.

Charlotte's soft form in his arms had an immediate effect on his body. He caught a delicious scent of lavender as her hair brushed his lips. She was lovely, quite lovely to look at. Her skin was pale and creamy and the curve of her lips more beautiful than anything he had ever seen. Her blond hair, like glossy wheat kernels, lay thick and curling on her shoulders.

"Ian," she said playfully, pushing him away, "why didn't you write that you were coming?"

"I had no time. The Spanish are on their way back to Florida after we soundly defeated them in battle last month and my commander thought it safe to give me leave. It's hurricane season and I doubt they will attempt to return soon, if ever."

"How long do you have?"

"A two week leave."

She looked at him with a happy smile. The lids over her large, brown eyes seemed to droop slightly, provocative, seductive. "You look very handsome in your uniform."

Ian felt his face grow warm as her gaze lingered on his legs.

"You can stay for dinner, can't you," she asked suddenly, seemingly unsettled by his knowing look. "I'll call Elsie and have her set another place. It's only Mother and me now." Her lower lip trembled and tears appeared in her dark eyes.

He reached out and took her hand. "Darling, I am so very, very sorry about your father's death."

Charlotte dabbed her eyes with a lace handkerchief. "It was so sudden . . . there was no warning . . . It's hard to believe he's gone. Mother grieves deeply, she keeps to her bed most of the day but I know she will be cheered when she sees you. She was always fond of you."

As your father was not, he thought savagely. But he did not say those words. There would be a better time. His lips curved in a mocking smile. "Aye, I'll be glad to stay for dinner. 'Twill be good to taste some good home cooking and when I'm not filling my stomach I can feast my eyes on you."

"Where are you staying?"

"I haven't secured lodging yet. I came directly here, anxious to see you. I thought I would inquire at Mrs. Wilkes Boarding House."

Charlotte nodded. "Dinner will be at six. That should give you enough time to get settled." She took his hand and led him to a brocade camel-backed sofa standing against the wall. "First, though, we must talk. Tell me everything that has happened since you last wrote."

For the next hour Ian recounted the details of the battle for St. Simons Island and Cory's death while Charlotte filled him in on the details of her father's passing. Finally she inched closer to him and put her arms out. He gathered her close and kissed her hungrily, his blood aflame. Charlotte had the sweetest tasting mouth he had ever encountered. "Till tonight," he whispered. "I must go, now."

"Till tonight," she promised, smiling wickedly.

Charlotte managed to steer a safe course through the dinner conversation bringing Ian up to date on their mutual friends and happenings in Savannah. Mrs. Bruner sat ramrod stiff in a straight-backed chair and regarded him with watchful eyes. She was still a woman of remarkable beauty and she had lost none of the grace and style of London society where she had spent her youth. She was dressed in dove gray this evening, with a long rope of pearls around her neck, glowing softly in the flickering candlelight. Ian thought he detected a look of disdain when he answered her questions about life in the military. *Well, let her look down her nose,* he thought savagely, *her husband is responsible for it, and I don't doubt for a minute that she was unaware of his actions.* He suspected that she undoubtedly shared her late husband's views on his suitability as a suitor for her daughter's hand, but for the most part she was silent and withdrawn.

"Well, Ian," she finally said as the desert dishes were cleared and the meal drew to a close, "you seem to have fared well since your departure. I trust that when you return to your post you will advance rapidly in your ranking." She regarded him soberly with slightly raised silver eyebrows and for an instant he dared to think that she spoke with a trace of empathy.

"I will try," he answered politely.

"I have enjoyed talking with you. If you ever get to Savannah again, please feel free to call on us. Now, I am tired and must retire. Charlotte, please look in on me after Ian leaves. I trust it won't be late."

"Yes, mother. Of course!" Charlotte said, darting an amused glance at Ian.

With that Mrs. Bruner rose and walked regally from the room.

With a twinkle in her eye, Charlotte placed her hand on his arm. "Let's take a stroll in the garden. We've so much to talk about."

There was the first rosy flush of sunset in the western sky turning the stone bench where they settled to pink marble and painting Charlotte with slanting rays of golden light. With a groan Ian pulled her into his arms and bent his head to her pouting lips in a long passionate kiss. He felt he was drowning in their sweetness.

A hot wave swept into his belly and it was all he could do to control himself. He kissed her again and again.

"I've wanted to do that all evening," he finally said, grinning roguishly.

"So have I, dearest. But we must be circumspect in front of mother. Give her time to get used to your presence."

"I sensed her disapproval."

Charlotte hesitated. "To be honest, she is concerned about our financial security . . . now that Father is gone. She would like to see me marry well."

"You mean someone with more money that I possess or

am likely to possess."

"That is a rather blunt way of putting it . . . but, yes. Only, darling, it is you I love. You I intend to marry. Once you take over the business I'm certain that we will have more than enough, if not more, to keep us all."

Ian grimaced. There it was again—the blind assumption that he was ready to change his life and step into her father's shop. No discussion as to what he wanted.

"Why the frown?" Charlotte asked. "Don't you want to marry me?"

"Of course I do." She looked so frightened he crushed her to his chest and sought her lips once more. He could feel her heart throbbing and his own soon began to beat furiously. He had to have this woman. Conversation about their future could wait.

Charlotte writhed in pleasure. He could feel her body pressed into his. Their kisses became deeper and more passionate and lasted longer. His hands became insistent.

She pulled away suddenly, pushing both fists against his chest.

"No, Ian. Not here . . . not like this."

"It's not wrong, dearest, we love one another. We're almost married."

"But we aren't. We haven't even talked about it."

"That's what I'm here to do, Charlotte . . . to plan our future." He grinned mischievously. "I can't help it that I'm so starved for your kisses I get diverted and end up in your arms."

"Stay in Savannah then. Desert the stupid army. You were forced into it anyhow and I apologize for my father's actions, but I need you to help save the business. I take care of the finances and Johnnie, our apprentice, has been keeping up with the repairs but he's only fifteen and certainly not a master clockmaker. If someone with your skill and ability doesn't step in I fear we will loose everything. We could be married during the season."

"The season?"

"Savannah society. The better class has adopted many of the English social customs, among them a Winter Season. In fact tomorrow night there is a dance to—"

"Whoa . . ." Ian said sharply. Suddenly he felt incurably sad. Desert the army. Become a clockmaker. Join Savannah's society! This conversation wasn't going the way he intended. "Let's back up a little. First of all—"

Just then there was a discreet cough from beyond the garden bench. Ian looked up and watched as Agnes approached Charlotte.

"I'm sorry to interrupt, mum, but your mother is ill and asking for your company."

"I'll? She was fine at supper."

"Yes, mum. She thinks it may have been something she ate. Her stomach is quite upset."

Charlotte's brows puckered in exasperation. "Tell her I'll be right up." She turned to Ian with a forced smile. "I'm sorry, darling. Mother has become quite demanding since father's death. We'll have to continue this conversation tomorrow. I must be at the shop in the morning. Why don't you stop by and see for yourself how things are going?"

Ian regarded her with cold speculation. Charlotte was different somehow, more assertive than he remembered her. He didn't like the feeling that he was being maneuvered. He grabbed her—a little rougher than he intended—and gave her a hard kiss.

"Ian!" she sputtered.

He let her go. "Now, go up to your mother who became so conveniently ill. We'll continue our discussion tomorrow. I do have a few thoughts of my own on the subject."

"You're angry."

"Aye, a little." He saw her look of confusion and felt himself weaken. "I'll see you in the morning," he said pulling her to him gently this time and kissing her on the top of her head.

Charlotte turned her face up to look into his eyes. "Agnes will pack us a picnic lunch. I'll take the afternoon off and we'll go to Tybee Island. I know a lovely, quiet spot where we can be alone."

"I'd like that." He kissed her warm lips again, then turned and strode from the garden into the street. He felt vaguely disquieted. Tomorrow was all mapped out and again she had made the plans without asking for his input. *I suppose,* he thought, *becoming head of the household and taking charge of the business has forced her to mature. She's no longer the fifteen-year-old girl I fell in love with.*

Yet . . .

Ian woke up in bed the next morning with the sheets a tangled mess, thrown every which way and damp with sweat.

He lay in bed for a few minutes, thinking about waking up alone, imagining what it would be like to find Charlotte beside him when he opened his eyes each morning. With a soft sigh he slid out of bed and began to dress for the day ahead, striding to stand in front of a clouded mirror that hung from a nail above a wash stand. He removed a straight razor from his travel kit and stropped the blade until it was honed to a fine edge. Briskly he applied lather to the stubble on his face before carefully gliding the razor over his jaw and cheeks.

After completing his shave Ian slipped a soft shirt of bleached linen over his broad shoulders. He removed the long length of red and green tartan from the back of a chair by his bed, then wrapped and belted it around his waist creating the knee-length kilt. The balance of the material he draped over his left shoulder and fastened with his favorite broach. After donning red plaid knee stockings and soft leather brogans he walked back to the wash stand to comb his hair. He parted it in the middle and combed it back causing deep waves to fall forward onto his forehead. He ran the comb through it once more, patted it into place, and with a satisfied grin, placed his tam firmly on his brow, adjusting it to his characteristic rakish angle.

Ian smiled at his image in the mirror and bounded down

the stairs to join the other borders at breakfast.

He had been lucky to get a room to himself, not just a bed, at Mrs. Wilkes Boarding House, but he was hungry to talk to the other boarders about current politics.

He sat down in the last empty chair at the table and was soon engrossed in the comments flying back and forth. The English Trustees had divided Georgia into two counties, Savannah and Frederica. William Stephens was the executive of Savannah and talk was that he would become their first Governor. The town now boasted four beautiful squares: Johnson, Wright, Telfair, and Ellis with two more being planned. Many of the men were concerned about the occasional alligators that passed through the streets of the new city. Besides Savannah, colonists had settled several nearby areas. There were now French families at High Gate, fifteen German families settled at Hampstead, and there was a sizeable settlement of Scots at Abercorn about fifteen miles up the Savannah River. In addition Savannah had become home to large groups of persecuted religious groups: Moravian, Saltzburgers, Jews, Lutherans, Puritans and Quakers. The only ones not welcome were Roman Catholics who Oglethorpe and most of the English in Savannah viewed as being the persecutors of their religious freedom.

Ian was on his second helping of sausages when the lively conversation at the table turned to the subjects closest to their hearts—slavery and rum.

A barrel-chested Englishman with shaggy white hair, a wrinkled face and an untidy mustache fixed his rheumy eyes on Ian and stated loudly, "Slavery is the most divisive issue we face in Georgia. The people of Savannah want . . . no they need Negroes, while you Highlanders and the Saltzburgers at Ebenezer want to be slave-free."

That statement brought forth a flurry of tempers and did not abate until everyone had expressed their feelings with much shaking of heads and hands.

"Ah, enough of that despicable subject," an old man in a muslin shirt, black breeches and a goatee sputtered. "Let us tell this fine Scotsman who has joined us at table, the welcome news received just last week. Parliament has finally repealed the "Rum Act". We are now free to import rum and whiskey as we see fit. Welcome news is it not?"

Ian grinned and raised his coffee mug in a mock salute. It was welcome news indeed for the settlers and the traders but he could not help but wonder what effect it might have on the Indians who had shown a marked inability to handle the more potent brews of the white man.

As the mantel clock on the dinning room buffet bonged the hour, Ian pushed back his chair and sprang to his feet. Much as he was enjoying the conversation, he was eager to see Charlotte and talk more about their future.

Once again he walked along Abercorn Street to the Bruner's. The street looked curiously empty in the golden sunshine of late September. A large black cat crouched motionless before a clump of asters, its tail twitching in concentration.

Instead of calling at the main house Ian went directly to the attractive little cottage housing the clockworks. He entered the shop to the familiar smell of freshly cut oak and walnut, flaxseed oil and varnish. Charlotte greeted him with a warm smile and immediately introduced him to her young apprentice, Jimmy Walpole, a tall skinny youth with severe skin blemishes, who looked at him with anxious eyes.

Ian spent most of the morning examining the various works in progress, answering numerous questions the young boy had and actually helping him with a troublesome repair on a fine pocket watch belonging to the local magistrate. Charlotte watched with ill-disguised satisfaction. Ian could practically see her brain working. Everything was playing out as she wanted. He chuckled to himself. Well, she was in for a surprise.

He finally mentioned lunch.

"Of course, dear. Agnes packed us a delightful picnic hamper. Let me get it from the house and we'll be on our way. I had Jimmie hitch the shay and we can leave it at the dock when we catch the ferry. The beach should be practically deserted this time of the year."

The day was just about perfect, mid-eighties, sunny, the air clear and crisp with a cloudless blue sky. He took Charlotte's hand and pulled her to the crest of the dunes. The ocean was just beyond them, less than fifty yards away, only partially hidden by the constantly waving sea grass.

"A little further up there's an inlet that's almost completely hidden from view," Charlotte said. "Let's go there."

They climbed over the dune and walked hand-in-hand along the shoreline to the spot she had in mind. After she spread the cloth Agnes had tucked into the hamper she began to unwrap the sandwiches. Ian unfastened the broach holding his plaid in place and removed it from his shoulder. With a dexterous swirl he twirled the cloth and let it settle on the sand for them to sit on.

He liked the scene stretched out before him. The quiet, pretty beach was soothing and he relaxed with a deep sigh. Sea oats, morning glories and pennywort anchored the dunes. A gentle breeze carried the smell of ocean, but also the scent of sea lavender and asters. Dozens of gulls glided up and down, in and out, cavorting in swirling eddies of wind. His eyes studied the girl beside him. Her golden hair was pulled back and secured with a wide ribbon leaving tiny tendrils to curl around her face. Her face was flushed and her brown eyes sparkled. She looked lovely. It was just about perfect. The temperature was just right and so was the picnic lunch Charlotte unpacked, and the view of the ocean was definitely breathtaking. Now all he had to do was convince her to marry him on his terms—not hers.

Ian sat cross-legged on the sand looking out at the ocean, marshalling his thoughts. Charlotte averted her eyes when a sudden puff of wind lifted the corner of his kilt, then she began to giggle.

"Aye, 'tis a fact I know what you're wondering," he said with a knowing leer. "But there's only one sure way to satisfy your curiosity."

He saw the heat rush to her face and playfully reached over to place a chaste kiss on her cheek. "Before we lose our heads and fall into each other arms again I think its time we talk about our future. I know you don't want to hear this, but I love the military. Your father did me an unexpected favor. I'm proud to be an officer in the Highland Company. They are warriors of the first caliber. Charlotte, I don't want to be a clockmaker."

"But—"

"Hear me out, please. If I marry you and let you mold me into what you want in a husband I will be miserable and our marriage doomed to failure."

She began to clasp and unclasp her hands. "You are turning down a respected business that will make you a wealthy gentleman and secure you a place in Savannah's emerging social structure for a low-paying position on a desolate military outpost in the middle of nowhere. I can't believe you're serious."

"It's not a desolate place at all," Ian retorted hotly. "Darien is a vibrant community situated at the mouth of the mighty Altamaha River. Someday Darien could be as important a port as Savannah."

"And who settled it, Ian? Who lives there? Men of breeding and their families, as we have in Savannah, or impoverished debtors imported for colonization?"

Ian looked at Charlotte as though seeing her for the first time. She was a snob. This discussion could escalate into a full-fledged fight if he let it. He didn't want to fight. He wanted to convince this beautiful girl to marry him. Didn't he?

He cleared his throat and took her hand. "Do you forget that imported colonists were the first to settle Savannah? Do you forget that I was an indentured servant in your father's household? Do you look down on me as well?"

"Of course not. You come from a good family in Scotland. Only death and misfortune put you in a position of servitude.

You are a handsome man with a strong presence. With the proper backing you can become anything you want."

Ian's stomach clenched. He had yet to tell her of his plans for MacGrath Bluff. "What I want is to remain a soldier and make my home in Darien. Listen to me, dearest. Let me tell you about this piece of ground I have found to build our home." For the next few minutes he described the land he had his eye on, the spacious home he planned to build facing the sweep of the river and the ocean beyond. Charlotte sat silently listening, her face a mask, and when he finished he pulled her into his arms.

They kissed, softly at first then more warmly and deeply. He ached with an inner longing for this girl. He laid her back on the sand and took her mouth with a growing urgency. When they were breathless, he moved his lips down her throat, nipping and kissing gently.

He raised himself on his elbows to look deep into her eyes seeking permission. Instead, what he swore he saw was a look of calculation. He had the uncomfortable feeling that he was the one about to be seduced instead of the other way around. And that would give her just the leverage she needed to get her way. With an oath he pulled away.

"Don't stop," she implored. "I want you, darling."

"And I want you—more than I've ever wanted a woman. But we have issues to settle and I won't compromise you."

Charlotte jumped to her feet her brow wrinkled in agitation. "I must have time to think about what you said," she said coldly. "Now we must get back. The ferry leaves at four and I've the shop to close and mother to tend to. There's a small dance tonight at the home of Major Regor and his wife. You remember him, don't you? You worked on the beautiful grandfather clock father made for him. Many of your old friends will be there and it will give you a chance to see them."

"Won't they object to an uninvited guest?"

"Not at all. I had Elsie deliver a note to them this morning telling them of your unexpected arrival in Savannah."

Once again Ian had the feeling of being maneuvered. His jaw tightened in rebellion.

Charlotte saw it and rose on her tiptoes to plant a kiss on his cheek. "It will be a lighthearted, fun evening. Do you good. Besides, I'm dying to show you off to my friends in your handsome uniform. My girlfriends will die with envy."

"Will my name be the only one on your dance card?"

"We'll see," she said with a coy smile. "We'll see."

The parlor of the Regor home had been cleared for dancing and about twenty young people filled the room. Ian had to admit he was having a good time. He knew most of the men and answered their questions about his abrupt exile with lighthearted lies that seemed to satisfy.

Charlotte was more beautiful than ever, able to garner the attention of every male in the room and very much aware of her effect on Ian. However he felt unsettled, there was a subtle change in his fiancée's personality. Her youthful softness had a harder edge to it. Her eyes had a shrewdness he had never noted before. He stood at the punch bowl watching her dance with Jeremy White, an old friend of his. Jeremy led her in the waltz with a proprietary air, obviously displeased with Ian's presence. Charlotte, the little vixen, flirted openly with him. *Trying to make me jealous,* he thought grimly. *Well, two can play that game.* He walked over to the Regor's pretty daughter and wrote his name on her dance card twice.

The evening flew by amid much laughter and drink. Ian's head felt fuzzy from too much rum and he was thankful when they finally bade their farewells and settled themselves in the fresh air of the open coach for the ride home.

Charlotte cuddled close to him and he caught the heady fragrance of her perfume.

Ian leaned his head back on the seat. Maybe he was kidding himself. Maybe life in Savannah wouldn't be so bad after all. With the proper training the young apprentice at Bruner's could probably carry most of the workload freeing him to do as he wanted. He would have a beautiful wife at his side and financial security.

Or maybe this was just the rum talking and his pent up desire for this provocative girl. Maybe this was just lust talking.

When the carriage stopped in front of her home Charlotte turned her face up to his for a goodnight kiss. "It was a nice evening, wasn't it," she murmured.

"Yes, it was."

"Ian I won't leave Savannah. I love you but I can't abandon my mother or the business my father spent a lifetime building. You are asking too much of me."

"Love asks a lot."

"More, then, than I'm willing to give."

He looked at her intently and suddenly it was all clear. Aside from the conflict over where they would live there was the startling realization that Charlotte was not the girl he fantasized. As an only child she had always been spoiled and petulant but maturity had hardened her. She knew exactly what she wanted from life and her goals were not his goals. He had never given her a ring. There had been no opportunity when he was unceremoniously banished from her presence. They were engaged by a verbal commitment only, but he was an honorable man. How could he go back on his promise? His stomach contracted like a fist. Wouldn't it be far more dishonorable to enter into a marriage that was doomed to failure?

He took her chin between his fingers and looked deep into her eyes. "Charlotte, dear one, I'm not the man you should marry. You can't mold me into the husband you want." He kissed her gently on the cheek. "I think we should say good-by. Treasure good memories of what we felt for one another, but move on with our lives."

"You've had a lot to drink," she said, her eyes wide with alarm. "Things will look different tomorrow. Besides, you have a week of leave left. Maybe we can work things out."

"No."

"Oh, Ian, don't you see. I need you. You need me."

"Need, Charlotte? What you need is a man you can control and fit into your business. Your father was right. I'm not the man for you."

Charlotte's lip trembled and a tear ran down her cheek. "I guess . . . I guess I know you are right. I wouldn't be right for you either. Somewhere you'll find a good girl who will treasure a life with you at Darien. It just isn't me."

She hopped out of the carriage before he could help her and ran into the house.

"*Yes*, he thought somberly. *Someday I will. And I think I know just who that girl might be.*

Chapter Twenty-One

"A woman's fate is determined by the love she accepts."
-Old Italian Proverb

Ian set sail for home the next afternoon. He had been lucky to book passage on a mail cutter headed south, and, now as they clipped along the Inland Passage, he leaned against the rail of the little ship, staring at the crest of small whitecaps. A storm was brewing and occasional small waves rose and splattered against the wooden bow sending droplets of seawater onto his face and hair. Sails snapped and ropes lashing the deck creaked in the wind. Despite the fact that he had hoped he would be returning with a bride, or at least an agreed upon wedding date, he felt strangely at peace. Shackles to the past were gone. He was now free to pursue his own future.

He suddenly sensed the gaze of a man standing beside him at the rail. The pleasant, open-faced older gentleman smiled at him. A smile Ian recognized as almost angelic, strong even teeth, full well-formed lips and dark eyes so large and kind they seemed to embrace him.

"Reverend John McLeod," the man said, extending his hand.

"Lieutenant Ian MacDonald," he replied grasping the hand in return.

"Are you one of the Highlanders garrisoned at Fort King George?"

"Yes, sir. I'm on my way back to the fort after a visit in Savannah to see my fiancée." Ian's face sobered. "Ah, my ex-fiancée that is."

"Oh, my. I can only assume then, that the visit was not an entirely happy one. But forgive me, I do not mean to pry into your personal affairs."

Ian did not reply at once. It was not in his nature to speak freely to strangers. Especially to men of the cloth who were certain to begin spouting well-meaning platitudes. "The visit did not have the outcome I anticipated but I am content with it," he finally said. He looked at the Reverend quizzically. "You minister at Darien, don't you? I seem to recall seeing you there."

McLeod nodded his head. "I've been at Darien since '37 but I'm being transferred to Charleston. I'm returning here to tie up a few loose ends. Do you attend church? I don't remember seeing you at any of my services."

"I'm afraid I've grown lax in that matter although I do consider myself a Christian."

"Well, I'll be here for several weeks and we'd love to have you come if you can. There is no church building, but I hold services in my home. I know a soldier's life is pretty well regimented. Were you involved in the recent battle on St. Simons Island? I hear our forces were victorious."

"Aye. We sent the Spanish cur home with his tail between his legs." A gust of wind lifted Ian's kilt and he slapped his hand on his thigh to keep it in place. "We were outnumbered three to one but we turned them away."

"I see God's handiwork in that story."

Ian smiled. "I remember the biblical stories of God always leading the outnumbered and downtrodden to victory. My mother took us boys to the kirk in Glencoe when we were small."

"But now you have drifted away from the church?"

"I always thought I could go it on my own, that if I was strong enough I could defend myself—could rule my life by the sword. But my friend was strong and his sword failed him. I wonder though . . . does religion really improve your life?"

"Religion makes life more difficult. God makes life

bearable."

"It never seemed to me that God was very involved in my life. My grandparents were massacred, my mother died when I was little, my father was unjustly imprisoned. I was shipped to America as an indentured servant and then shanghaied into the Crown's army. It doesn't seem as though He cares a fig for me."

The Pastor reached over and put his hand on Ian's where it rested on the rail. "And now you have apparently broken off your engagement and feel adrift in bitter waters. I can see how you might feel abandoned. There are times in a man's life when he is particularly vulnerable. This may be one of them. But son follow your faith, as weak as it is, rather than your doubts, as strong as they seem to you right now. You do that and leave the rest up to God."

The boat rocked suddenly as the storm broke around them and Reverend McLeod scurried for cover. Ian pulled his plaid over his head and let the cold rain lash his face. Maybe church was just the place he needed to be to lick his wounds. Lately he had been feeling disquieted, like the rudder in his life had been jarred loose.

If he was going to build a new life perhaps he was going to have to build new habits. Maybe the church would be a good place to start.

The next thing he had to do was to contact the owners of the piece of land outside of Darien that he had his eye on. He admitted to himself that somehow Charlotte had never quite fit his vision of the mistress of a home on what was still the frontier. Someday Darien might become an important port city but for now he had to admit it was really only a small village of less than two hundred hardy Scots and the fort.

And then there was Tabitha. The thought of her brought a sudden lurch to his heart. She had none of the vibrant sex-allure of Charlotte but he was slowly realizing that a woman's appeal lay not in the luster of her skin and the curves of her body but in what was revealed by her eyes. And Tabitha's eyes had always spoken volumes. She had never been far out of his thoughts and he couldn't wait to discuss with her all that had happened in Savannah. She was a good listener. There had always been a spark there, he was deeply attracted to her, and now that he no longer had an obligation to Charlotte he was free to develop that feeling—to see where it might lead.

A smile played across his lips as an idea crossed his mind. He would not leave the boat at Darien as he had planned. Instead he would stay on board until it reached Fort Frederica. Surely she should be back from her trip with General Oglethorpe by now.

Once at Frederica Ian found himself undecided as to how to find Tabitha. He did not want to waste valuable time hoping she might appear at the dock in the evening as she had in the past. He guessed the most logical place to look was the Calwell's chandlery where he knew she worked most afternoons, so he headed there.

Mrs. Calwell looked up in surprise when he entered the shop. It was obvious that Highland warriors were not among her usual customers. She was alone. Tabitha was nowhere to be seen.

"How may I serve you, sir?" Mrs. Calwell asked.

"Actually I am not here to purchase anything. I'm looking for your servant Tabitha Plummer. It is an important matter or I wouldn't bother you. Do you know where I might find her?"

"You'll not find her here," Mrs. Calwell snapped. "The ungrateful girl is no longer in our service."

Ian stepped back shaken by the vehemence in her voice. "I'm sorry," he said. "Then where—"

"I suggest you talk to General Oglethorpe," she retorted, cutting him off and turning away.

"Aye, I'll do that." He turned on his heel and left the tiny shop, closing the door a little more emphatically than necessary.

Ian stood in the middle of Broad Street trying to decide what to do next. On both sides of him the street teemed with activity as people went about their daily activities. A small girl rolling her hoop ran into him and her hoop careened to the ground. Her cry of dismay aroused the curious stares of several small boys playing marbles at the side of the road. The Parade Grounds were empty except for a few soldiers. Perhaps he could find someone at the Barracks who would know Oglethorpe's whereabouts. He set his jaw and turned up Barracks Street.

George Mohr, a soldier Ian remembered from his days at Frederica, was sitting on his bunk, one hand holding a clay pipe while he unbuttoned his red wool jacket with the other. Despite the summer heat he was dressed in full uniform. As Ian entered the room the soldier looked up and acknowledged him with a nod.

"Good to see you, old chum."

"And you, George." Ian looked around the barracks where several soldiers lay on cots in various stages of undress. "Where is everyone? The post looks deserted."

"The general took a crew out to his farm. He's building a new barn. George's eyebrows shot up. "I'm surprised to see you. Have you been reassigned?"

"No, I'm on leave. I'm actually looking for General Oglethorpe . . . I have several questions I'd like to ask him."

"Then you better trot out to his farm. He won't be back for days. The jolly barn is nowhere finished."

"Thanks, I'll do that. Take care, lad."

It was only mid-day and Ian thought it best to approach the general after the evening meal, when he would likely be alone, so he meandered down to the dock to pass the time. He sat there deep in thought.

Why was he doing this? His encounters with Tabitha had been relatively few but they had always been deep and satisfying. She listened to him—really listened. He felt he could unburden his soul and she would understand. She was attracted to him, he had always known that, though she tried hard to hide it. He remembered the night their hands accidentally touched and the spark of desire that had shaken him deeply. Yes, he had to find her . . . had to pursue this relationship to its natural conclusion. He had been falling in love with Tabitha for some time even though he was just now admitting it to himself and that with deep reluctance.

Ian glanced at the sun. It was time to seek Oglethorpe and find some answers as to Tabitha's whereabouts.

The general's three hundred acre parcel, known simply as The Farm, lay not far to the southeast near Harrington Hall, home of Captain Raymond Demere. He set out on foot, crossing a narrow bridge over Gully Hole Creek. The tide that floods the coastal area twice a day was running high. A well-marked wagon path led through groves of live oak, southern red cedar, hickory, holly, loblolly pine and sweet smelling bay. In the fall sweet gums would turn a brilliant vermilion, the hickories and bullis grapevines a lemony yellow but for now all was a verdant green. The trail ran along Oglethorpe's golden-leafed vineyards, their vines hanging heavy with sweet muscadine grapes, then turned into an open yard to reveal Orange Hall, his modest frame cottage.

Ian found him sitting on a porch that ran the length of the house affording a clear view of the fort and nearby village. He was pushed back in a rocking chair, smoking his pipe, dressed casually in a homespun shirt open at the neck and minus his powdered wig. It was the first time Ian had seen the general without his wig and he was surprised to see that he possessed a full head of wavy hair the color of old brick.

Oglethorpe's eyes squinted in annoyance as Ian approached and saluted.

"I see you are a Highlander from Darien . . . uh . . . Lieutenant MacDonald, as I recall," he said, his gaze sweeping over Ian's uniform. "Is there trouble there?"

"No, sir. I'm on a private mission. I seek only a few minutes of your time."

The general continued to look at him intently then waved to an empty chair beside him. "Of course, I recognize you. You were at the marsh when we turned back the Spanish."

"Yes, sir."

"What is it you wish?"

Ian cleared his throat. "News of that Indian girl, Tabitha Plummer, who recently acted as interpreter for you on your trip north."

"And why do you ask about her?"

"Oh . . . ah . . . we became friends during my posting here at Frederica. I would like to see her again. She was indentured to the Calwells but Mrs. Calwell tells me she is no longer with them. She suggested I ask you about her whereabouts."

Oglethorpe drew deeply on his pipe, his blue eyes staring intently into Ian's. "You say friend. Was there more than that?"

"No, sir. But . . . I . . . I think I would like it to be more." Briefly he recounted his prior commitment to Charlotte and the break-up of their engagement.

"And how long have you known Tabitha?"

"Since Ft. Mosa. You may remember that it was my life she saved by going for help."

"Oh yes. I do remember that incident. She was a very brave young girl. In fact that is what compelled me to seek a home for her with the Calwells. You continued to keep in touch with her, then?"

"Not really. It was only after our Company was ordered to Fort Frederica in June that I made contact with her. We became friends and spent many evenings on the dock talking. Of course, I was engaged, so it was no more than friendship."

Wisps of smoke rose from Oglethorpe's pipe. The sound of a harmonica drifted in the air from the nearby servant's quarters and birds called their evening song as they settled into nearby trees for the night.

Oglethorpe finally removed the pipe from his lips and looked at Ian shrewdly. "I noticed you asked about *that Indian girl*. I take it you think of her in that manner—as Indian not white."

Ian could feel the heat rise in his neck. That was his real problem, wasn't it? He did think of Tabitha as Indian.

"I admit I do, sir. My prejudice against Indians has always

colored my thinking where she is involved. My former employer told me many stories of their brutality. Then my best friend, Cory MacGrath was scalped during our reconnaissance at Fort St. Simons."

"I remember that incident. But son, the white man has likewise scalped many Indians in greed for bounty and God only knows we are guilty of many acts of unbelievable cruelty. This land belonged to the Indian nation and many a night I don't sleep well knowing that we are unjustly pushing them from it. You should not think despairingly of them . . . they are loyal and courageous people. I considered Chief Tomochichi of the Creek Confederacy to be a true friend. You are wrong, Lieutenant MacDonald, to judge all by the actions of a few. And wrong to think of Tabitha's Indian heritage as inferior to yours. Both white man and Indians have committed atrocities."

"I know you are right, sir, but old hatreds die hard."

"Well, let them die. As long as you hold onto your anger, you'll lead a mean, bitter life. Leave it here. Now, about Tabitha . . . you wish to know her whereabouts?"

Ian nodded.

"Before we left on our journey to Singing Spring I promised the girl I would compensate her for her services. She was an excellent interpreter and a valuable asset to our party. After a new treaty was signed with Chief Walking Stick she asked that her compensation be rendered in the form of freedom from her indenture to the Calwells. She said she wanted to return to her native village instead of Frederica. I detected great sadness in her eyes but she seemed quite determined."

Ian flinched with regret. "I had told her I was going to Savannah to ask Charlotte to marry me."

"Perhaps that accounts for her sorrow. However, she also indicated that Broken Arrow, our Cherokee scout, had asked her to wed."

Ian felt his stomach tighten. "Did she . . . did she tell you her answer?"

"Not in so many words but I rather suspect that was her intention." Oglethorpe smacked his clay pipe on the palm of his hand knocking the ash to the porch floor. "I like the girl—like her immensely. She is very intelligent and deserves more from life than life in an Indian village can give her. I think she is making a mistake and now I believe I know the reason. If you think you love her go after her before it's too late. Don't let that fine child get away from you. But Ian, go find that girl with an open mind."

"I don't even know the name of her village, nor where it is."

"The village is named Tustacatty. It's at the headwaters of the Altamaha where the Oconee joins the Ocmulgee Rivers west of Savannah. How much leave time do you have left?"

"A week."

"Do you have a horse?"

"No, sir."

"You would make much better time if you travel by land instead of waiting for passage on a ship. I have a yearling in the barn that needs to be ridden. His name is Dash. Take him."

Ian jumped to his feet. "I don't know how to thank you, General Oglethorpe."

Oglethorpe's face suddenly took on a haunted look. "Had fate been kinder to me and I had not let convention stand in my way I would not be a bachelor with only memories to keep me warm." He stood. "Let me draw you a map before I take you to the barn. I'll have one of the men saddle Dash." He smiled. "This is only a loan you understand. I expect my horse back in good condition."

Ian grinned. "Of course, sir."

Ian followed Oglethorpe's map carefully, keeping to the trails that followed the Altamaha as it flowed southeast. Wild grapes, warm in the September sun, filled the air with heavy fragrance. He held the reins loose in his hand careful not to ride the horse too hard and tire him, his only companions the scurrying wildlife. Deer, rabbit, squirrel and opossum were plentiful in this part of inland Georgia. As he rode along he found his mind was imprinted with memories of Tabitha. He remembered how kind she had been to listen to him talk of his love for Charlotte. How she had maintained her dignity when in his grief over Cory's death he had lashed out at her Indian blood. He smiled to himself remembering her spunk as she battled an alligator to save a man's life and the courage she showed when as a mere child she risked her life to seek help for him where he lay injured at Fort Mosa. Most of all he remembered the warmth and understanding in her amazing blue eyes when she looked at him. Her eyes held a regal serenity, yet they could take on a passionate fierceness when her ire was aroused. Perhaps more importantly, he remembered the attraction between them that he had refused to acknowledge.

He had been besotted with Charlotte's beauty, by the intrigue of their clandestine affair, by the thrill of wanting what was forbidden and all the while Tabitha, plain, gentle Tabitha, was right there in front of him listening to his selfish prattle with remarkable patience.

His hands clenched on the reins. What if he could not find her? What if he was too late and she was gone forever? What if she had already married Broken Arrow? He dug his heels into the horse's rump and urged him on.

Tabitha's mind was in a whirl. After promising to give Broken Arrow an answer to his proposal she tried to calm herself by entering into the work of the village.

Somberly she squatted on the bare ground using a heavy pestle to crush freshly roasted sweet potato roots that would be formed into cakes and roasted for dinner. Wilimico hovered over the sweat oven, a hollowed-out hole in the ground lined with small rocks. The oven was topped by a mound of clay, like a butterfly cocoon, with an opening at one end for smoke to escape. Aluste tended the fire pit where a side of venison suspended from a bone hook on a tripod of poles dripped tantalizing smelling juices that caused Tabitha's mouth to water and stomach to rumble.

The central work yard serving their cluster of four houses bustled with activity. Everyone had a chore. An old man worked to shape a blowgun out of river cane for hunting squirrels. Several young girls were boiling fish skins in a pot to make glue while others were fashioning ropes of moss into fishing nets. Two young boys were playing a noisy game imitating the adult game of chungke where a small wheel-shaped stone is rolled down the street followed by the would-be warriors who threw spears toward the spot where they expected the stone to stop, screaming with delight when their spear was the closest. Horses nickered in a nearby coral. Across the way Shining Star nursed her infant daughter. Tabitha wondered about her, she had long flowing hair unadorned with oil, a sign that she was recently widowed. She, the baby, and four other children lived in a small chickee-home of wattle and daub with a roof of split river cane and mud.

Tabitha could not help a feeling of pride when she glanced up at her uncle's substantial buildings and fields planted with English wheat, Indian corn, peas and potatoes. An open lean-to covered with palmetto fronds served as a storage area and a large frame stood inside from which several deerskins had been hung to dry. She had been promised the largest skin, which she would have to chew to soften and then fashion into a new dress.

Smoke rose from the fire pit, and, from the well in the center of the clearing, a woman drew a bucket of water. It was a good life, a simple life. The problem was, Tabitha admitted she missed her home at Frederica Town with its formal flower gardens and neat lawns. She missed her translation work with Pastor Ulrich and her quiet times of devotion. It would be more difficult to practice her Christian faith here among the Muskogee. Silently she chided herself. God would be with her regardless of where she was. She had to believe that. She closed her eyes and mouthed a silent prayer, then, with vigor, began to shape the ground roots into patties for the evening meal.

That night she tossed and turned on her moss-filled mattress unable to fall asleep. It was unbearably hot in the one room hut and her body was covered with a thin sheen of sweat. A deerskin stretched across a pole for privacy was all that separated her from Wilimico and Bald Eagle who snored loudly in sated sleep. Earlier the sounds of their mating had caused Tabitha acute discomfort. She felt blood flush her face. Finally, in desperation, she rose, tiptoed across the room and pushed through the skin flap that led to the common well in the clearing behind the hut. She drew a bucket of water and splashed her hot face with its soothing wetness, then filled a horn ladle and drank deeply. The night was dark and quiet, without a cloud. The villagers did not bother to dig latrines and the faint smell of human odor drifted to her as a sudden gust of hot wind blew across the parched yard. Tabitha shuddered in disgust. How she missed the neat whitewashed privies behind the Calwell home.

She walked quietly through the village and several dogs followed, keeping their distance. Although the communal spirit was strong, people had earmarked their homes with their own personal touch. One woman had planted wildflowers around her hut, another hung colorful beads across her door. An old man had built a crooked porch where he spent his days in a chair fashioned from twisted tree branches.

She passed the communal workshop where they kept gardening tools, spades and hoes, bartered for from the Trading Post, past the ceremonial circle where they held their festivities and the barn where the corn from the summer harvest lay in large piles waiting to be shucked.

Distant trees were black silhouettes against the moonlit sky. Without thinking where she was going she headed for their beckoning sanctuary. When she reached the woods she sank to the ground and tucked her long legs beneath her, breathing deeply the rich forest air. Looking up at the pale moon hanging above her, memories of Frederica came flooding back.

This same moon had shone on her and Ian as he played his Jew's harp that first night they sat together on the dock beside the fort. *Was he watching the moon now with another girl at his side?* Her eyes misted at the thought and a dull, empty ache gnawed at her soul. She groaned and dug her hands into the soft forest floor. She should not be thinking of him. She was here to make a decision about Broken Arrow. But it was impossible to remember Ian dispassionately—the way he looked, the sound of his voice, his laughter and his hair of remarkable thickness that swept up and back from his broad brow. She had spent the early evening hours with her Bible seeking an answer to her dilemma. The Old Testament made many references to arranged marriages made for practical purposes. Love hopefully developed after the union of man and woman. Did this justify her temptation to take Broken Arrow as her mate knowing full well that her feelings for him were second to her feelings for Ian? Broken Arrow was a good man, strong of character and resolve and she did not doubt that in time she would learn to love him. Perhaps that was the better basis for marriage—not passion, but respect and honor. David married Bath Sheba out of a raging passion and look at the grief that brought him.

Tabitha felt incurably sad. God seemed strangely quiet on this matter. She could not sense His plan for her.

Soon a new day would dawn and her answer to Broken Arrow must be given. An answer that would determine the course her life would follow.

She put her chin up and smiled bravely. She would say yes. Her lips broke into a full grin as she visualized Broken Arrow's joyful reaction. She felt better already. He could speak to her uncle tomorrow and they would be married before the week was out.

Ian drew his lathered horse to a halt beside a tiny brook and jumped from the saddle. While the horse took his fill of the sweet water he sank to the ground and wiped the sweat from his face. The sun was at its zenith and he had been riding since sunup. Best to rest a while and let the horse nibble on the tender grass that grew close to the bank.

He spread Oglethorpe's map on the ground and studied it carefully. If he was correct he could reach the Oconee River by dusk, camp for the night and arrive at Tustacatty early the next morning. He realized he was hungry and broke off a stalk of cabbage palm to eat. It tasted like chestnuts. He drew a piece of dried beef from his knapsack to chew while he traced his route. A sudden stab of anxiety twisted his gut as he thought of what lay ahead—his meeting with Tabitha, how she would react to him, how he would react to her. He had always scoffed at men who prayed, but unexpectedly he felt drawn to bow his head. "Lord," he beseeched quietly, "please remold my thinking, reshape my heart, burn away the prejudice that has sunk roots of bitterness into my heart."

Quietly, and strangely comforted, he bent to fill his canteen and then rose to place his saddlebags, with one more days supply of pemmican and jerky, on Dash's back. Lastly Ian adjusted his bedroll of soft rabbit fur for what little sleep he would allow himself and sprang into the saddle eager to be underway. He intended to ride as long as there was light and on into the night if there was sufficient moon. Digging his heals into Dash's flanks, he set out at a full gallop.

Morning dawned, a golden morning, already warm enough to bring beads of perspiration to Tabitha's forehead. She felt sticky and craved a bath. It was best to bathe early before the alligators stirred. She gathered her supplies—soap, a bladder filled with steeped tobacco leaves to rinse her hair and kill any lice she might have acquired, a comb fashioned from buffalo horn—and headed for the river.

The sun cast its brilliance on the slow-moving water like a walkway of reflected light. The view was soothing and peaceful with low-slung trees draped with veils of Spanish moss lining the bank.

She removed her deerskin dress, draping it carefully over a staggerbush and stepped into the cool water. The river was shallow at this point, barely more than a creek, and tall as she was she could barely submerge herself. Holding tightly to the precious sliver of rosewood soap she had brought from the Caldwell Chandlery she moved it slowly over her body sighing with pleasure. She soaped her hands and then worked the lather deep into her scalp before rinsing it with the tobacco solution. A large, long-legged whooping crane stood regally in the shallows watching her with beady eyes and a turtle dropped into the water with a loud plop. She inhaled deeply, the familiar scent of rosewood causing a wave of homesickness for Frederica. She missed the little candle shop and the children, missed Anna and missed Pastor Reverend Ulrich.

When she finished her bath, she reluctantly left the refreshing water and sat on the bank to let the sun dry her skin. Her long black hair lay in abundance over her shoulders framing her face. Tabitha's mind skipped over the conversation she would have with Broken Arrow later in the day. Now that the decision had been made she was anxious to move forward as quickly as possible. Her skin began to tingle from the rays of the hot sun and she pulled on her dress and tucked the small piece of precious soap into the amulet that hung from a piece of sinew on her chest.

As she walked back to the village on a trail that paralleled the river she heard the sound of horse's hooves approaching from the rear. She halted and cocked her head. Thank heavens she had finished her bath and was fully dressed.

The horse drew nearer and Tabitha stepped off the trail to give the rider room to pass. As he drew abreast she heard the sharp intake of a breath. She looked up into the green eyes of Ian MacDonald with a gasp.

"Tabitha!" he stammered, reining his horse to a stop.

Tabitha was too startled to say anything. *Dear Lord, what was he doing here?* There was a roaring in her ears from her pounding heart and she felt almost faint. This couldn't be happening, not today of all days.

"Wha . . . what are you doing here?" she finally whispered.

"I've come to find you."

"Me? Why me?" she said searching his eyes, his face.

"We need to talk, Tabitha." He jumped to the ground. "Can we find someplace in the shade and sit down for a few minutes?"

"I just came from the river," she said weakly. "We can go back there and sit on the bank. It's shaded and cool." She turned away from the trail and began to walk briskly. Ian, leading his horse, caught up with her, and reached for her arm. She let him take it and as they walked she took note of every thing about him, the warm clasp of his fingers, the muscular bulk of his body, the self-assured firmness of his stride.

They reached the river and he stopped, looking down at her, shielding his eyes from the morning sun with his hand. He smiled. "You look as though you are afraid of me."

"I don't understand why you are here."

"I came for you."

"But . . . I thought . . . Charlotte . . . ?"

"I need to explain what has happened." He still had a hold on her arm and he guided her to a shady spot under an ancient linden tree and pulled her down beside him. "I went to Savannah as planned intent on asking Charlotte to marry me. She was more beautiful than ever. Able to garner the attention of men wherever we went. But I soon realized her beauty was all on the surface. I was too young before to see it. She has a plan for the life she wants and she intended to mold me into a husband that would conform to that pattern. Maturity has given her a hard edge, an edge I didn't care for. So I broke off our engagement."

"But you did love her, didn't you?"

"Desired her, yes. But that isn't love. It never was."

"I thought you would be married by now, Ian. I . . . I . . . ." Her voice trailed off. She looked into his eyes. Then, as if drawn together by some inexplicable force, their lips touched, as light as the landing of a dragonfly, then more deeply setting her blood aflame. She melted like butter into his arms, dissolving at his touch. She could deny her feelings no longer. She felt driven by a pulse of desire impossible to hold back. She did not know what it was like to mate with a man but she knew she did not want to live without love. She drank deeply from Ian's demanding lips, quenching a thirst that had been building all of that hot Frederica summer.

When they finally drew apart she was breathless, aching with an inner longing, her eyes unable to leave him. This should not be happening. But she did not care. She was unable to tear herself from his arms, unable to quell the tide of love that rolled over her.

Ian lifted his fingers to her mouth and gently traced the outline of her lips. He looked at her with deep intensity. "I love you, Tabitha. God only knows why I didn't know it before. I only hope it isn't too late."

She closed her eyes, happier than she had ever dreamed possible. "Just hold me," she whispered. "I have often imagined meeting you again. I don't want this moment to ever go away."

They sat cradled in each other's arms. Light streamed thorough the branches of the linden tree in wide bands across the forest floor. The luscious fragrance of the small green-and-yellow flowers and the droning hum of bees filled the air.

Tabitha finally stirred and turned to look up at the handsome Scotsman holding her so tenderly. "I am still of Indian blood, Ian. That hasn't changed."

"Love changes everything."

"Even a misgiving as deep as yours?"

Ian's face took on a haunted look. "I was acting like a wee bairn, condemning an entire race because of the actions of a few. I am sorry for my words, Tabitha. I know they hurt you . . . know that I have hurt you in many ways. I was blinded by my intolerance toward your people, although I have observed their allegiance to Oglethorpe and seen their bravery in battle.

I do not pretend to have put all my feelings behind me—you will have to help me—but I have changed and I promise I will try."

"That's all I can ask for, Ian. My mother taught me that one of the great arts of living is the art of forgiving. Your life will be different if you can make allowances for the differences in others. I don't believe that we are all meant to be alike. I believe that God puts people in our path whose journeys are interwoven with ours in a seemingly random pattern. We are not meant to walk alone in our life."

Ian stared at her intently. "I wonder if you know how wise you are, my dear."

Tabitha looked at his well tanned face, his unruly red hair, his firm jaw and sea-green eyes. She wondered how such a handsome man could ever be attracted to someone as plain as she. She didn't want to get hurt, but neither did she want to live without love. "But Ian, I am not beautiful like your Charlotte," she said, her voice trembling.

"You have dignity in your face. And serenity. To me that is true beauty. Oh, Tabitha, how you must have agonized at my foolish chatter about Charlotte. I didn't realize it was you I really wanted. I chose to ignore what was happening." His voice was soft. "I often watched you when you weren't looking. I loved the way your black hair fell like a veil around your face. You were quiet and your eyes were soft and you always listened to me. It makes me sad to finally realize that you are the one I love because I don't really know you. And these past two days I have been terrified that I misread your feelings for me, that I'd be too late and you would already be married."

"You almost were—too late that is."

"Broken Arrow?"

"I was about to give him my answer. To tell him that I would marry him."

Ian stood and pulled Tabitha to her feet. She went forward and Ian reached out his arms and she slid into them as though she belonged there. He embraced her, tipping her head back to kiss her neck. Her arms went around his shoulders, pulling him into herself. "Tell me you love me," he murmured burying his face in her hair.

"I tried not loving you. But I do. It is natural with me, like the wind or the rain or the stars. I . . ."

Suddenly she stiffened. Ian looked up, his breath ragged and uneven. "What's wrong, dear?"

"Did you hear something?"

"No."

She pulled away from him, her gaze searching the riverbank. Then she gave a startled gasp. Standing in the shadow of a near-by tree was the tall form of Broken Arrow.

Tabitha's trembling fingers fumbled to smooth her hair and straighten her dress. "How long have you been here?" she cried fighting to control the tremor in her voice.

He stepped forward. "Long enough."

His black eyes bored into hers like burning coals and his fingers moved to stroke the tomahawk tucked into the waistband of his leather leggings.

Ian pushed Tabitha behind him and started to speak but Broken Arrow raised his hand to silence him. He was scowling at them, his thick black brows almost meeting over the bridge of his nose.

"Tabitha is fine woman. I always know of her feeling for you. I hoped to make good life for her so she forget. It not to be. You the one she want." He took his hand from the band of his legging and held it toward Ian. "You the victor. We touch hands like the white man."

Ian grasped his hand and they shook.

Broken Arrow turned and looked at Tabitha. She sucked in her breath and met his gaze head-on.

"I like talk with you, alone!" His words were curt.

Tabitha looked at Ian standing at her side. "Do you mind?" she implored.

Ian shook his head. "I'll tend to my horse. Take your time."

He walked away and Tabitha waited for Broken Arrow to

speak. She hoped she didn't look as abashed as she felt.

Broken Arrow took her hand and placed it against his chest, then put his own hand against her breast. "You will return to the world you have chosen, and I will go back to mine. But our hearts have touched. I will never forget you."

"Nor I you," Tabitha said. She was close to tears. She found it hard to say good-by to this man who had become so dear to her. "I won't ever see you again, will I?"

"No. We have chosen separate paths to follow in this life. And you have found the man you truly love." He moved his hand to her shoulder and looked deep into her eyes. "I dared to think there was a connection between us, between our spirits. I thought in time your love would grow for me. But it not to be." He dropped his hand to his side. "Someday we may meet in another world. Till then, White Blossom, go in peace."

Tabitha felt incurably sad as Broken Arrow turned with dignity and disappeared into the woods.

Ian walked back to her and she turned her face so he would not see the tears in her eyes. He reached down and took her hand, standing silently until she could regain her composure. She looked at Ian with a shaky smile. "He is a good man. He never meant to harm us, you know."

"I know."

"I must get back to the village. Wilimico will be worried about me."

"Wait . . . there is more I have to say." Ian stepped back and looked deep into her eyes. "I plan to stay in the army, you know."

"Of course."

He took her by the hand and pulled her down to sit beside him on the soft grass. "Let me tell you about a piece of property I have my eyes on," he said as he cradled her in his strong arms. Her eyes widened with delight when he described the homestead, surrounded by massive live oaks with a view of the marsh and sea.

"It is in Darien, then?"

"Yes." He smiled

She smiled back at him. "Good. It sounds like a perfect place to settle." She felt a sudden stab of anxiety. Perhaps she was assuming too much.

"Tabitha." He reached over and drew her closer. But she pulled back and their gaze locked and unspoken words played back and forth between them. It was like a warm breeze brushing over her.

"Marry me." His voice was husky.

She saw the love mirrored in his eyes and her heart turned over. She felt she would split with love for this man.

"Yes," she said, smiling at him, her face flushed with happiness. She moved into his arms once more and put both hands on his face pulling it forward for another kiss that left both of them shaken.

The day had turned out differently from what she had planned. But then she had always known that God would reveal his will for her when she least expected it.

They had been so absorbed in each other that they had failed to notice the rain squall approaching but suddenly fat drops were pelting them in the face. Ian drew his length of plaid over their heads as they cuddled together and let the rain blow on them as they held each other in the swirl of wind and emotion. Ian's heart pounded, his eyes slicked with rain, certain that he could never want another girl as he wanted this one. His lips found hers, wet and warm and soft. They lingered a moment then caressed her eyes and slid down her throat. She smelled of soap and rain and everything clean. He held her and gently ran his hands through her wet hair.

"You smell good," he said as his mouth lifted in a tender smile.

She laughed and he joined her, filled with the joy of loving her.

The squall passed and he removed his plaid from her head, refastening it at his shoulder and rose to his feet. "Let me take you to your village to collect your things. We can be married at Darien. I met a Pastor on the ship that I would like to perform the ceremony."

"I would like that," she said softly.

And then without saying another word Ian took two steps and swung her up into the saddle behind him. Tabitha rested against him, her arms wrapped tightly about his waist. With the wind in her face and her hair streaming behind her they rode forward on the wings of morning . . . and the future.

It was time to end one journey . . . and begin another.

The End

Afterward

Anna Meyer and John Henney did marry but a year or so later Anna died in childbirth. By 1754 Constance Calwell was a widow and records indicate that she later married a MacIntosh and settled near Darien. Both of her sons, John and Henry, applied to the Crown and received large tracts of land.

John and Charles Wesley considered their brief sojourn in Georgia a failure and they never returned to America.

Within a few years James Oglethorpe was recalled to England and the military units were disbanded. With over half of its citizens gone there was no longer a need for a town site. In 1758 a great fire swept through most of the buildings and Frederica Town ceased to be.

The land was in private hands until recently when it was deeded to the National Park Service.

Printed in the United States
23159LVS00001B/61-174